I0611401

Past Life Press

Yellow Fever

Steffan Piper

Other works by the Author:

Novels:

Greyhound
Waiting for Andre
Black Night, Green Felt

Poetry Compilation:

Electronic Butterflies
Observations of a Dead Man
During the Apocalypse

ISBN 978-0-6152-4293-4

First Edition

www.steffanpiper.com

"This is the sound of my agitation ..."

\- Ludwig van Beethoven

From the lobby ...

You can kiss me, and you can touch my tits, but no sex.
You cannot finger me, but you can masturbate. Those are my
rules. Her mind was racing, trying to figure out what she was
going to have to say. Qianqian, pronounced like the jutting
facial appendage just below your mouth, not once but twice,
sank slowly into the soft cushions of the large burgundy couch
that found a place in the center of one the oldest hotel foyers
in Hollywood. She adjusted herself carefully trying to find a
little comfort. Her eyes moved across the folds and bends of
her black gown. She began admiring herself with her hands,
stroking the blonde streak in her silky black bangs, adjusting
her bra strap and crossing her legs, left over right.

She was nervous. She usually didn't put wine or spirit
to her lips, but she was creating tension just sitting still. She
could almost taste the tequila soaking into her gums and
moving across her tongue. Usually, alcohol was out of the
question. It created a blush response that she found

indignifying. Tonight though was different. She could feel herself unraveling slowly.

Qianqian had never met anyone outside of her club. She didn't think that anyone would ever find out, and so she saw no harm. She was stripping at the Industrial Strip Club in North Hollywood. It was a fully nude club that gave lap dances behind closed doors. The club had the reputation of the place to go if you wanted sex in return for a small amount of money. Most men felt that the risk at the club was lower than picking girls up off the street. She'd been there for almost a year. She wasn't sure if she was losing control, but the money was starting to change her and it was what put her in the lobby of the Hollywood Roosevelt. When the waitress had appeared and asked her what she wanted, she politely asked for a premium margarita. In the hope of subverting the waitress from asking for identification, she went into a routine of exactly 'how' she wanted it.

"Can I have a top shelf Cadillac on the rocks, no salt?"

"Absolutely," the waitress responded. "Would you like to start a tab?"

"I'm in 221, can you charge it to my room?"

"Sure, no problem," the waitress shot and then disappeared with a smile. Qian sighed in relief, glad not to be carded, and languidly placed her arm across the top of the cushion next to her and began admiring the room. The lights were soft and blending calmly with the cream walls and red carpeting. The building had class and was quiet enough for the type of rendezvous that she had in mind. At least, this was the idea she had romanced in her mind. She began to feel overdressed and she felt the eyes of the place moving in on her. Her neckline was low, the curve of her breasts were barely visible. Her nipples were thick and stuck out confidently through the sheer material of her gown. She felt no embarrassment. The waitress brought over the drink, smiled and left.

The man Qianqian was waiting for was sixty-one years old. His name was Layden Strausse, he had been married to the same woman since he was twenty but was long past any pretense of fidelity. He had met Qian several times in the club and became fixated, starting an everyday routine that quickly turned into a personal obsession. He had begun asking her to meet him outside of the club. She resisted, but finally broke drown for the offer of five thousand dollars. Quietly, she sat anticipating her evening, but mostly her payment. She sipped her margarita, and glanced around the lobby looking for Layden, trying not to appear nervous. They were supposed to meet at eight pm, but it was already ten after. She was feeling foolish and wondered if she was about to be stood up. Her ego started to grate against the side of her head, looking for a place to inflate for the purpose of self-preservation. The panic from inside quietly began.

"Qian, you showed!" Layden exclaimed. "Sorry, I'm running behind. The traffic was heavy." He approached her from behind and he placed his crumply hands on her bare shoulders. He squeezed her thin neckline and massaged her once with his thumbs.

She held her breath in bound and nervous apprehension. She was trying hard to remain silent and not start blurting things out foolishly. She didn't want him to sense her fear. In the year that she had been dancing, she hadn't felt this tense since her first day. The first day she was uptight about being fat, now she was frightened about losing control of herself and going too far.

Layden sat down beside her, only a few inches away. She had her hands in her lap and was looking at him from the side of her face. He put his arm around her and placed his hand lightly on the inside of her covered knee.

"No, Layden. Not in public," she admonished him, removing his hand away. The waitress appeared and gave them both a quiet once over with a raised eyebrow. The nature of their relationship was flamingly apparent.

"Can I get you anything?" she asked, looking at Layden.

"Diet coke, please."

"Anything more for you, Miss?" she asked, with impertinence

"No, I'm still fine, thank you."

The waitress hesitated for a moment before she left, any good mind reader could've figured out what she was thinking.

"Can we go up, people are beginning to stare?" Qian asked.

"I thought that you'd never ask," Layden responded oozingly, smiling from behind his silver moustache, his eyes gleaming with lust. His mind was focused on his purpose. The tablet of Viagra he had taken in the car before he had come in had begun to have a chemical effect on his thinking. When all the blood starts to move to one head it quickly leaves the other.

Qian stood up and trailed off alone towards the bank of elevators across the lobby. She glanced at the black and white photographs that adorned the walls, depicting old Hollywood as she headed towards the polished brass doors that portrayed her mirrored image. She reached out to a picture of the Roosevelt Hotel standing alone with flat ground on all sides surrounded by oil derricks, scattered mathematically. She thought it was better to stare at the pictures than her own reflection in front of her. Her cheeks were already flushing pink, she was lightheaded. She turned back to see Layden still at the chairs, paying the waitress. He was trying to find something smaller than a hundred, amongst a larger stack of the same. In a rush, he gave up and told her to keep the change. Qian felt cheapened by the way Layden was handling the money and his desire. He was moving quickly to catch up as the elevator doors opened and swallowed Qian whole. Finally, they were alone. She pushed the button to the seventh floor for the room she had reserved earlier. He pushed the button to the penthouse suite. He moved in close to her and placed his hand on her hip. The thin material of her gown made it apparent that she wasn't wearing any underwear. She leaned against the wall. Layden pressed against her and moved in to kiss her.

The bell dinged and the doors slid open, it was the third floor. They quickly moved away from each other to avoid being seen. Fortunately, no one was waiting. When the doors closed again, Layden moved in again, Qian put up her hand and stopped him.

"You can kiss me, and you can touch my tits, but no sex. You cannot finger me, but you can masturbate. Those are my rules," she spoke firmly, but it just made him smile. She was letting him know where she stood, or where she thought she wanted to be standing.

"No sex, huh?" he queried.

"You heard me," she laughed. He looked at her carefully from the corner of his eye, slightly askew, and chuckled. "Okay," he replied in disbelief.

"I'm serious," she insisted. Qian quickly became aloof, and tried to behave in an unconcerned manner. Layden was a bit taken aback, but still single-minded. When the doors opened again, she walked out ahead of him. He was happy to watch the swish of her figure. Qian was extremely well proportioned. She was endowed with the figure of Salvador Dali's wife. Her smooth back, majestic, and strangely wide hips and firm breasts had the dangerous formula in them that could make men kill each other in the deserted city streets like a scene from a Charlton Heston movie.

He slid the magnetic card through the electronic door lock. It clicked and he pushed it open. He allowed her entrance into the room first but she recognized the room immediately. He was trying to throw her off as fast as possible and he succeeded. It was the same room from the movie 'Pretty Woman'. Qian set down her drink just inside the door, on the glass table in the entryway. Layden slowly moved in behind her and pushed himself against her backside. She arched herself outward and moaned. She let go of her purse and gyrated against Layden's erect member. She was no stranger to it. Every time he had come to the club, she had given him at least a handjob. It was her way of making at least three hundred dollars from each customer. She could always bank on going home with close to a thousand bucks if she was willing to make the sacrifice.

Layden moved his hand up the inside of her dress he knelt down on the tiled floor and buried his face into her crotch. He found what he was looking for. She allowed him to please her for a long twenty seconds, and then abruptly moved away. She was moaning and panting. Within a few steps, she was on the other side of the room. Layden was still on his knees wiping the smile from his face.

"Leave the money on the table next to my purse, please," she instructed him. The word please was more of an afterthought. She found herself looking out the open window into Hollywood and lighting a cigarette. The windows had been left ajar and the blinds had been pulled back, Los Angeles at night was beautiful and absolute. From the fourteenth floor of the city, the noises had faded. She stared at the lights coming from the boulevard below. As usual, the Mann Chinese Theater was setting up outdoor lights, bleachers and white tents for yet another meaningless awards ceremony that would only interfere with traffic and bloat the streets with tourists. She thought of Sebastian working on his reports and listening to 'Charles Mingus among us'. She believed Sebastian was deeply predictable, especially on weeknights. His face faded into the slow current of distracted reality that she found herself stepping out of.

She looked behind her. Layden had done as he had been told to. The money was sitting neatly beside her purse. She looked over at him again. He was pouring himself a drink and had removed his blazer, which he had tossed across the back of the couch. She felt safe with Layden and never thought that he would mistreat her. Layden provided an immediate sense of security for her, and there was no denying the path that she was now following. She wondered if maybe it was his age that made her feel so secure, but he was actually older than her own father. She felt comfortable, but she told herself to be cautious. She repeated to herself what she had told him in the elevator. *"Those are my rules, those are my rules, those are my rules."* Her mind Xeroxed what she thought important for the moment. *"And don't get arrested,"* she added as she glanced at the money across the room, lying neatly on the table.

"Did you bring any music or a change of clothes, Qian? If there's not going to be any sex, I assume that I'm at least in for some kind of show?

"I am providing the entertainment, stop worrying," Qian chided. Layden began dimming the lights around the room. She slipped into the bathroom to change. "Wait there in the chair, and relax." She closed the door behind her. She saw herself in the reflection of the mirror as soon as she hit the light switch. Glancing back at the doorknob, her instincts told her to lock it, but she ignored them.

She kicked off her shoes and dropped her gown via the spaghetti straps and began admiring herself closely. Her dress fell to the cold tile floor like a whisper and bunched up around her feet. She cupped her breasts in her hands. At twenty, she was already preoccupied with sagging. She wasn't in need of a bra and refrained from wearing one on most occasions. She pulled her hair straightforward in front of her face with her fingers, let it fall as it wished, and then moved it outward to the sides for effect. It was a personal distraction. It was her way to find sensuality in moments when she didn't feel sensual. Her skin glowed like deep honey from the countless hours inside a tanning bed against the stark white walls and silver fixtures of the tiny bathroom. Rifling through her purse on the counter, she retrieved the lip-gloss and applied a small amount. The light taste of kiwi that was embedded in the wax made her smile. She thought of all the times as a girl when she had savored the wax across her tongue, and couldn't fight the temptation of eating it. Her large almond shaped eyes were common in her province where she was from in China, but uncommon to most Westerners with their mal-formed stereotypes of squinting half-closed sleepy stares. As an Asian woman, she always stood out and she knew it.

She deftly applied a little more black eyeliner. Finally, she crumbled a breath mint between her teeth and checked the shape of her pussy and examined the crevice of her ass for flakes of toilet paper. She had learned the hard way, as all dancers do, that toilet paper glows luminescently under the black-light when on stage. No one wants to find it gliding across the surface of their tongue either. Now, it was just a customary habit of nature. Again, she glanced at the doorknob. There was no sound or movement from the other room. She opened the door slightly to see what Layden was up to but found him leaning against the doorframe of the bathroom waiting for her. He had already begun to disrobe and looked down at Qian's naked body. She looked him over slowly. He stood six-two, pale, his chest hair was white like TV static and he had a personal scent that was as close to Stetson as anyone would ever be able to identify without saying so for sure or having to testify. He wasn't tone, but his torso was supple rather than fat or saggy. For a man of his age, he had been given a little grace in his posture, but it was fading and Qian thought he was now reminiscent of someone's uncle. The chemical aid had restored his confidence, and his eagerness gave everything away to her that he foolishly believed remained secret.

He was no stranger to Qian's kisses. Kissing was the highest form of arousal for her, whether she knew it or not. His fingertips brushed the outer edge of the curve of her breasts. He caressed her lovingly and slowly. It was all in a single pass. He stepped closer and kissed her forcefully, she thrust her tongue into his mouth and began moaning again. They stood together naked, pressing against each other on the tile floor. She was slowly forgetting herself. He placed his hands against her hips and pulled her soft frame into him. Gripping her by her ass cheeks, he lifted her up onto him, she straddled her legs around his waist, and he sank slowly into her. She wrangled herself into a comfortable position as he took her off into the bedroom.

"God," she moaned, "Layden, I shouldn't be doing this," she sighed. She was confused about the sensations. Somewhere in the back of her mind she felt guilt, but it wasn't enough to stop her from indulging in the overpowering moment. He laid her down on the hotel bed and made love to her. When they finished, his mind was completely blank. She was merely agitated and exhausted but they were both speechless, if only for a moment. Qian began laughing as they lay there naked against each other.

"What's so funny?" Layden asked, finally breaking his silence.

"Nothing," she responded. She bounced out of bed and began dressing. She searched her purse for her cigarettes and lit one. "Hand me the ashtray," she commanded.

"What's the magic word?" Layden taunted.

"Now!" she replied. She was sinking back away into herself, realizing the gravity of the moment, sensing her compromise.

"Where are you going, Qianqian?"

"I've got to get home. I have some things to do," she lied. She just wanted out of the hotel. She didn't feel dirty or disgusted, she just wanted to go home and count her money.

"Can I come by the club and see you tomorrow?"

Qian inhaled on her cigarette, pulled the straps of her dress over her shoulders and looked at Layden blankly. "No," she answered. "Why don't you give it a few days before you come back in?" She couldn't help but smile trying to get his cooperation.

"I'm leaving for San Francisco on Monday, for three days. Do you want to come along with me, or not?" he asked. "Why would I go to San Francisco with you, Layden? Don't you have a wife for that?" Qian looked at him with an eyebrow raised as she picked up her money and put it away.

Layden stretched out on the bed casual, and exposed. He rested his hands behind his head and smiled. "I'll pay you three thousand dollars. Is that reason enough? That's a thousand a day. That should more than compensate you for your time away from your club, your patrolman or whatever else you spend your time on. Don't you think?"

"I'll have to think about it, I'll call you tomorrow in the afternoon with an answer." She was already holding the handle of the bedroom door. "You're paying for the airfare?"

"Sure. Why not?" he replied.

"I'll call you Thursday, then." She disappeared into darkness. He listened for the slamming of the door, and then called for room-service.

Qian chain-smoked for the rest of the evening. She was telling herself that she had done well, and that the money would be well spent as she pulled away from the Valet stand in the rear parking-lot of the old hotel. She squirmed in her car seat and felt the wetness starting to ooze from her, slowly being evicted. He had cum inside of her. Nary a condom, foam, diaphragm, pill, patch or surgery. Only Russian roulette was a good enough credo for her to adhere to. Her heart raced from the panic of the situation. She had already undergone five abortions, her first one at fourteen, and she didn't know if she could take another trip to the doctor. She turned up the stereo and opened the sunroof, which she rarely, if ever did. She had been listening to the same music for the last three weeks, and it was still going. She realized that she had compromised 'somewhat' on the rules, but convinced herself that she needed to be flexible. The city lights cast a burning glow up and down the entire boulevard. The street was thick with people on all sides. She looked in her rear view mirror at the tall building she had just left, watching it fade and grow smaller. She thought about San Francisco. She thought about the three thousand dollars, but she never once thought about what she was doing.

Yellow Fever

From a rain soaked world ...

I was stuck inside my Hollywood apartment working on reports when the phone rang. It had been raining all morning and I was locked in due to activity concerning the Los Angeles Marathon. I could hear the combination of pelting rain on the window and the soaking wet runners being urged forward by supporters on the sidewalks.

"Hello" I answered, blunt and cold.

"Can you come out to play?" The voice on the other end beckoned, playfully. It was Qianqian. Her voice clutched at me, I was immediately under some form of mind-control that was beyond my ability to consciously resist. I was one of the people that would possibly kill someone in the deserted street to stay next to her. It was madness, desperation or something that I didn't have a name for yet.

"Of course, Miss Mao" I replied, feeling like I was falling under her spell all too easy.

"How about now?" she asked.

"Why don't we at least wait until we're face-to-face. Phone sex with you can be a trifle one sided," I gibed at her, amusingly. She laughed. Sucked in, I forgot about the large amount of work that desperately needed attention. "I'm turning onto McCadden Street now. Why don't you put your shoes on and come down?" I glanced down at my bare feet and examined myself in despair. Across the room, I caught a reflection of myself in the mirror, I looked like a young Humphrey Bogart in winter. I tussled with my hair. I was still wearing my pajamas.

I had worked through the night once again. I felt madness stirring just below the surface of my skin.

"Why don't you park and come up, it's been too long since I've seen your naked body, I need you ... and besides I have a surprise for you," I responded.

"Oh joy ..." she wearily replied. "Another surprise. I wonder what it could be this time, maybe a kiss ... or something you found laying in the street?" She had grown wise to my schemes and impromptu romanticism. I laughed.

"You're so lucky, Sebastian Raines, there's a parking spot in front of your building."

"Good then, I'll see you in a minute," I replied.

She clicked out, without need to say goodbye. I got up and went to the bathroom to brush my teeth and wipe my face with a hot washcloth. Just as I was finishing, her key hit the door lock. I still had my face in a steaming, cotton hand-towel, but I managed to hide myself, quietly, before she saw me from the hallway. I stood statue-like inside the bathroom. I heard the slamming of the heavy, reinforced fire-door close behind her. I listened to the sound of her wooden clogs scrape across the hardwood floor as she crossed through the small blue colored entryway and into the pale green front room. She was heading for the office, where she must've thought I was working. I crept up slowly behind her, tip-toeing. I wandered through the maze of my apartment trying not to be seen. When I got to the office, she wasn't there. I was a little shocked but now, I was on the hunt. It was only right.

I maneuvered back into the front room and headed for the closet door. I opened it quickly and laughed, she was flinching against the wall wearing a wide-mouth smile and indulging in her own laughable hysterics.

"Aagghh. Damn you!" she screamed between giggles. I stared at her for a moment as I began to fall apart. She glowed a deep hue of tan from inside her white linen dress. Her teeth gleamed pearlescent beneath her large, half-crazed expression. She swore a few lines at me in Chinese as I reached in and socked her on the arm and pinched at her flanks. She tried to run out and escape, but I caught her from behind as she tried to slip past. She became hysterical as I tickled her. Some people have extreme aversions to being tickled, she was one of them. My hands found their way around her curved body, her hips resembling a pear. I had already started salivating for a small, carefully placed bite.

She ran to the bedroom, I focused my eyes on her birthmark about the size of a half dollar in the shape of the 'Black Sea' on her right thigh. It was showing through her thin dress. She ran to the solace of my large king-size poster bed. I jumped on behind her and grabbed her foot. She screamed, not wanting me to tickle her any further.

"Don't touch me …" she bellowed, laughing.

She was on her knees crossing the countryside of the fully-clothed mattress. I slowly pushed up her dress and held onto her shoulder with my left hand, I began my motions to mount her right then and there. The intensity was burning, I was fully consumed. As I rubbed up against her backside, she sighed, as I pressed harder, she moaned. I cupped her left breast in my hand and turned her over onto her back. I slowly began removing my pajama pants, pushing them away with complete disregard. I inhaled and took in the smell of her skin. She smelled of vanilla. She moaned loudly as she lost herself next to me as our tongues met. We kissed like a hundred salmon jumping upstream, with only one purpose. I cradled her head in my hand. As my right hand searched down and felt her, she was wet. From all the hours of drinking tea, my senses were completely dulled, and for that I was a thankful. We made love for what felt like most of the afternoon.

"Would you like to play a game?"

"Of what?" I asked.

"Take your pick …"

"What, like chess, or something?"

"No … not like that," she answered.

"Ohh … I see." She was intimating a game of words. It took a moment. I was exhausted, but I figured it out.

"How about '*most unforgivable thought*'?"

"All the way to the bottom, huh? No '*confessions*' or '*pick your favorite year*'?" I queried.

She pulled the covers over her bare skin and leaned on her side, watching me, happy to see me, smiling.

"As you like to say, everything to lose and so little to gain."

"Why not," I responded. "But you go first."

She bit on her bottom lip to think for a moment, I wondered if she was just dreaming something up to shock me, or if she was actually going to admit her most unforgivable thought that she had in the last day or so.

"Every time I see a homeless man, who's filthy, bearded and bumming a cigarette, I want to have sex with him. It's like an urge that I can't explain. Men fantasize about screwing most half-decent women that cross their path, but I just wanted to put his filthy cock in my mouth."

"Sweet, sweet Jesus. How can I make a move on that? That's putting my senses on 'tilt'. How can I forgive you for scarring my brain with that?"

"That's pretty unforgivable, huh?" she blushed, laughed and slipped under the sheet, trying to pinch me.

"I don't have anything even close to that."

"Oh no. You aint' getting off that easy," her head popped up from under the sheets with a comic-seriousness.

15

"The most *'unforgivable-thought'* I had all week ..." I slipped into silence contemplating something worthwhile. I could've lied and said anything, but it was about being honest, practicing open communication.

"I thought about quitting the department, turning in my badge. Moving somewhere far from Los Angeles."

Qian looked at me with a serious but concerned look. "I don't believe you. You love being a cop."

"If you believe that, then you don't know me as well as you think you do," I sighed, quietly. "I could do without it let's just say."

"You don't get off on carrying a gun, wearing a uniform, having a prowl car?"

"Well ... I've always liked the cruiser. I can't lie about that."

"See," she replied. She was shaking her head at me, mocking me. I reached over and grabbed her, planted my face on hers and pecked at her lower lip like I was meditating against the great wall.

The rain outside fell steady all afternoon, I could still hear the crowd clapping for the runners down on the street. The stereo was washing them out slightly. Tom Waits was playing on repeat, in the front room. We held each other and laid silent for over a half-hour. A love affair is nothing without the comfort of being firmly in the grasp of your partner in the middle of the afternoon. My orange cat, Fuzzbody, was lounging in the window ledge against the wet screen cleaning his paw. He had been watching us, and I felt sad that he had no mate.

I got slowly up off of the bed, Qian laid there motionless. I suspected that she was watching Hollywood moving in and out of fogged obscurity. The wind pushed under the open window and toyed with the curtains. The buildings seemed to melt into the dark and heavily billowed sky for the entire length of Los Angeles. I felt that it was magnificent outside, but I knew the rain just made her depressed. I crossed my rented-rooms and found the kitchen amongst the mess of paperwork, half read books and what not. The kitchen's pastel blue was warm and just being there always increased my appetite. I put the kettle on and prepared the tea service on a mahogany tray. The cat had wandered in and sat in front of his bowl crying about the crumbs, and of course, that just wouldn't do. I made the tea, fed the cat and left for the bedroom.

Qian was laying on her side, smoking a cigarette with the covers off, her eyes lit up when she saw the tea service.

"Oh yes, that sounds good, I could really use a cup."

"Really?" I asked, quizzically. I thought she might have been teasing me, tea was not an addiction to her, as it was to me. I had lived on the Eastern seaboard of England during my formative years as a youth. I attended a public school in a small seaside resort town. Felixstowe was known for its crumbling churches, day-spas run-down theme parks and coin-slot gambling. Through the years many people have remarked upon my English accent, which has always seemed out of place. But tea was ingrained upon me and anyone in my own direct influence. Tea had currency, warmth and familiarity. Tea gave me something while everything, including the day, did nothing but take.

I had also brought us both a shot of whiskey and a side of lemon, which of course, prompted a 'definitely not.'

"C'mon now, sweetheart, old Deep South cold remedy, I heard you sniffing over there ..." I prodded her to take the shot and the lemon. I really just wanted to see her turn pink one more time. I used to think that plying her with alcohol would open her up and make her talk, spill all of her carefully hidden lapses in judgment. I felt she had too many secrets and could've been well-served to loosen up. She was always tense, even if it didn't show. The alcohol just made her more defensive and standoffish. I had never seen it, but I would've bet she was a mean drunk. I believed that was the price of too many unresolved issues and secrets. Her eyes lustily scanned the surface of the lemon from behind the solace of the white tea cup.

"You gotta take the shot, Qian. If you want the lemon, you got to take the shot."

"Damn it, Sebastian. I don't want to." She pulled the blanket up over herself. The sky was getting darker. I pushed the windows down to the half-closed position. Gratefully, all my downstairs neighbors had their heaters on, allowing me to save the effort and money of ever having to mess with mine. It was an antique as old as the building and I never had it serviced. The one time I did turn it on the smell of burnt hair lingered for hours. I spent the next day wiping every surface of the sooty ash that had invisibly covered the entirety of my apartment.

She finally drank the shot. After all, it was only one. "Very good ... here," I handed her the fruit. She bit down on the opened end and sucked out all the juice. Her face didn't ball up into weird expressions like some people's faces do upon the taste of citrus. She had an addiction to only a few things that I knew of, lemons were one, sex was another and I would find out later that lying was a third. Some thing's you just never see coming, although it does help to keep your eyes open. I took my shot and ate my lemon whole. The rind, having more vitamins than the actual fruit itself, was something I never shied away from.

"Care for a game of chess?"

"You can't be serious?" she asked, between sips of tea.

"Why wouldn't I be? You've been playing so well lately."

"I never win when I play you."

"Do you always have to win to enjoy it?"

"Probably," she answered. I set the up the board in front of us, using a few books to steady it from underneath. I behaved predictably and opened textbook e4.

"How was work today? Was the club busy?"

"Ugghhh," she groaned. "I don't want to talk about it. Would you like it if I asked you to tell me why you like being a cop? Or whose privacy you were violating today?"

"I hate being a cop," I replied, looking straight at her.

"Really?" she responded, curious.

"I've never really fit in with the other boys and girls, so to speak. They're some pretty useless excuses for a collection of dried turds."

"Ouch, that's rough."

"I'd never violate your privacy," I answered with a wink.

"You can violate my privacy anytime, Sebastian."

"Not much use violating your privacy on the payroll, but I do have some thoughts about violating you elsewhere …"

"I bet you do."

"So, answer the question. Do you like being a stripper? I've asked you this many times before and I always get a different answer."

She looked at me again with a glint in her eye. "You know I hate stripping, but it's hard to say no to the money. It's even harder to walk away after you've been sucked in."

"Tell me about your shift," I volleyed.

She relaxed gracefully, chewing on her lemon, tossing the rind down on to the tray. She had already memorized several openings, knew two ways to checkmate in under thirty moves and understood that the Knight was vastly more powerful than the Queen, a lesson most people don't realize until after several decades of playing. At first she was reluctant to believe this, until I played against her without a queen for quite some time. She always preferred playing black as she found it fashionable, and was always happy to allow you to go first.

"Ok, fine, I'll just drink my tea." I kept quiet, knowing better to back off. I messed with the fading creases of my dry-cleaned pajama bottoms and stared into the board deeply.

"I did thirty dances. They were all two-for-ones, so I really did sixty." She sipped her tea and met my standard Pawn opening with a textbook response of developing a knight.

"What did you leave with?"

"Take a guess." She was now playing with me again, as usual.

"I'd say around seven fifty, eight hundred".

"Nope. Guess again," she sipped.

"A thousand even," I ejaculated. "I wouldn't be surprised if it was more, though."

"No, but you're getting closer."

"Twelve and a half then?"

"Very good, twelve sixty. I'm glad I went in to work, that's a lot of money for one day."

"It just depends upon what you gave back in return, I guess." As much as I was being silent about the obvious truth of her activity, I tried my best to only be subtly aware. Madness is sometimes easier to wear warm than the cold reality of truth. I advanced a Bishop.

"Dude, this guy I was dancing for was wearing jeans and he wanted me to grind on him really hard. My pussy is really sore now, never again. No more jeans."

"Never say never," I laughed at her. I lost myself for the moment in the comfort of the cotton sheets and down pillows that adorned my king size bed. I leaned against the headboard and searched for the cigarettes.

Qian grabbed them from my hand, "Get your own," she insisted.

"Why should I, when I can just smoke all yours?" I responded. I had known Qianqian for almost four years, she had been stripping for two, and I had seen her change. For all the *good* there was, she had been moving into some very obvious *bad*. I didn't think that she was seeing any of it though. The forest through the trees was on fire, and no one suspected a thing. She moved in on my side of the board aggressively hoping to make me sacrifice pieces early. She loved having the advantage, even if she couldn't hold it for twenty moves.

"Some of my regular customers came in. Layden came in again. I pulled him into the booth and kept him there for ten songs." While she continued talking, my heart sank a little upon hearing that name.

"Are you planning another trip with him?" I asked her, hoping that she'd say no.

"He asked me to go to San Francisco with him for three days. Does that bother you?"

I didn't know how to answer her. I relaxed my mind for a moment, trying to let it all pass. I sipped my tea again, the water was extremely dark. It had fully steeped.

"Are you mad at me?" she asked again, with a slight hint of insecurity.

"Of course not, Qian. I just wish that he wasn't a factor in our relationship. It's just a bit too creepy. It just doesn't make me feel right. Besides, he's older than both of our fathers," I laughed.

"You have nothing to worry about. There's no sex involved between us," she said. I looked over at her with a raised eyebrow, but she missed my meaning. I was readily accepting of her lie, which she ham-handedly put down for me to digest.

"He's going to pay me three thousand dollars just to spend the weekend with him up in North Beach." I took her Queen from her, leaving her in bad shape. I began wondering if she was trying to play a Pawn game against me, trying to stall me and wear down my attention span. I tried hard not to think about her with other men, and so I instructed myself to believe her. When you witness someone lying to themselves, it seems obvious to you that no good can come from it. When you start lying to yourself ... well, that's just a whole other set of sad circumstances.

"Why can't you understand that it's just business? Falling in love and having a relationship are two different things" She remarked, sharply. I said nothing, and this just made her more infuriated and defensive.

"Ughhh," she grunted, "I don't know what your problem is!" She rolled over and set down her empty teacup on the side table. I moved the chess board off the bed and set it out of the way on my side table to finish later.

She had her back turned toward me. The cat popped up onto the side of the bed and sat in front of her staring at her in a way that almost seemed confrontational. The cat had his own thoughts. He was like the great bodhisattva from the East, all knowing, all seeing, everything but amused. He treated Qian like he knew her well. It was that way from the first. But that's not saying that the animal was fond of her either.

I took a sip from my tea and sat it on a Conan-Doyle volume that she had picked at a flea market. I began kissing her back and pulling on her foot. Most women have a certain amount of self-consciousness concerning their calves. Qianqian of course, was no different. All it took was is a single comment or even just a touch to spark a bad mood. I began to kiss her on the inside of her calve.

"Mmmmm, … soft calves." Silently, I felt like Hannibal Lecter.

"I hate my calves," she replied automatically, it was almost a knee-jerk reaction. I kissed her tattooed string of flowers. I slowly began caressing the outside of her thighs. I then buried my face in between her legs. She moaned and arched her back at my touch as I licked her. She was clean-shaven and wet. She began making even louder noises, I tried hard not to laugh. The splendor of any woman moaning at the slightest touch is an interesting and rare experience. I was fortunate, and I was smiling from one side of the room to the other. She arched her head upwards and back, moaning as I slowly took her over. I rode her in that position for twenty minutes. I was playing matador, she was playing bull, or rather cow. Her moaning was guttural and continuous. She bucked me and became louder than I had ever heard her before. She pounded on the pillow and screamed my name out. I was beginning to get scared, but I laughed a little, nonetheless.

She came three times. The first and second time I could actually see and feel her coming, the third time I just felt the same muscular contraction. The final time I had told her

22

that I was about to come. I thought she had finished, but she ordered me to hold out because she was coming again and she wanted me to wait until she was completely through it. She was being selfish not letting me enjoy it, but I had grown used to it. She was a victim of the 'Dildo Culture' that had unnecessarily desensitized her to real sex. She was probably more interested in imaginary sex and masturbation then having a partner.

Holding off and controlling ejaculation is probably one of the most difficult tasks for any man to accomplish at any time or any age, regardless of the situation. Most women today don't appreciate that fact. They just want to wait for the tail-end of the reclension to start again.

I rolled Qian over onto her back and positioned her legs against her chest. I pushed back into her (very carefully – with softening penis) and grasped a hold of her breasts. She began laughing again, of course I couldn't help it, the more she laughed, I laughed.

"Why are you laughing?" she managed through her own laughter.

"Stop laughing," I answered, barely, "I'm trying to finish."

She kicked me off in a hysterical fit and I fell over the side of the bed unable to stop. I hit the floor hard, but we were both still laughing. My leg was tangled up in the bed sheet. When she saw me get up off the floor, she wasn't laughing.

"You're not hard anymore?" she blurted out, both surprised and unhappy. I couldn't stop laughing now, and I had lost my train of thought, so to speak. She grabbed her cigarettes, jumped from the bed and ran to the toilet. I listened to the sound of her feet crossing the old creaky hardwood floor. She moved as if she was responding to a schedule. I moaned in frustration when I realized the episode was over and I didn't get to finish. I did a few push-ups on the spot to channel my energy elsewhere. Most of the time, I couldn't watch her while having sex, her mouth would make an expression as if she was grasping for air and her eyes would roll into the back of her head. It was too exhilarating. I found solace in picturing the grimacing face of Gene Hackman. If I had been able to patent the idea, I could've made millions. I would've called it 'The Gene Hackman Method'. I admitted defeat, got up, got dressed and was proud that I had done my country honor, at least in figurative terms anyway.

She was dressing now in the hallway mirror. She watched herself as she threw on every piece of clothing. In my mind, she had been in dress-rehearsal all day. It didn't take her long. Within a few minutes she was ready to leave. She was singular amongst all women in that regard. She looked striking at every turn and needed no preparation.

"I'm going home," she stated, without any other words of explanation. I glanced at my watch. It was just after seven. Her words gave me chills, I was feeling abandoned.

"You're not going to stay the night?" I asked, pleadingly. I could sense that she didn't want to. She wouldn't and I knew it.

"No, but do you want me to?" she answered, ambiguously.

"Of course I do, I was hoping it would be just the two of us alone tonight." I was tying my shoe, sitting in the darkened front room.

"I've got things to do at the house, but you're welcome to come over." Her words made me feel like an afterthought. I wondered why she couldn't find a little sensitivity and just ask me to come over first.

"I'll come over with you," I said, quietly falling into the trap and releasing a little more of my control.

"You want to follow me in your car, since you have to work in the morning?" she asked.

"Sure," I answered. "I'll follow you."

I had been working on the force for three years. I only spent a year on the streets. I was promoted to a highly classified post, listening to cell phone conversations on top of Mount Lee at the old antenna display. I spoke three languages fluently: Arabic and Korean. The department either valued me or didn't trust me. I could never decide which. The department is everything that it's cracked up to be concerning its Internal Affairs. I didn't mind being a cop, but I never felt it in my blood. It was probably more accurate to say I didn't mind collecting a cop's paycheck. I had family on the force who had carried a badge their whole lives and never thought or wanted anything else. From birth, I had wandered from one servitude into the next. I had joined the Academy during my last few months of enlistment in the Marine Corps. After the Persian Gulf, I felt another uniform might help me keep my sanity. Looking back, I thought it was the most natural thing to do in the world, but I should've joined the Post Office. After so many years, I had slowly developed a distaste to being a subordinate. There was always too much room for insubordination. Most of the time I just couldn't relate to bureaucratic thinking patterns and their inertia-infected reasoning. The need to crush another under the weight of a supposed success to obtain an obtuse, oblique goal that internally never had merit, had absolutely no curb appeal for me at all. I had little interest in Managerial Statistics, and it probably would've been better in the long run to develop '*The Gene Hackman Method*.' Most of the police forces around the country operate under these systematic and antiquated modalities of non-thought hoping to achieve peace through force, or rather nullification through over-stimulation. Good luck. To me, it just seemed like another bad John McTiernan movie come to life.

Moonlighting is usually an officer's only escape and it pushed me to seek the refuge of higher ground. I had been writing a column under a pseudonym for the *L.A. Weekly* newspaper for six months. It was a free trade press that found its way into small red boxes around the city like clockwork every Thursday. I never gave myself a name, I just described myself as an appendage pointing myself directly at celebrities and local officials spreading gossip and nefarious accusations. However, both entities had no idea I was working for the other. It was a precarious position to be in, one wouldn't allow the other. After all, it was only gossip that I was publishing, but it was in direct violation of my agreement with the Federal Communications Commission as laid out by the regulations in conjunction with the L.A.P.D. '*Under no circumstances would any information derived from the activity of monitoring private citizens be repeated to any outside entity in any form of communication whatsoever*', and so on and so forth. Signed documents to follow ex post facto.

When most people look up and see the Hollywood sign in Los Angeles, they might think of the symbolism that it stands for: actors and actresses, production sets, the history of movie-making and so on. A few people take note of the structure just above it and to the right, wondering what it really is. Fewer people know what the structure is used for and most would cry constitutional infringement if they did. Having to shorthand all conversations heard and recorded, I became an adept and voluminous writer. The Police Academy had made me engrain *Gregg's Shorthand Manual* into my brain. Later, I found it to be an excellent tool for stream-of-consciousness writing. The kind that either makes you a good writer, a bureaucrat, or a kook. I had been writing for the magazine for only a short time, but the article I wrote was well received. In the beginning, the staff always questioned my information but would be astonished when the same information would surface elsewhere within a week at another publication or on television, and usually in a much more 'progressed' form. Having the heads up by a whole week in the media world is solid gold. My response would be something about journalistic integrity or a saturated look that implied 'Sorry,' or 'Yes, I am related to Stonewall Jackson.'

Little by little, they stopped questioning the source and just ran what was written. Time would bear out the truth. Was I ashamed of taking advantage of my fellow Americans and trampling their constitutional protection to privacy just to pay my rent and squander it over drinks in *Boardners Bar* on North Cherokee? Absolutely not. Most of the people I published information on not only deserved it, but probably craved extra press. Did I actively make an executive decision about that though? Everyone was fair game as far as I was concerned. Lenny Bruce had once stated that in this society, everyone's ass is up for grabs. It's an unfortunate but balanced truth. It's the American Way.

Qianqian sped along, and I followed behind her, having some trouble keeping up. The drive into Burbank from my house was almost thirty minutes with traffic. She could always do it fifteen. I watched the red taillights of her BMW 735i move in and out of traffic as she slipped like mercury between speeding cars traveling North on Highland Boulevard. The back end of the BMW is pleasant and classic. It's almost sexual and pleasurable to stare at. I could see her silhouette lighting a cigarette through the darkened back window. I began working on the congruous task of making anagrams from her license plate. 2LVA666. It was a tough one. To love a demon, a devil … to live like a demon? I just couldn't tell. She pushed through every amber light unflinching, and even went through two red ones. I gunned it through both just to keep up. I wondered if she was trying to lose me. She would criticize me later for driving dangerously. It was a given. She was doing sixty in a thirty-five.

I settled beside her at the next light. Rain began to fall across my windshield. I looked over and watched her talk intently into the telephone. Her posture was unbecoming, hunched over in the seat. From my vantage point it looked as though she might be gnawing on a piece of leather. My mind drifted back to my unfinished writing that I had left on the desk and open on the computer. I couldn't remember saving it. I had told myself too many times to bring it with me regardless of where I went. I could see that she'd be on the phone again, most likely for a large part of the night. She was probably canceling plans that I was unwittingly trampling on. I listened to the radio, a song by *Steely Dan* that played earlier in the afternoon, came on again. It was the lyrics that caught my attention the second time around. The singer said:

You'd been telling me you're a genius, since you were seventeen,
In all the time I've known you, I still don't know what you mean.

I chuckled when I realized the song made me think of her. Even the name of the band seemed appropriate. The cell phone on the seat beside me rang. I thought that it was Qian, but from the caller ID, I could see that it wasn't.

"Pronto?" I answered.

"Sebastian?" Abbey, ex-wife. I exhaled.

"Good evening, darling. How's things?" I asked.

We had been separated for almost nine months. Our relationship had failed because we had just both stopped trying to keep it together. More self-fashioned servitude. Sometimes it's harder to do that, than to just walk away. She had pushed me away as time passed and I stopped coming back. I eventually fell in love with someone else. I had mixed feelings about the way things had ended between us. We had a solid love together, which was as well-formed as any could be, but the differences were far too great. She came from a traditional Korean background - Buddhism, family restaurants, over-bearing parents, financial schemes called *Ket-dongs*, (or Joy Luck in Chinese), church meetings three times a week and sacrificing your life for your parents poorly constructed whims. Her family was lost in a country with less footing than the one that was left for a dream that never panned out.

I wandered the earth alone from city to city my whole adult life. My independence was too great for a matriarchal culture where the women run the show, without question. There was still a great deal of love between us, but we weren't about to start trying to salvage anything. Especially not after I had fallen in love and had sexual relations with her best friend behind her back. Having done the unthinkable, I was immediately written off by her as untrustworthy and barely tolerated. Abbey despised me, and I deserved it. She was still concerned for reasons that are usually too difficult to explain rationally.

"I haven't heard from you in over a month, Sebastian. I was a little concerned about you." I had to tread delicately with her. She was still stripping in the same club as Qian, but she had gone down to part time and was spending more time in her job as a tarot card reader at the Psychic Eye in Venice Beach. Abbey had worked as a stripper two years longer than Qian. Abbey always made good money, and it had eventually influenced her long time friend from High School to do the same. Qian had always told her that the work was demoralizing, prostitution and everything else, but through the years I realized that Abbey's price for her job, wasn't as high as I had originally thought. Qian, on the other hand, went much farther than Abbey and for a whole lot less, but that was the shape of things in the stripping business. Qian had practiced on me, as her first customer, when I was still married to Abbey. She gave me her first lap dance in my front room on the sofa. It became a moment in my mind frozen forever, and most-likely the impetus for everything that was to follow. Some religious scholars would say however that it's just remnants of a previous life repeating itself one more-time for the camera, with the same actors again and again. When I saw the expression on her face when she touched me, my mind became hideously pregnant with envy and desire. In chess, it's called Castling. Covert sacrifices made, both large and small.

I followed behind Qian as she passed an enormous billboard of Jay Leno that was attached to the NBC building where the show was broadcast, pre-recorded.

"Doing good really," I answered. "On route to a friend's house for a little while. How's everything with you? Still stripping at the club?"

"Yeah, I haven't walked away from it yet. It's hard working with Qian. Every time I see her I want to punch her in her smug fucking face. She's such a cunt. You have no idea." I pondered that last statement inwardly. I laughed a little to ease the tension she was creating between us.

"I really figured that one of you would have quit by now to tell you the truth. Just from sheer tension alone," I feigned my ignorance, sheepishly. Abbey knew we had previously slept together, but she didn't know about my relationship with Qian and Qian wanted to keep it that way. I also didn't bother to tell Qian that Abbey still called me. I was playing both sides dangerously, and reluctantly.

"She's going to have to quit first. Not me. She keeps giving me these stupid looks all day. I swear it's going to come down to blows. It's just a matter of time. Everyone in the club hates her anyway. They all know that she's fucking her customers in the booth." The images ran through my mind of her being fondled and fucked by strange, unknown men. I swerved in and out of a few cars. I slowed behind Qian as we passed an accident where a motorcycle lost to a minivan at the corner of Olive and Buena Vista. People were looking on from the stoop of the Mobile gas station. The Police and the ambulances had yet to arrive. Qian slowed as she passed to get a good look. Within moments I was doing fifty again behind her. I realized that she was a psycho behind the wheel - and would probably die behind the wheel. I would never mention it to her myself, but I'm sure that she'd tell me one more time before the day was through how reckless I was.

"How's your so-called anonymous job at the paper going?"

"Everything it's supposed to be when nobody knows your real name," I answered. I noticed the scambler light blinking to the adapter on my phone, all Department issued equipment. Someone else was now listening. Work checked up on me often, if for no other reason, than just to listen. That was the dark truth of surveillance. While I was listening to the thugs, someone else was listening to me.

"So, what are your plans?" I asked, looking to change subject. Hanging up would be too suspicious.

"I'm flying up to San Francisco on Monday for the week. I'm going to a gallery opening with a friend."

"Be careful that you don't run into Qian and Layden."
No sooner had the words left my mouth had I regretted
uttering them. I thought for sure that she was going to grill me.

"Yeah, I don't want to run into that whore, I'd just
embarrass her. Maybe if I see them, I'll take pictures and mail
them to his wife."

"Some unresolved tension, and bruised feelings?" I
asked, relieved. Thankfully she missed the opportunity to lay
into me over it. She did suspect the two of us, I could tell.

"Nah ... well, just a little maybe," she laughed on the
other end. The scambler light went off. I was only a block
from Qian's house on Scott Road, when she turned into the
parking lot of the *Ralph's Grocery Store* on San Fernando.

"Hey, I'm here, I've gotta go. Call me sometime?"

"Okay, take care of yourself, please eat, I know how
you are." Ex-wives know your habits better than your own
mother.

"Yes, dear," I quipped. Just as I put the phone down, I
pulled up beside Qian's car. She had stopped in the back of the
lot and was still on the phone. She was staring into deep space,
oblivious of me. I stared at her, waiting for her to
acknowledge me. When she finally did look over, her
complexion was glassed over. She was nodding her head
slowly, miles away from where she was. Finally, she hung up
after I had waited for what seemed like an eternity. I rolled
down my window on the passenger side, she rolled down hers.

"I've got to get some tampons and stuff, okay?" she
announced.

"You're not starting are you?" I could hear the
desperation in my voice. I was definitely snagged and
pussywhipped. For any man it's a sad state of affairs and not a
good position to be in.

I roamed the isles, selected some import beer from my
country of origin, some cat food, and stopped at the magazine
rack. Qian had gravitated to it every time like a small moon
lost in space, finally finding a passive orbit. I never
appreciated magazines for their pulpy substance, the glossy,

empty longing that they created in the souls of young women the world over. It was abominable. The magazine stand was where the disease of gold-digging begins. It's just a more popular delivery-system for feminine greed. No one could ever be what the magazines asked. No matter how hard - all would die trying, just to find a miserable, breathless crash upon the wheels of subscription. Her phone rang once again, and I couldn't help but send her a disapproving look.

"Andrew," she grunted, unhappily, and then shut it off and smiled at me. There was definitely a first time for everything. I moved in closer. Something instinctive took over, I pushed her magazine aside and kissed her. She placed her hand on the back of my neck and when I pulled away, she was looking at me as if I was crazy. Maybe it was her? I couldn't tell.

When we got to the house, it was still and a little cold. The heater had been off all day. When Qian saw her mess one more time, she huffed "I really need a maid."

"I thought that was why you were seeing me? I come early and clean real good, cheap too!"

"Promise?" she asked, seeking clarification of my point.

"Don't know the meaning of that word," I shot back at her. She hit me on the arm.

I poured a hot bath a little later. A nightly ritual that we had shared from the very beginning of our relationship. It was the most natural way to dissolve into sex, sleep and the end of the day.

"You don't need to worry about Layden or Andrew, Sebastian," she answered, opening up the subject herself. I tried hard not to bite at it. I just continued with my task of gathering up towels and washcloths.

"Don't I?" I asked, falling in head-first like a fool.

"No, I just said that you didn't."

"I'm glad, Heiness, that's very reassuring," I quoted a line from *The Princess Bride*. She hated the things I loved. She was aware of my sarcasm and I knew it. Qian was now staring at me in a very disapproving sort of way. I sat on the edge of the tub with my feet in the water gauging the temperature as it filled. I watched the yellow sodium bicarbonate soap ball, spin and dissolve in the bath water. I was shocked that it wasn't jasmine. Every item in her bath-tub arsenal was jasmine scented. I surveyed the territory and counted twenty-three bottles of different shampoos, conditioners, body soaps, facial scrubs, deep pore facial cleansers, etc. I shook my head at her excessive and overtly American nature. I once told her that she reeked of condescension. She got pissed off at my remark and made me recant my position. She never delved that deep into the meat of what I truly meant. I always wondered if this was her attempt of "getting it off". It was like something right out of Macbeth. It gave me chills.

"Have you ever read Macbeth?"

"Is that the one with Mel Gibson?" she answered. I gave up.

She came down beside me and sat in the same position. She was naked and her leg were pressed up against mine. I touched her hand, and realized at that moment that I felt trapped inside that bathroom. I was her prisoner and sought confirmation, wanting her to touch me. I wondered in that split second, how it got to that point, that place, that deep?

"I'm now open for Confession," she said, musically. Another bathtub ritual. "Your sins first, then mine." She was staring at her toes in the water and groaning from the heat. She had painted her toenails black again.

"Baby ..." I laughed.

"What?" she looked me over. I watched the desire in her eyes swimming towards me.

"You know damn well that I've been living a confession free life since I've been with you. You know all my secrets." I grabbed the loufa sponge and submerged it under the surface of the water. She leaned forward and kissed me on the cheek with her eyes closed. She slowly placed herself in the water, making noises the whole way down.

"Ohhhh ... my God, it's hot!" "ah, ah," and so on.

"Please, it's adequately hot, stop fussing."

"And what exactly does 'adequately' mean to you then?" she asked, curiously.

"That, perhaps, it could be just a little hotter?"

When she was all the way in, she farted and giggled. She was the gassiest chic that I had ever laid eyes on. She farted every chance that she got. I always felt that she needed more meat in her diet. She had a paranoid disposition regarding meat and starches, although '*Sizzler*' was her favorite restaurant. I left it alone for my own good. I had told her that we hadn't climbed to the top of the food chain eating vegetables. She didn't find it amusing. She thought my argument was antiquated.

Candles flickered in the other room behind me. I got up and turned off the bathroom lights and turned on the antique wall heater. It cast a reddish glow across the white tile walls before I sank back into the water.

"I'm not bothered by Layden at all, Qian, really. It's just what he represents."

"Meaning?" she plied.

"Meaning ... that I wish you didn't have to see him at all." I had something on my mind, but was unable to force the words out of mouth.

"You don't seem to understand and I don't want to talk about it."

"This is so predictable. May I ask why not, Qian?"

"Because, Sebastian, you're pissing me off."

"Ok," I gave in and resigned myself to shut up. She quickly became defensive and retreated further inside herself, the one place she felt safe. Having me on the outside was preferred. I sunk into the large tub and soaked while she scrubbed herself. I watched her cross the entire surface of her body with a sea sponge. She went through the familiar process of cleaning her face with several different products and then gradually slipping down to soak beside me. I thought she was going to continue the conversation, but she just remained

34

silent. I knew that if I pushed it, there was bound to be either an argument or me leaving in the middle of the night to go back to Hollywood to spoon with Fuzzbody. It's not that I minded leaving on principle, I just didn't want to. I was reluctant to disturb the status quo and become the enemy.

I watched her as I rested in the warm water. She began tapping at the hair on my leg with her razor, watching it slowly come off in small clumps. I wondered how far I really was in this with her. Deep down though, I already knew. She spat water at me and told me that I was finished. I washed my face and got up from the tub.

After I found my robe, I made my way into her office. I opened the drapes and sat down on the leather swivel chair and looked out the window. I didn't turn on the lights as I wasn't in the mood for anything so illuminating. I had seen enough for one night and sat quietly by in the dark.

Outside the tiled patio was lit by moonlight, I noticed that the vines crawling up the bricks that we had planted earlier in the summer looked weak and needed water. The sound of the stone fountain in the center of the yard, just below the orange tree made me close my mind for a moment and relax. I leaned back and reclined, putting my feet on the stool. I lit one of Qianqian's *Stone Forest* import cigarettes that her father had brought her from China. I had tried for a long time to quit but without having another habit to replace it, I knew that I was doomed to addiction. I thought for a few moments about the words 'stone' and 'forest'. An image of a cemetery loomed up in my mind from the sketch on the front of the cigarette pack. I wondered why any one would've chosen that name. It seemed almost obvious. I felt like quitting immediately. My concentration that had been affixed on my assured demise was broken by the sound in the bathroom of Qianqian pulling the bath-plug.

"Sebastian …?" she called out from inside the tub. I could hear water droplets sliding off her body.

"Yes, What can I do for you?" I answered her. I almost didn't even hear my own voice. She soft-footed across the floor and sat on my lap. She was still wet, but wearing the towel. She cocked her head to the side and began to slowly brush her hair. I watched her do this for what seemed like ten minutes. Her hair was always badly tangled, and in need of rescue. She had removed her contact lenses and had on an old pair of glasses that looked as if they were a style that was popular in nineteen fifty-two and purchased from a plastic turn-style rack at Woolworth's for a dollar forty-nine. I slipped my hand inside the robe and placed my finger on her belly button and kissed her on her exposed breast. She watched me, but didn't say a word. She kissed me back and I finally felt as if she had registered me as a separate presence, outside of everything else and all the bullshit. She usually treated me with more kindness after a bath. It was as good of a feeling as any to end the day on.

From a dimly lit restroom stall ...

I strolled into the offices of the LA Weekly on Sunset Boulevard. The office was just around the corner from the apartment. The place was under the spell of a dull hum for a Saturday morning. I waved at the Mexican girl answering phones at the front desk. She just smiled and continued talking on the phone in Spanish.

I made my way up the stairs and on to the editing floor. Saturday was the day that I had picked to work on the column. The one day that I would have to contend with the least amount of people possible. The publication hit the streets on Thursday morning. The 'regulars' were still enjoying their days off. The remaining eyes followed me as I crossed the carpet and headed toward my desk. My work space was was completely absent of the usual junk and detritus that cubicle heads would surround themselves with. I had no family pictures, pen cups, name tags or manuals on editing, or style. I kept only a dictionary in the drawer and I chose to write everything on a 1961 Underwood typewriter. The sound of the old machine made my associates look at me with curiosity as they involved themselves at their PC or Mac's reading chain letters and searching through free Asian porn sites. Qian had secured the typewriter months earlier for me as a gift. I kept it locked in the large bottom drawer with an extra spool of ribbon on standby. I was always graced with a bag of mail from readers of the article and a few post-it notes from my contemporaries. I looked down and thumbed through some of the letters, I was only interested in the writing on the envelope and not what was in them. Only when I saw a truly remarkable sample of handwriting, would I investigate the letter further. It may have seemed elitist, but there had to be a process.

I began to block out the distractions of the office around me. Movie posters littered every inch of wall. Fuzzy, Disney-esque animals and knick-knacks abounded around in chaos thanks to the cubicle heads.

Writers can be a tremendously pretentious group of people once they start getting paid for their ability. The pretentious ones compete at out-doing each other with their far-out individualism. Every Gen-X'er seems to believe that the pinnacle of intellectual elitism is to be folded into the quickly expiring baby-boomers hippie sub-culture like it's the underground old-boy network. Far too many times these young lemmings would believe that the secret code of admission was their dress code, which was slacker centric or post-punk and not their frame of mind. I'd thought on several occasions how much fun it would be to put a signed photo of old Tricky Dick Nixon on my desk, in plain view. When I contemplated getting a General William Westmoreland nameplate made, I realized I'd probably gone too far with it. The worst kind of person is the one who builds a montage around their work station, generally spending more of their time doing that, than actually being productive. Officers in the department are exactly the same way. Straight shooting, rookie officers collect pictures and articles of boring statistical crime data, each one trying to be more intellectual and seemingly cluttered than the other. I live in a dichotomy - a pool of people crying out trying to find themselves amongst their own work but lost upon some ever-useless endeavor that takes them further away into oblivion.

I rolled my thick bond paper into the machine and started banging away at the keys. The fingers had to get used to the smaller keys. But after a few moments, I pounded the latest gossip into the page, sheepishly. I felt the guilt, like sweat run down my back and I felt the eyes of my contemporaries, unattuned and unaccustomed to the noisiness of my device. All the readers wanted to know what the real truth was. It was all about feeding more paper into the aged beast who had become my friend and the way I was paying off my student loans. I was just looking for an easy way to make money. So far it was working. '*I am not a crook.*'

After an hour or so of editing and retyping, I disappeared with my twelve perfect pages into the latrine, where I felt more comfortable locking the door and making all the phone calls necessary concerning the submission and the content. I've found that public bathrooms make wonderful offices if the stall is equipped right and the foot traffic is minimal. The lighting in a public shitter happens to be a little more carefully thought out than the lighting in most general work areas. The restroom lighting is always at a lower wattage to give the feeling of being relaxed, unless of course, you're in Wal-Mart where it's always glaring. Shitting is all about the comfort. This is of course, being key to having a successful movement, or even a few moments away from your work associates.

Before vacating the premises, I engaged myself in a little light poetic reading, scribblings left behind by my cubicle headed buddies. The only redemptive piece was the simplest:

'*Please keep the gasket between both holes.*'

'*The space shuttle blew up due to a faulty gasket, ours are for when you do.*'

Below that, a different hand had written in an addition: '*Gaskets are for assholes.*'

I capped the pen and put it away, satisfied.

Yellow Fever

From the back of the stage ...

       The club wasn't open yet by the time she got there, but the backdoor was already unlocked. Jose, a young Mexican boy that had been hired by the club to watch the parking lot and collect three dollars from the customers for parking, was putting on a red vest and getting ready to sweep up trash from the night before. Qian pulled her small, black travel bag with wheels from the trunk of her car and headed inside through the backdoor.

       At first glance, the club, from the outside didn't really look like much at all. Just a small dark gray building, three quarters of the way down the block, surrounded by machine shops, unfinished pine furniture outlets and storage warehouses. Most strip clubs in North Hollywood are easy to find and usually conveniently located. You wouldn't have to walk too far before bumping into the next one. As time passed, the clubs became more and more prevalent. Strip club franchises moved into the neighborhoods in groups, like pawn shops, liquor stores or laundry mats. Most had names like Gentleman's Club, Gold Palace or harbored an endangered species that roamed the African plane in its logo.

Qian took her usual seat in the back-room next to Erykah, who was eating left-over Chinese food from a Tupperware container. Erykah was completely naked, smelled like cocoa butter and the Nag champa incense that was burning beside her. The room was a mirrored vault with round, white light bulbs; like the kind you might see backstage in a theatre. Several plush velvet couches and multi-colored chairs adorned an area below the mirrors forming a sitting room. There were a lot of cast-off and half-filled cups and beer cans from the night shift girls.

"David really should pay his Mexicans more money to keep this place clean. If the customers saw this place with the lights on, they'd be horrified and leave."

Erykah was the only black girl that worked the day shift. She was stunning to look at, mostly behaved herself, but had an attitude that oozed out from underneath her that was darker than her own shadow. She had been a fashion-model in New York for several years and had near perfect curves, lips, eyes and delicate soft skin. She had no problem getting past David's cold demeanor when she applied for the job that was always posted in the paper, as the club was *always* hiring. Girls, willing to get completely naked and make a spectacle in front of every man in town including their own fathers, were always a valuable but copious commodity. But at some point along the way, she had decided that smoking weed was more important than her modeling career.

The club was run by an Israeli, David, who didn't much care for black girls. He tried hard to keep them out of the club, but Erykah was the exception. Saying that he was a racist was putting it lightly. He was very selective of the girls that worked the day-shift. Most of the girls were forced to work nights, clocking in at four in the afternoon to deal with the multitudes of cheap dollar-laden dregs that wander through the plastic car-wash blinders over the front-door addictively to perv-out and observe, but not spend any real money. The best money for the girls was in the day. It was a sure bet. Local businessmen and entertainment executives would usually come in for the 'lunch buffet', spending twenty's and hundred's in exchange for a repetitive addiction. The best money for the club though was at night, it was just a numbers game after eight pm. Ten dollar admission, three dollar parking, and a two drink minimum were pretty stead-fast recipes for success.

"Well, Erykah … I don't think the men are coming in for the décor."

"Don't fool yourself, Qian," she said between mouthfuls of noodles. "We're nothing more than another piece of furniture, honey. We're just one more thing for those greasy bastards to put their filthy junk on." She got up and stood next to Qian, looking closer into the mirror at blemishes that weren't on her face.

"This place is a pig-sty though, we're just the rotten fruit in the slop, baby. And this carpet, it always feels like it's wet. That's how really nasty this place is."

"I know what you mean."

"Who said this place is nasty?" David came through the dressing room from the back-door entrance. He had his hands full of black plastic cases, and was being followed closely by Rullo, a bald Armenian man, who shadowed him everywhere he went.

"Good morning, Qian. Good morning, Erykah. Make me some money today, okay girls?"

"Hello," the two girls answered in unison, but quickly bored. He slid off into his office though the main room of the club and closed the door. Several other girls filed in and got ready to go on the floor by eleven, despite the ten-thirty opening. The girls had often protested about starting so early, but David didn't want to hear it. Ignored, the girls had pressured the DJ to come in fifteen minutes late everyday and take his time in setting up. The money he made directly from the club was only a dollar per head for every John that came through the door so he depended heavily on their tips. He was in no position to refuse them.

Qian turned off her phone, put her purse in her locker and secured it. The girls that had already showed up were in no mood to start dancing. Several were sitting together closely on couches, smoking cigarettes and gossiping about last night, their boyfriends that they were supporting or another dancer. Strippers, throughout time, have had an unnatural habit of supporting men in their non-successful ventures, whether they were musicians, meth-chefs or movie extras. Most girls will tell you it just seems like a curse that comes with the job. Common men seek common girls that they can take home to their common parents in some common small town just to prove how different they've become. Strippers, hookers and troubled, dope fiending ex-fashion models were not the kind of girl you'd want to make that trip back home with. Qian felt that she was better off than most because Sebastian worked and supported himself and wasn't looking to take her back home anytime in the near future. It would've been easier though if she had felt the same way about him as he did about her. She didn't love him and she wasn't upset about it either.

Abbey came in with the DJ and had disappeared directly into the bathroom as soon as she saw Qian. They hadn't spoke in almost two months and the feelings brewing between them became more intense with every passing day. Qian and Brittsy had tried very hard to convince David to not let Abbey work the day shift any longer, but he wouldn't be pressured. He would also do absolutely no favor at all for Brittsy, who he considered to be washed-up, white-trash. He teased her every chance he got because she lived in Sunland, a part of Los Angeles reserved for low income, mid-western transplants that were either methamphetamine addicts, prostitutes or the out-right homeless. The problem though was more to do with cold hard reality, than it had to do with white-trash Brittsy, who had just pushed the cusp of forty-five years, and was trying hard to keep whatever white light that was shining on her focused. Abbey consistently made per shift, more money for the club, without breaking the law than any other girl. For David, it was impossible for him to agree to her ousting.

Qian's reputation amongst the other girls wasn't very good. She had already been accused of stealing their customers away, which was *rule one* of what you never do in a hen house. Fucking men in private booths, and cheating the club out of money were number two and three. Breaking any of them would usually result in consequences. Several of the girls had already stopped talking to her, one had keyed her car and another, as a final act, had poured a mop-bucket of dirty water on her when she was dancing on stage. The atmosphere between Abbey and Qian, was the most intense, was quickly coming to a boil.

Britts had been standing in her transparent platform heels and dark-red panties with her face jammed into the receiver of the dressing-room pay-phone, talking loudly to the phone company about her interrupted cell-phone service. She was hunched over, inhaling cigarette after cigarette, trying to get the service restored without a deposit. She had neglected to mail in the bill for the last three months.

In the main room, the music began playing, the clock on the wall read ten-forty-five, and David was already prancing around the dressing-room, checking out his day-shift inventory. He and Abbey had gone out to the parking lot to talk, smoke a cigarette and get information about a girl who had gotten drunk and passed out in a booth with a customer during the fiasco that was the night before. Abbey had the most charming personality of all the girls and had worked at the club the longest. She was the most motherly and understanding, and she rarely, if ever, stopped smiling. For this and a few other reasons, David had put her in charge of the girls shortly after Qian and Brittsy's coup had failed. Officially, she was just another dancer, but unofficially she was the Madame. Most of the girls not only understood this, but preferred it. All the girls except two. Abbey was a darling, and this irritated Brittsy to no end. She couldn't even stand to look at her. All the problems that any of the girls had, went through Abbey first and then later filtered forward to David.

By the time she and David had come back in, Qian had already found a seat in the back of the darkest area of the club. She had hid herself in darkness, veiled by black vinyl booths, black velvet drapes and diminished lighting. The single red eye of her cigarette was the only sign that someone was there. On the dance list, she was fifth out of six girls to get on stage and perform. Dancing was the part of the job that Qianqian hated most. She had often said that if she *'didn't have to dance on stage, it would be the perfect way to earn money.'* For every reason that came to mind, putting herself on display felt demeaning, and with or without clothes she hated dancing.

She sat quietly with her legs crossed and watched the second girl-of-the-day, Abbey, perform her set of three songs. Abbey was wearing an all-white, fringed, thong bikini that barely covered her goods at all. She had loosely draped a see-thru white shawl around her and was wearing calf high boots, which normally would've come off during the second song had anyone been in the club, but no one had yet walked through the door.

Abbey rolled around on the stage on her back, slowly moving her hips and kicking her legs in the air, and finally slipping off her panties to Isaac Hayes' *'Walk on By'*. Abbey was dark-skinned for being Korean, big breasted and voluptuous. If she had any fault at all, you might think she was stocky, but that would be too cruel to go that far. Someone had once told her that 'her body was built for pleasure' and she never forgot it. She was the quintessential woman that most men fantasize about and have advertised to them in men's magazines or old-school adult films. She had a nicely shaped round ass, that jiggled just enough, and in all the right places. It was her shining attribute as an Asian female. She had proportions in spades.

Her 'stage show', as it was known, was one of the best in the club. Both the girls and the customers were usually mesmerized. Customers would take the girls into booths for private lap dances at either twenty or twenty-five dollars per song, depending on the day of the week. The club collected eleven to fifteen bucks back for each dance and during a usual shift, the typical girl would get anywhere between fifteen and twenty dances. Abbey would always manage at least thirty-five dances, but would make a lot more in tips. Abbey usually left the club holding five to six hundred dollars a day, minimum. No other girl in the club save Britts, then Qian, in that order, made that much money regularly or even came close.

Britts had the worst reputation of any girl. She was blamed squarely, for corrupting Qian. To everyone, but Qian, it seemed obvious. Brittsy had been caught buying drugs in the parking lot, selling drugs to another girl in the dressing room, soliciting customers in the booth and arranging rendezvous outside of the club, thus cheating the club out of a lot of money. The club frowned on the girls meeting the Johns out of the club for private shows. They saw it as theft of their clients and impinging on their profits but they couldn't do much about it, except for firing them when they'd had enough. Most girls could usually get away with it if they kept quiet about it. Problems became apparent when the John's would show up and not spend money, drop them off and pick them up after their shift or a litany of any of the many tell-tale signs that the club kept tabs on.

David was always on the brink of letting Brittsy go. He knew that she was one more police-raid away from being history. He had even made up his mind to point them in *her direction* next time he was faced with the prospect of the police in the club. The money that she brought into the club as the number two earner was the only thing that kept the door open for her in the morning. She had also decided, for her own best interest to work five days a week. Her money probably paid for the lights and the air-conditioning. One person's nightmare is another person's nightmare with mixed drinks, AC and naked women. Brittsy's was just the extended version.

After Abbey was done with her set, she vanished backstage, but judging from the looks on the girls faces sitting around the club, any one of them would've quickly paid the twenty bucks to take her back into a private booth for awhile, smooch, get it on or be entertained. Several other girls went up and slowly but surely, men started appearing magically on the club floor. It wasn't as if what was going on inside the club was a secret, some days it just took longer for kick-off than others.

The first two 'targets' that wandered in off the street should've been stopped by the bouncer, George, who had still not showed. Rullo was behind closed doors in the office and had been ever since Abbey's set ended. While there were no hard and fast rules on dress code, wearing work bibs, being covered from head to toe in sheet rock dust and spackle dabs should've been red-flags for a hard and fast eighty-six bounce-out. Several of the girls wanted nothing to do with the two Mexican day-laborers and wouldn't even acknowledge them when they made long leering gestures at them. They looked as if they had just walked off of a job-site to drink soda and stare at naked women. Brittsy however, didn't need an invitation. Boldly, but coyly she approached them and put on her scared pussycat routine she saved for desperate, end-of-shift stragglers eager for something, just as long as it was naked and wet. She stuck her butt out, arched her back, put her hands on her knees and bent over while slowly gyrating her body to the music above, with a look on her face of wantonness or ecstatic pain.

"Do you want me?" she begged, wooingly. They didn't answer right away, which Britt took as a good sign. She didn't even bat an eye, or wait for a response. She sat between them, loosened her top and picked up a hand that belonged to the older of the two, who was on her left and placed it in her bikini top on her titty, and let him rub her nipple. She handled the man's appendage like it was some inanimate object that had been lying around absently, collecting dust on her coffee table at home.

"Sure, okay hon-neee," he blurted out. Then as quickly as it began, she disappeared with him into the most remote booth in the back of the club, next to where Qian was sitting, hoping to keep him in there for as many songs as possible, no matter what she had to do.

After awhile, Qian had to pick up and move due to the racket Brittsy was making in the booth, getting it on with the Mexican day-laborer. After hearing the sounds of what could only have been him coming out of his clothes, pounding her relentlessly from behind and the statement from Brittsy's mouth: *It's a hundred dollars more if you want to stick it in my ass,* was more than enough for Qian to get up and move to another empty part of the room. She had noticed that Abbey was sitting with an elderly Italian gentleman that usually came into see her once a week. She had her arm around him, and was tapping his knee with her index finger and happily telling one of her stories either about church, her sisters or another girl in the club. All that, of course, after an introspection into the way she felt about herself which would illicit a counseling conversation with her elder patron, making him feel useful and coming back for more. Rarely would there be a lap dance, rarely would they ever disappear into the booth and rarely would he ever give her anything less than four hundred dollars. Alphonso was one of Abbey's regular's, and she worked hard to have them all come in on separate days. Most of her dealing that afternoon was spent out in the open, on the center couch in the middle of the room much to the bewilderment of all the girls and David included, doing nothing more than talking and occasionally laughing. Making money hand over fist in the most unorthodox way, in one of the most unorthodox places.

Qian was relieved, when Layden appeared beside her out of nowhere.

"Oh, thank God you're here. I was getting ready to fall apart, leave or set the damn place on fire."

"Are you alright, darling? What on earth is the matter?" Layden asked, exceedingly polite and well-mannered. For a sixty year old, no matter how he behaved, he always came across as an over-polite, socialitic baby-boomer until he took his Viagra.

"Well, I'm better now that you're here. Just another day in Fantasyville," she sighed, resigning.

"Have you given much thought to what I asked you the other night, regarding San Francisco?"

Several of the girls eyed Layden hungrily, dying to pry him from the clutches of Qianqian. He reeked of money, more than any other man that had ever walked through the doors of the *Industrial Strip*. From head to toe he was outfitted in twelve thousand dollars plus, and on him it looked normal and inno way out of the ordinary. He had told Qian, after visiting her several times in the booth that he worked as an investment banker in Encino. The mundane repetition of his day consisted of pouring millions into well-qualified, high-tech start-ups. She knew that he was married, had been most of his life, had several children, a few Qian's age, which had given her the creeps and made her feel inadequate and remote.

He also spent a large amount of his time traveling, which was the most attractive facet of who he was to her. She had a feeling of restlessness that had strangely brought her into the club in the first place. It was the same feeling that allowed her to give into him. Frequently.

"Can you get me a drink, Qian? Got to keep up appearances, y'know."

"Sure."

"Meet me in the back, usual place?" he queried.

"Actually head to the other side of the room would you? Booth 14."

"Something up?"

"No, Britts is in our booth with some construction worker."

"Sounds riveting. Are they replacing the carpet?" he joked.

"Probably. See you in a second." Qian paid for Layden's two drinks from her own money and headed back to the booth, closing the door behind her and sitting down beside him. *Bono* was moaning away in the background about wearing a velvet dress, the moon being a Mirror-ball and God knows what else.

"On your lunch?" she asked.

"Of course."

She moved in around him, and sat on his lap facing him, holding his glass of coke and slowly letting it wet his lips.

"Did you already eat?"

"Of course," he repeated. She slowly untied the bow holding her bra top closed. Her breasts fell out and he could see that she was already aroused. Although the air-con was going full blast making her nipples firm, he didn't suspect that it had nothing to do with him.

"Feel like having some of me for desert?" she quizzed him, smiling and suggestive. He began massaging and suckling on her titties while she slowly grinded away on his lap. He became rock-hard beneath her within a few seconds. She pushed her tits into his face and wrapped her arms around his neck. Layden moved his fingers past the elastic of her panties and began toying with her wet underside, slowly beginning to finger her, Qian moaned quietly in his ear for several minutes as she let him play with her. Layden kissed her neck softly, as his fingers reached deeper into her, soaking her underwear. Pausing, she quietly and subtly removed them and placed them on the bench. Qian moved back towards the door, in order to block anyone from peeking over the low cut saloon doors as Layden quietly undid his pants, and pushed them gently down around his ankles. She moved in, put her mouth around his member and slowly worked around in his crotch while he laid there and enjoyed himself. When the next song began, she got back on his lap and engulfed his penis inside her and slowly began riding him. This was now the pattern of her day, anytime Layden came to the club. She felt powerless to resist him and the longer their afternoon visits continued, the less she felt that she had in common with him and found it more difficult to keep a good conversation afloat. After several minutes, her knee-jerk reaction was just to resort to sex. She turned her head as George, the floor bouncer walked by. Thankfully he failed to look in the booth to monitor what was going on. Maybe he did and she just didn't see him looking. Most likely, he just didn't want to know. Regardless, she would find out from him later after Layden was gone and he would wag his thick head at her disapprovingly. After an hour of playing around with each other, they slowly dressed, talked about San Francisco, and he paid her two hundred and fifty dollars.

"Is that all you're giving me?" she asked dumbfounded and stupefied.

"Sorry, Qian, that was all I brought in. I didn't think we were going to ... you know?" he responded, sheepishly.

"Ughh," she grunted. "Then why did you just conveniently come in with a condom, married man?"

"Look, I'll make it up to you in San Francisco. I promise." After she settled down, and accepted it, he kissed her, headed for the bathroom and then left. She was thankful to have made the money and didn't mind having sex with him either. She just knew that it was better if she kept it to herself and told no one, especially Sebastian. He was suspicious of Layden, and rightly so, but she wasn't going to give him an inch to work with. Her having sex with another man wasn't any of his business.

After Layden had left, she had gone to the toilet and cleaned herself. Thankfully he had worn a condom, so there wasn't much to clean up. Her new plan for the day was to rest for awhile, maybe have a cold drink and smoke a few cigarettes. After a good twenty minutes or so the DJ nodded that she was third on the list and would have to go up in about fifteen. This meant that she couldn't pick up a guy and head into a booth until *after* she performed a stage show.

Qian quietly primped herself and waited for her name to be called before going back out. When she heard her name, she slowly made her way out of the dressing room and up the ramp. Unlike the rest of the girls, Qian didn't see the point in using a fake name. Abbey's name wasn't Abbey, Erykah's wasn't Erykah and Brittsy wasn't Brittsy. Being not bold, but stupid and reckless didn't seem to phase her. She always thought that no one would ever find out about the life she chose and if they did who would really care?

She glided easily out onto the stage like the unmooring of a virginal vessel getting ready to mount the tide. The music rose and moved slowly across the room. The patrons, who by mid-afternoon were twenty-odd strong, lingered upon the periphery of the stage. The commitment of sitting down in the front row, on stools, was a sucker's game and would turn any well-dressed spender into an immediate mark, who would probably spend more money on soda than girls.

Qian was snugly fitted into her thong bikini and a dress made up entirely of small mirrored tiles. The lights above reflected off each small piece and sent thin beams out across the expanse in search of attention. She grabbed the pole, spun around, wrapped it around her left leg, leaned back and slowly slid to the floor. As the music continued, she meticulously undressed piece by piece, her top, then her panties, all the while trying to remain calm. As she moved around, swishing her hips and flipping her long black hair to the side, she became short of breath and had difficulty keeping pace. Nervousness was slowly overtaking her the longer the song played. Her hands trembled as she pulled the long black feathered boa between her bare crotch, and then gathered it up in a ball around her breasts. When the song ended, as instructed by law, she quickly left the stage, replaced her thong panties and returned to collect up the single dollars and the few fives that littered the stage. Los Angeles Municipal Code forbade any girl picking up money on stage in the nude, as that was considered prostitution. The L.A. Board of Supervisors must've worked all night on that one. A few of the men clapped, but a dull murmur of talking stirred the dense cigarette laden air, as if something coming was to be expected.

"Let's welcome back to the stage, for her second song the lovely and luscious … Qian!"

The DJ played Foreigner's *'I want to know what love is'*, as requested by the dancer. On queue, Qian traversed her lithe frame once more to the music, removing more clothes and massaging herself stiffly and visibly trembling to the point of obvious and uncomfortable fear. Slowly, her muscles hardened and her joints locked-up. The look on her face went from calm to absolute horror. Several faces in the crowd started to show their surprise at the obvious strain besetting the fair and sensuous paid underground ballerina. As she moved around the area of the stage from the pole to the center, she wobbled on foot, trembled further and suddenly fell hard to her knees. It was a routine that Abbey and the girls had already seen unfold several times a week. A couple of the girls grunted in disgust and half-heartedly tried to conceal their laughter. No matter how long she danced, she would usually stutter and fall and then spiral out of control on a regular basis. Her movements became robotic and she prayed for the song to end. Every set of eyes in the place was transfixed on her aberrant behavior and trying to figure out exactly what it was that they were watching. The sympathy in the air was palpable. Abbey rolled her eyes in disgust at the display which she saw as nothing more than cheap antics in order to receive attention and make quick money. Even before the song ended, naked and crawling off stage like a stroke victim or an extra in a zombie movie, Qian just wanted to get out of sight and be able to breathe again. Her chest was constricted and heaving, tears had welled up in her eyes and were now beginning to flow down her cheeks. She couldn't bear to go back out there and round up the second batch of dollar offerings, which now scattered the stage in great abundance like rose petals. Even the thought of having to perform a third song was now completely out of the question. Brittsy appeared beside her, bent down and wiped her eyes.

"Holy cow, Qiannyqianqian, it's alright, baby. You'll be okay." She held her for a few seconds before disappearing quickly out onto the stage as a replacement to collect Qian's pull. Struggling to light a cigarette behind her trembling hands, tears and sobs, she caught David's reflection in the mirror shaking his head at her in frustration.

"Just so you know, Qian. This isn't a circus. Whatever you're doing out there, it needs to stop."

"Fuck you, David. I don't give a damn," her voice cracked. He understood in that moment just how messed up she really was. He had once thought it was an act, but now knew that she was falling apart.

"What the hell is it? Fear of failure? Daddy beat you too much?" he asked. She ignored him and didn't feel his taunting justified a response. "It's probably your ego. You probably think you're too good for this job, but you keep coming in anyway. You should probably get it in check."

"Talk to the back of my ass, you fucking terrorist!" Brittsy interrupted. Qian was nonplussed over her meltdown and David's ranting.

"Here … now go calm yourself for ten minutes backstage and then get back out there. I swear to God, I've never seen men salivate so much in my life." Britts shoved the crumpled bills into Qian's hands and went out on stage as Qian was introduced for her third and final song. Brittsy was next up anyway, and didn't mind a few extra minutes out of the booths.

By four in the afternoon, quitting time, Qian had long forgotten her embarrassment of the earlier hours stage show. She had drifted away mentally taking John after John into the dark confines of the booths. She had stopped worrying about Abbey who had been able to post more dances on the tally board than her as usual, and with only half the number of men. She quickly wondered if Abbey wasn't better suited to be a lawyer rather than a stripper with all the talking she did. In the course of three and a half hours she had performed thirty private dances and as usual, Brittsy had showered several times during the day. She had gotten cross looks from David when she emerged from the booth in the morning with her ass covered in white sheet rock-powder and sweat. Qian was beginning to wonder if Brittsy's pussy was made of rubber rather than flesh as she had seen her disappear into the bathroom on two occasions carrying a box of *Summer's Eve* douche. All one could do was raise an eyebrow at the spectacle of the thing.

When enough girls from the evening shift began showing up, she decided to slip away with her entire earnings before she was forced back onstage for yet another miserable self-constricted suicide. 'Never leave without tipping out in the cash-cage' was rule number four and grounds for dismissal, but she didn't care. She peeled out of the parking lot, after slipping past Jose and just missing David's clutches in the doorway by mere seconds.

From the freeway, speeding ...

Qian white-knuckled the steering wheel of her car as she wedged in and out of traffic while discussing flight arrangements with Layden on the cell-phone. Traffic was moderate, if not standard, for Saturday afternoon. She was traveling South, through Laguna Beach.

"I'll fly up Monday afternoon and I'll stay until Wednesday, no later."

"Why can't you stay until Friday?" Layden asked.

"I can't, Layden. I have plans. Besides, staying until Friday would be a whole week and that would be five thousand, plus my airfare. Do you still want me there until Friday? Or do you have to check with your wife first to make sure that you can spend the money?"

"You're really not that funny, Qian."

"I'm completely serious. That's life, so deal with it." Qian's face contorted into a weird smile as she inhaled from her cigarette. She checked herself in the mirror. The bloodshot eyes were a clear indication of needing to have some rest and relaxation. Her eyes hurt adjusting to the new contact lenses she had replaced earlier in the morning. Up until the previous evening, she had left the last pair in for over three weeks and had been suffering behind the same deteriorating prescription for the past eighteen months. She was ashamed to make her Optometrist appointments because she had been overly flirtatious with the Doctor during her last visit. He was young, smart, Chinese and everything her parents would've approved of. Unfortunately, he wasn't interested in her at all. As was her custom, she hadn't worn any underwear under her dress and after she had caught him looking a few times, she had decided to splay herself which made the man run from the room in a nervous sweat. The one time she called for an appointment, the receptionist said they were fully booked.

"I'm spending the rest of the weekend with my parents, so don't call me until I call you from the airport. No exceptions, do you understand?" she spoke to him seeking his submission and wanting him down where he belonged. Manipulating Layden was an easy task to her, although he never really resisted. As long as he knew what he was getting, he was compliant.

"What happens if I get lonely, Qian?" he asked, boyishly.

"Deal with it," she blasted clicking out on him without another word. She focused her eyes on the highway in front of her. The afternoon sun was gold across the edges of the trees and the sky was a clear and light blue. She passed a steady stream of Harley riders on her right that were all pacing each other at seventy miles per hour. She rolled down her windows and waved at the men who were all smiles from under the beards, leather, and in front of their tired blonde wives. Some of them waved or honked, a few of the women flipped her off. One showed a tit. She sped up to over ninety passing everyone on the road. She merged over to the right and took the off ramp into Del Mar and downwards to the beaches. She was late for dinner but her parents expected no different. She traversed down the PCH watching the surfers lining the road. She wanted to jump out and blow through a few rolls of film of all the half-naked men emerging from the water with their surfboards, but the camera body was empty and without a soul. She drove by drooling at five miles an hour, gawking at the boys stripping off their wet-suits next to their parked cars. She thought she was a purist and had failed to switch over to digital, resisting it at all costs. It was in this moment that she regretted it.

Later, when she pulled into the subdivision where her parents lived, she was astutely aware of the difference in life-choices that she had made versus most of her friends and her parents. Everything in suburbia was different. She could feel it moving through her like a bolt of electricity. The rows of identical houses and manicured lawns made her shiver. Her parents had absolutely no clue as to what she really did for the money and she preferred to keep it that way. She had told them, as she had told everyone else, that she was a documentary photographer and that she was involved with the Los Angeles Times Travel Section. Nobody questioned her story, but her parents always wondered why their daughter never got credit for any of the photographs that were in the paper. Her usual stream of lies usually began with the whopper that she worked in lay-out and editing, and that it would be a few years before she would be able to put up her own stuff for consideration. It was adequate cover for her with her trips to Morocco, Costa Rica, Tibet, China, England and the large amount of disposable income that she raked in. She had no qualms spilling bold face lies out to her mother, but she could always see suspicion coming from the eyes of her Father.

"Ni Hao!" She announced as she walked through the door. She wondered if they had eaten without her.

"Ohh . . . Ni chile ma?" her mother, Su Ying announced as she floated over to greet her at the door as she entered. Her father greeted her with a smile from the kitchen tending the soup. "Come, come Qianqian, we waited for you," her mother suggested, helping her with her bags.

"I thought Sebastian was coming with you. We made food for the four of us," her father, Chen, spoke slowly and never seemed to be upset or in a hurry.

"No, I had to leave him in Los Angeles, he had to work."

"That is too bad, we haven't seen him in several weeks. I was going to have him translate some French for me."

"He's not French, dad," Qian wagged her head, disgusted.

"Oh … I thought he was French this whole time."

"I kind of wanted to have some peace without him for a change," she sighed. "May I be so bold and ask what we're having?"

"Your Mother has made some bao zhu and zhi tang. You can help set the table."

The soup smelled of onions, cabbage and chicken broth. Qian ignored her father for the moment and walked out onto the patio to pet the cat that her parents had to adopt from her. She had almost starved the poor animal to death from neglect when she had it in her apartment in Los Angeles. Her parent's house was a mix of eastern things scattered along the walls and western furniture covered in every kind of colored cloth imaginable. The sofa was 'decorated' with three different clashing fabrics, each one a completely different texture. The room looked like a Patrick Nagel nightmare come to life. Several prints and random pieces of art hung in peculiar places throughout. Chinese calligraphy scrolls, embroidered lions, and pink and blue art deco paint splotches all filled the same space. The whole house made you feel as if you were probably better off if you were wearing ray-bans and a white fedora.

"Hey, Scooter!" she scowled, as she picked the cat up in a swoop by the chest. Scooter dropped the bug from his paw that he had trapped against the concrete and hadn't yet decided to eat. Qian sat down with the cat and lit another of her Stone Forest imports, she got in a few strokes on the cats head before he shot off growling in disgust and fear of the cigarette.

"Qian . . . help your mother, please," Chen asked her again, in the exact same way he did the first time. She was fortunate to be the only child.

"Is Li Anne coming over from China this summer?" she asked her father, remaining motionless, smoking. She became still and statue-esque in the garden chair.

"She said that she wants to come over and spend the summer with you. Haven't you spoke to her on the phone? I'm sure it is a good excuse for you to spend a few hours on the telephone," he responded, laughing to himself amongst the cutlery as he ladled out the soup into three bowls carefully. "Now ... stop posing for the magazine and help."

Qian put out the cigarette, walked in and sat in the nearest chair to the patio door. Her mother looked at her and laughed.

"Is everything good with your work? You didn't call all week?"

"Yes, mother, I'm going to San Francisco on Monday to photograph the St. Francis Hotel. I'll be there until Wednesday. I'm getting paid three thousand dollars for the job, so I'm going to do some shopping too. Should I get you anything?"

"Maybe you should begin to save some of that money, instead of buying used German luxury cars with 100,000 miles on the odometer, and seven hundred dollar raincoats?" her Father suggested.

"Who told you I bought a seven-hundred dollar raincoat?"

"Your Mother found the receipt on your bedroom floor last week while running the vacuum."

"Mom! I can't believe you told him!"

Her Father guffawed at the extravagance, "So, for seven hundred dollars, does the coat give you special powers or something?"

"Maybe I should go to Mexico next weekend for a few days, instead of sharing my weekends with you, Dad. What do you think?" she responded. She made sure to smile after she said it and look cute. The remark cut deep, but he said nothing more to her about her finances for a few minutes.

Her mother wisely changed the subject. "Did your father tell you that he wants to buy a motorcycle now? I think it's so dangerous to be driving on the road with all those people, so easy to get into an accident," her mother spoke with caution and trepidation at the thought of it.

"There's absolutely nothing to worry about. You just have to watch were you're going," he rang in, smiling after sipping his soup. He watched Qian carefully from across the table with an expression of curiosity. Qian reached over, grabbing a fluffy white bao, ripping it open, exposing the red, porky heart. Examining the dumpling, she thought of Sebastian in that instant, and laughed.

"What is so funny?" her mother asked. Qian didn't even look up at her to answer. "Mother ... you don't want to know."

"So ... Qian . . ," her father continued. "Exactly when will you be finishing your last credit of college and getting that degree? I wonder why, every day, you stopped one credit from the finish line."

"I just haven't had any time, dad," she sighed, as she ate her bao. "What am I supposed to do ... drop everything?"

"Sometimes ... it is the smallest things that have the greatest importance in life. Whether it be a grain of sand or a single elective for a foreign language requirement. That's truly the way it is, you must know that."

"Next semester," she replied. Chen turned to Su Ying, "She said that last year, dear." They both chuckled as they slurped their soup. Qian joined in with the slurping, loosened up, and laughed with them.

After dinner, Qianqian moved cautiously around the two-story house looking for things to accomplish. When she had finished washing the dishes, which her parents sat at the table and watched her do in awe, she wandered upstairs to the office. The small room that was made smaller by painting it blue, was littered with foot and back massagers, three different computer workstations and walls of books, journals, and medical texts. She began checking her email, but she thought of the wooden stump that she was carving into a face downstairs on the patio. Her eyes rested on the chess board on the far end of her battered and cluttered desk. The game had been interrupted with her having an advantage for a change. Three moves from a mate. Rook moves up one, bishop to the center and the knight to close. She considered it an obvious attack and would be better executed in the opposite order. Sebastian was a better player, more aggressive and rarely lost; but he did make impulsive decisions at the wrong moments, which was usually all she needed. Having a clear victory in sight made her smile, even if it was slight.

　　Her cell-phone rang, interrupting her thoughts on the game. She ignored it after looking at the caller ID, it was Andrew again. Persistent as always, she turned it off. He probably would beg her to come back to Los Angeles and pose for her in some elaborate but boring set that had too much to do with fruit, her being naked and him getting high. She had no desire to speak with anyone outside of her parents, including Brittsy. They never expected that Qian would ever move back home, but they had prepared a permanent room for her just in case. Inspired, she left the office and went looking for her camera. Her old Minolta sat on her clothes dresser that she had since high school. She had used the camera when taking classes at the community college. The camera had thousands of rolls through it and in every mechanical action was loose. She loved it for all its flaws and would probably never part with it.

　　Refreshed and now smiling, she was pleased to see that the camera still had a roll of film in it. She ran down the stairs and wandered back out into the yard, past the un-carved wood stump, and began setting up her tripod to take a few exposures of the sleeping cat. A single ray of sunlight had found its way along the concrete and stopped just short in a point at the tip of Scooter's nose. The cat languorously faced East during every nap he ever took. Her father had noticed the cat's compass like qualities.

Qianqian's mother came out and sat in the steel garden chair with a cup of tea. The cat poked its head up and watched Su Ying for a very long moment. She waved at the cat and smiled. Scooter yawned and went back to sleep, but did so with one loving eye on his beloved mother. Su Ying gave him milk in the mornings, and she was the one that fed him the fish paste and the chicken pieces. He gravitated towards her every opportunity he could. He stayed away from the younger one with the burning stick in her hand. That much, he had already learned. Qian listened for any noises coming from the neighborhood, but there was nothing. No barking dogs, no sounding horns, no traffic intersections or even children yelling in the street. She thought that maybe this was why she loved spending time here; away from the over-crowded city, that always held the constant flow of life in every inch of the eye.

"Oww," she mumbled in pain. She forgot about the bruises on her knees from dancing on the stage. She blocked out her most hated task in the world. If she didn't have to dance on stage, she knew that she would love every aspect of what she did and never seek another career until her looks went. She stood up, brushed the grass from the knees of her jeans, and started singing under her breath.

"You look very pretty today, Qian. Why did your boyfriend not want to be with you on the weekend? That doesn't seem right." Her mother always spoke with a sense of curiosity when it came to her daughter. She knew that Qian was very cautious about what she told them and that had only made her father suspicious.

"I don't know what to say about Sebastian, Mother. He seems to be in his own world most of the time. I don't know what his deal is," she answered, continually messing with the tripod and looking through the lens. For a second, Qianqian stopped and reconfirmed in her own mind, that she had used Sebastian's name and no one else's. He was part of her cover.

"He adores you, I can tell. That should be pretty obvious to you, no?" she said, prying at her. Qian was oblivious to her mother's deceptively subtle ways, although it ran in the family.

"Whatever," she answered. She snapped off five or six shots in the matter of a few seconds. She didn't see her father sit down in the chair beside her mother. They were both watching her carefully, not in a suspicious way, but in a way of admiration of their only daughter, the person responsible for carrying on the family blood-line. Qian finally looked up from the camera and turned back around to face her mother. She jumped, "Agggghhh." and screamed when she saw her dad. He laughed at her.

"God, Dad, you scared me!" He said nothing but continued laughing at her. Her mother smiled.

"You always were a very nervous child. You still are. What are you afraid of, dear?" her mother asked, in a mockingly concerned tone. Su Ying sipped her tea with the same loud slurp she made while sipping her soup.

"No, I'm not, I'm not afraid of anything," Qian adamantly disagreed.

"Ohhhhh, please be careful now," her father spoke to Su Ying, touching his wife lightly on the arm. "Qian may want to put this one to a debate."

"But it's not true, Dad. I swear it," Qian proclaimed, smiling with her hands on her hips from behind the Minolta.

"Let me remind you when you were only eight, you were always so afraid of riding over dog droppings on your bicycle, that you would run over it anyway, even though you'd try so hard to avoid it. I could always hear you from ten feet away saying 'Ohh no, dad, there's dog stuff coming up', and then you'd get it with both tires. You never failed to run over it." Her parents were both chuckling hard and trying to sip their jasmine tea. Qian walked into the kitchen past them shaking her head, remembering the events. Looking for her own cup, she started the kettle.

"I was just very afraid of dog shit dad, that's all," she answered from the kitchen. Her mother turned around in her chair, now getting in it herself, "And you know why that is ... aww?"

"Don't even go there, mom. I've already heard this a million times."

Chen turned again in his chair, to speak to his wife, glanced over at Qian who was watching on through the patio glass, "Do you remember how bad she smelt when they brought her home that day?"

"Awwww" Her mother exclaimed, "I was so embarrassed that my daughter would ever play in the horse manure. She had it all over her. I never got the smell out from her dress." Her mother looked back her daughter who was leaning against the counter with her arms folded, shaking her head.

"Please ..." Qian tried to act disinterested. The water quickly boiled, as the kettle was already hot. She poured herself the water and placed in a Lemon Zinger teabag from the cupboard. Her mother used fresh tea leaves, but she kept a box of Qian's favorite processed American tea in the cupboard, special. Chen stood up, leaning against the patio door and popping his head in the kitchen, and spoke. Qianqian knew the punch-line was coming from him.

"You know, Qian, I've never said this before, but I have to tell you ... that you really are the shit!"

Qian laughed with both of them now, she punched her dad in the arm as she carefully carried her porcelain cup out onto the patio again. Scooter was sitting up, facing all three of them now. As a girl in China, Qianqian had once played in a pile of horse manure left by the police patrols in the town square, thinking it was dirt for her flowers. A neighbor, who was shocked at the child's behavior, had brought her home.

"Gee thanks, dad. I feel really special now ... maybe, next week ... I will go to Mexico," she announced, then turned to her mom. "And mom, dad is definitely not allowed to have a motorcycle. Okay?" her mother shook her head in agreement. "Yes, Dear. Very true."

"That is between your Mother and me, Qianqian. You will see me riding on the freeway in the opposite direction next time you're coming down," he advised, poking her in the arm now as she stood next to him.

"Dream on, Dad," Qian told him. She looked away and walked over to her wooden stump, which caught her interest. She knelt down beside it, and placed her tea down on the warm concrete. The summer sun's rays were now filtering off, but they were becoming longer as they stretched across the yard the later it became. Her father sat back down. Qianqian put on her carving gloves, picked up the small chisel that she had left sitting beside the stump and began chiseling away. She forgot about the Minolta.

"What are you digging for?" her father asked, looking in the opposite direction. His tone had changed and the words caught her attention directly. His voice sounded like he was issuing a challenge.

"What do you mean by that?" she asked. Her mother looked over at her now, with a raised eyebrow. Qianqian was now staring at her father confrontationally. She realized that he was talking to the cat that was sniffing something in the dirt. As the realization of that washed over her, she looked away and began chiseling.

"I think he was talking to the cat, Honey," her mom confided.

"Artists are said to know what it is already that they are in the process of creating, even before they have finished," he answered, in a much gentler voice.

"And where did you read that, dad?" she asked, in an unfriendly tone. Chen and Su Ying both acknowledged that they were getting under Qianqian's fur and winked at each other.

"I didn't read it," he replied, with a smile.

"It sounds extremely flaky first of all, which artist told you that then?" she continued carving away at the wood block.

"Your current boyfriend told me that. I found it profound enough to remember it." Chen had emphasized the word *current*.

"Ah-hah! I should've figured, it is absurd, and I'm not surprised that it's something out of Sebastian's mouth."

"You two having problems, are you?" Su Ying asked.

"Sebastian is just more ... politically difficult, than he is a problem, Dad. You just don't know him as I do." Qian was pulling a splinter of wood from out of her stump.

"That is very vague, should I ask you to explain that?" her mother toned in.

"No!" Qian responded. "Definitely not."

"He still working for Police Department?" her father asked.

"Yes, of course, why wouldn't he be?" she replied.

"Whatever you do with your life Qianqian, just remember - do whatever makes you happy. Whatever it is." Chen was going into uncharted territory, but his intentions were honest all the same.

"Whatever," she repeated. "Can we not talk about Sebastian, please?"

"You cannot be happy with yourself, doing something that either you or others may find disintegrating to your soul and your life. If your friends cannot respect what you do, then surely you will not either, whether you realize it or not," her father spoke slowly and with confidence, but he seemed to be thinking of something else. Su Ying was nodding her head and making sound in agreement. "Aww-huh" Qian knew that no matter how old she got, her Father would always lecture her about her life.

"Why do you say that? What are trying to say, dad?" she asked, stopping her carving again.

"Only because it's true." He was becoming more animated and louder again, but he was still exuberant to be talking with his daughter.

"He's not bad as far as boyfriend's go, Qianqian. He is definitely the most patient with you," her mother pointed out, knowing her own daughter as well as she possibly could. "I'm still confused as to what happened with his marriage to your best friend? That is a sad thing to say in the least."

"What can I say but, we're in love, Mother. He needs me and I'm there for him."

"That is the nicest thing you've said about him all day," her mother stated for the record. The sun was going down and the tea was either cold or gone. Her father wandered inside without saying a word and disappeared up the stairs. He told his wife in Chinese that he was going to do some work on the computer. The cat popped inside and disappeared under the couch.

Qian and Su Ying went back inside too, and moved through the house turning on the downstairs lights, the television and finally closing the screen door to the patio. The cat appeared by the edge of his bowl, looking in at the emptiness. Qian pulled its tail and drug the poor little guy across the linoleum.

"Hungry? You little fucking bastard," she whispered to it, not letting her mother hear. She held the cat by the head, but he was trying to wriggle away. He finally gave her a disinterested and a very low growling meeoow.

"Are you feeding the cat, Qian?" her mother asked, innocently.

"Sure, I am," she replied, peeking over the kitchen counter that separated her from her mother who was sitting on a sofa across the room watching the television and working on her needlepoint. She looked back down at the cat. He was still in her grasp firmly, and giving her an equally filthy look. She pushed him down on his side, spun him around on the floor, and finally let him run off.

Qian looked back up at the television, the actor Carey Elwes was on the screen listening to a story narrated by the actor Mandy Patinkin. Qian recognized the movie as *The Princess Bride*:

Inigo Montoya:
When the six fingered man appear and request a special
sword, my father took the job. *Draws sword.* He slave a
year before he was done. *Hands to The Man in Black*

The Man in Black:
Admiring the sword. I've never seen its equal.
Returns sword.

Qianqian turned back away from the television in
disgust, grabbed her cigarettes and went back outside to the
patio to make phone calls. She was disinterested in that
particular movie, with tormenting the cat and socializing with
her mother.

From a coffee bar in an airport terminal ...

I had a sharp pain in my chest as I watched her disappear down the boarding ramp to the airplane. I had dropped her off at the airport tens of times already, mostly when we had been friends. I was always her ride to the airport and always her way home. I thought maybe there was some significance to being the first and last person that Qian saw when she came and went from Los Angeles. Her carry-on was the only bag she was taking, which was light tan, leather and perfectly matched her shoes. She always wore the lightest shades of tan when flying. She was magnificent. She attired herself in a cream DKNY gown that covered her form well, but gave her an elegant stature, hiding any imperfection of build. Maybe that's what Mrs. Karan had intended. Her hair was down, and her jewelery collection was going full tilt. It took her several minutes for her to remove everything and get through the airport security scanner. I stopped and watched the guard check her with his toy. She was covered in silver and jade, mostly bracelets.

She turned around and blew me a kiss before she vanished around the corner. I smiled and stood there feeling rather silly, but desperately in need of coffee. I had an addiction to tend to. Airports always made me nervous. People always leave you there, and you have to patiently await their return. My mind always asked the question 'what happens if they don't?' I kept that thought to myself however, seeing that Qian would find me too insecure if I ever let on. I didn't ask her when she was coming back, I just told her to email me with the instructions of when to pick her up.

I found my way to the Starbucks counter and sat there for almost an hour waiting for her plane to take off. I drank two double macchiato's and watched South American Futbol on the overhead. A large Korean family sat grouped together tightly and taking up lots of space in the line and at the tables around me. I listened in on the conversations that ensued. For some reason, when people speak in their native tongue, they have this belief that they have a certain amount of secrecy or privacy around white people. In Los Angeles though, it just isn't the case.

"I didn't ever care for that woman. She was the most spiteful person I ever knew." Two small, pudgy ladies in striped shirts were talking to one another, speaking in Korean.

"Well, as you know," the other woman replied, "you can choose your friends but you cannot choose your family. She was your mother but you shouldn't feel so bad about her. It's not right."

"Do you think that I want to go all the way to Busan, just for her funeral?"

"Be thankful that you don't have to pay for the ticket, it's a free vacation."

"I wouldn't go otherwise." I heard all of this through the harsher syllables of an older dialect but understood most of what was said. When I bored of the drama and the crowds, I headed out of the terminal and back home.

I got up and found my Explorer where I had left it. Then I remembered that Qian had driven, which accounted for the doors being unlocked. I contemplated the exact length of what three days of jonesing for her would do to me all alone. Something told me that her trip would probably be longer. Nothing was ever what it was supposed to be with her, it always required just a little more commitment than originally thought.

Driving out of the parking structure and into the mid-afternoon sun, I noticed that she had left a letter for me on the seat. I recognized the stationary stock. The stationary was made to resemble a recycled brown paper bag. There was a black string tie at the end of the envelope and they were in the shape of airline tickets.

I paid the three dollars to exit the parking garage and sped my way back onto Sepulveda Boulevard, I raced next to a taxi and a limo followed close behind me. I didn't care. Los Angeles traffic is singular in that it can make you feel as if you're a part of some Nascar event at the drop of the hat. Having a powerful V8 under the hood also helps in keeping up and overtaking the competition, most people either can't drive or are just too damned afraid to.

I pulled over at a gas station, and decided to read the letter:

Dear Sebastian,

As I'm leaving again, just for a few short days, I realize how fragile everything is. I never have told you this, but I have loved you from the first. The last several months with you has been beautiful. Please forgive me for being so erratic and irregular. Never give up on me, because I do love you.

My Best – Qianqian.

I had to read the letter one more time. It was the most personal thing she had ever sent, stated or let me know of. I must've went over it repeatedly for what seemed like a half an hour. All the previous thoughts of throwing in the towel and disposing of my relationship with Qian began to fade, even though I knew, deep down, that I was playing the fool. I wondered if she was thinking of me now. The odds were heavily against it. She was on the plane, heading out of town, sitting in first class and quite possibly with Layden beside her. I got out of the truck to buy some cigarettes and get another cup of coffee, when I heard someone shout my name.

"Sebastian Raines!"

I turned around and looked, but couldn't believe me eyes. Michael Schiavo was standing pumping gas adjacent to my truck. He had the dubious honor of being Qianqian's ex-boyfriend from high school and beyond. They had been together for some time and they had separated because she was infatuated with every guy that ever seemed interested in her. He eventually grew tired of her wandering and I suspected that he never got over her. He had a habit of behaving like he was her father.

"Porco miseria, amico." I was a little put-off at his presence from nowhere. I began to wonder if he had heard about my relationship with Qianqian through my ex-wife, but this was the first time I'd seen him in several years. It was very unlikely that he knew. My next thought was whether he was stalking one of us.

"Sebastiano, how are you? I've heard so much about you, and I must tell you, man, that I'm shocked."

"You mean concerning 'her', yes?" I asked straightforwardly, smiling. "And what sources would those be?" I added.

"I have to say that I was shocked at first to hear that you two were seeing each other, but after a while it makes sense. You both are perfect for each other." He grabbed my shoulder and held on to it firmly, all the while looking directly at me. His hair had grown long and curly, he resembled the thin faced model in all of the Caravaggio paintings. I didn't trust his intentions at all. Something wasn't right. I had the feeling as if I was on the verge of being shot. I already had the feeling of being stalked.

"I don't quite know how I should take that, Lucas. Are you mad at me or something?"

"You realize that after having absolutely nothing in common, we finally have something to talk about?" His words rang true. The two of us together had always occupied some kind of awkward space in the universe, even though I only saw him on the rare occasion when he came by to say hello to Qian. High School sweethearts all have a place, I figured.

"Where are you coming from?" he asked.

"I just dropped you-know-who off at the Airport, she's going on a trip for a few days."

"Is she still stripping?" he wondered. I looked away, and found myself watching the traffic rumble down Sepulveda before I answered.

"Of course." I knew that he detected the sadness in my voice upon the answer.

"I can't say this for Abbey, but that job is going to destroy her," he stated.

"I believe it already has, partner, it's just a matter of time before the bill catches up with her," I answered.

"And you'll do nothing about it?" he questioned me in a way that made me suspicious. I began to wonder what his motivations were.

"It's not my place, and besides ... you never seemed to do or say anything." Suddenly we both stood looking at each other in a way that bordered on conflict. I put the pump away and we both just stood there staring each other down.

"You should be ashamed of yourself. You have no business with her," he finally began speaking his mind. "Your relationship with her is disgusting!"

"She's the one who finds you disgusting."

"Keep stalking me and I'll have you picked up and sent on a vacation courtesy of the County. Got that?"

I just wanted to leave, I didn't see the point of having conflict with someone that I rarely saw or thought of. We both left and went in opposite directions on the road. I didn't think I'd bump into him again anytime soon. It was a fluke as it was. I was still agitated nonetheless. I chewed gum, turned up the radio and finally started making phone calls when I could no longer stand the isolation. The voices inside my own head were bad enough, having to listen to random public banter about the decisions I was making was annoying. I made a mental note to do a background check on him later.

By the time I got back to the apartment, showered, changed, had several more cups of coffee and fed the cat, I noticed that I still had an hour and a half to be at work. Anxious to be outside, I left early. Fuzzbody was in desperate need of attention, but I figured he'd just have to wait. On the way past the bedroom I noticed the unmade bed from the day before. In a flash I saw her again, in my minds eye, naked. Doing her best to get herself off. I had left the bedroom and the bathroom lights on, but I just couldn't force myself into either of the two rooms to shut them down. As I stepped out into the hallway, I shut the door behind me, casting the apartment and its emotional triggers aside. Walking away I could smell one of the other tenants cooking food. I passed the landlord going down the stairs, who only ever seemed to say 'hello' these days. He desperately needed a bath.

"Gave up bathing, Mark?" I commented.

"Go arrest somebody, Sebastian," he answered flippantly.

"Oh come now, aren't we in a bad mood?" I replied, stopping to continue our little tryst of words. He was sweating profusely and obviously bothered.

"I just had to give Melanie her eviction notice and that bitch just started swearing at me. Like her financial problems are my fault? Somedays, I wish I didn't have this job. I'm everyone's fucking enemy," he continued mumbling as he slowly climbed up the staircase.

"You're not my enemy, Sweetheart," I said, as he disappeared around the corner.

"Hey, did you hear those gun shots behind the building the other night?" he asked, from the stairs above. "What are you going to do about it?" he asked, probably calling me an asshole under his breath.

"Which night was that, I hear gunshots almost every night. I think my cat has Post Traumatic Stress Disorder," I replied. He laughed and was gone.

I contemplated my police laden universe for a moment, realizing how much heavier my wallet was with my shield attached to it. I wondered if I had remembered to bring my gun. I grabbed for the small of my back and recalled having clipped it on. I always had a tendency to forget where I put my wallet and keys through the years. So far, I had lost only one gun. I was fortunate that it hadn't gone on my record. I hated the whole service revolver thing or even having to carry one to begin with. I hadn't pulled it all year and hadn't fired it in almost eighteen months. The department reminded me that I had to carry a weapon that was a nine millimeter or larger. For the sake of continuity, I carried a Beretta 92F, just as I had in the Marines. I usually kept the bullets separate and never had one in the chamber. I hated having to check it at every damn metal detector in the greater Los Angeles region, passing through security stations and airports. If I wasn't in uniform, it usually stayed locked in my safe. Putting my wallet on the conveyer belt was enough. They always met me with a side-ways-glance when they saw the shield in the monitor through the x-ray machine. It was a habit that was carried over from my military days when I had been assigned to the State Department in Washington D.C. I was unorthodox as a cop, and I knew it. I just tried to make sure no one else did for my own self-preservation.

The ride up the hill on this evening was a different one from all the rest. I was leaving behind a riot in Hollywood. A free 'System of a Down' concert hadn't worked out as planned and had caused some emotional unrest and a lot of riot police. I wanted nothing to do with it. Jamming up Citizen Joe over a pop-culture melt-down wasn't my idea of productive law enforcement. I would've been the first to fire tear gas and shoot rubber bullets before I had to manhandle the filthy masses and forever tarnish their record.

When I pulled up to the rusted gate at the end of the road, I was feeling the pangs of hunger again. Ordering food was strictly prohibited, due to the level of secrecy that surrounded what was going on behind the fence of a very innocuous looking building, which was only accessible by a forest service road. Pizza delivery was completely out of the question. The gate finally squeaked open enough to let me in. There was only one other vehicle present.

Officer Kim was the only Korean assigned to the unit. He'd been working the 'phone-lines', so to speak, for almost two years. He was familiar with the criminal activity in Koreatown. He kept logs in Persian out of paranoia that something that he wrote might be read by the wrong eyes. Namely mine, and the other three people on duty, who rotated out of what was commonly referred to as 'the shack' or 'the hill'. He was aware that I spoke and read Korean fluently. He shared food with me and sometimes volunteered to drive down for late dinner. I'd known him since the Academy, but I wouldn't say that we were friends. He was always open to having lunch with me, mostly because I never objected to having kim-bap, bulgogi, kalbi, kimchee soup or bee-bim-bop, the latter being one of my favorites.

"How's it going over there, Glenn? Still listening to that same girl?" I asked, looking over his shoulder to read his log. I was halfway decent at Farsi, but I wasn't letting him know.

"Ay, Ahn-yung, Raines? Still involved with those Russians over in Glendale?"

"I thought you had that Ugandan or Nigerian thing. You still working on that?"

"Yeah, just drug activity it seems. I'm going to send it over to vice and wash my hands of it. I can't believe half the things I heard coming from those folks."

"Are they setting up a raid?" I asked

"I don't think so. The risk assessment report stated that there wasn't enough direct danger to life or some such nonsense."

"Who writes these recommendations?" I balked. "It probably cost the County too much money."

"You mean the tax-payer?" Kim interjected.

"No, I mean the County. The tax-payer is going to pay, either way. Just because the County has the money doesn't mean that they're willing to spend it on a gang of retards that are only going to suck even more resources once they cop a bid and get assigned a CDC number."

"Half these people that we turn over, always end up making plea deals, or bargaining out with the feds once they're willing to turn over," he added.

"I'm just collecting a check, kiddo," I joked.

"Really? Is that County money or tax-payer contributions?"

"Take your pick," I grunted, lighting a cigarette. I busied myself at the large pile of paperwork at my desk, admitting to myself that I would have to pull a few early afternoons downtown and get caught up. I was hours away from being able to get on the computer and check my messages. I had court dates coming up and still had to prepare briefs for each trial. I was slowly becoming overwhelmed.

From a window seat in Cafe de la Presse ...

Qianqian found her way through the streets of San Francisco with relative ease. The tightly packed rows of shops, cars and restaurants spun their way up Grant Street, into Chinatown, and made her feel much closer to who she thought she was than the drab flat buildings of Los Angeles. She casually strolled up sidewalks, gazing through every window, stopping at some, passing others. She caught her reflection many times and felt proud of the way she appeared. She noticed the way people were looking at her, especially the men. She felt as if she was exuding something foreign to the environment that everyone appeared to be picking up on. She immediately saw the differences between herself and the other Chinese girls that passed her on the street. She felt as if they looked childish compared to her. She stood out in the crowd, and of course, it did nothing for her humility.

She was enveloped safely in her infamous seven-hundred dollar raincoat that was starting to catch the first few light drops of rain. The weather was overcast, but it definitely wasn't summer. She hid behind a shield of dark sunglasses and flowing black hair, which she'd created with her accoutrements. To her, it was a visible, physical shell that protected her from the world. It helped to keep her tethered in to her fragile reality, and it helped her from loosing herself completely or giving too much away. Every reality has its reasons for existence, material objects were a large part of hers.

The smell of lunch rose from the streets and billowed out from open doorways. It became thicker the farther up the hill she traveled, but the farther up the hill she got and deeper into Chinatown, she started to feel uncomfortable, and out of place. Her heart began to race. She squinted under her brow at her own discomfort. At the corner of Pine and Grant, Qianqian was surrounded on all sides at a traffic signal on the sidewalk. Chinese ladies adorned in polyester pants, plastic shopping bags, bobbed haircuts and umbrellas were waiting to cross in groups. She loomed over them all in size by at least a foot. She noticed the polite smiles and the friendly gestures. They all had turned a little and had noticed her, she was too afraid to say anything in reply to any of their comments. Something was telling her that she was overdressed, but she let it go.

"You sure are a pretty young lady," exclaimed a small elderly woman in Cantonese, who was closest to her. With her free hand, she was pulling on the sleeve of Qian's seven hundred dollar coat.

"Oh ... thank you, that's so nice," she replied in Mandarin, just to be a snob about it. Her face froze after that, and retracted into a smile. She might as well have told the woman that she was a slave and to go fuck herself. It was as far as her veneered performance would take her. She felt relieved and headed across the street when the light changed. A French Cafe on the far end of the crosswalk had surfaced, and a desire within her for a Café Au Lait pulled at her. She usually shied from coffee, but it made her think of Sebastian, and for once, she missed him. She wandered inside off the street after a few drops of rain began to fall more purposefully. The man behind the counter waited on her immediately.

"Yes miss, what can I get for you?"

"Café Au Lait ... for here please."

"Anything else?" he asked her coyly, flirting with his eyes.

Qian responded warmly and openly and began to ask the young fellow what the soup of the day was, what was on special and finally what he might recommend. She felt more capable with him than she did with the woman at the traffic signal. She quickly read the man's name tag, but had to do it twice, which made it obvious because she immediately forgot it just as she was opening her mouth to speak it.

Robert recommended that she try the soup of the day, which was minestrone, not her favorite, but she feigned as if it was, with the importance he was putting on it.

"If you're hungry for something more, I'd say the fettuccini with parsley flakes and butter would be the lightest way to go."

"That sounds really good," she added.

"What's your name?" he asked, politely.

"Qian . . ."

"That's a really pretty name," he complimented, "I'll get your coffee, okay?" Robert was full of old-world charm and service. He was what was expected in a San Francisco restaurant. She looked him over, feeling jubilant at what she had found.

"Okay, that'll be great. I'll have a seat." Qian found an open table at a window that overlooked the street that she had just escaped from. The restaurant was quiet. There was only a few other people scattered inside, despite the weather. Qian became mesmerized by all the people on the sidewalk, swimming around each other under their multi-colored umbrellas. The Chinatown Gate was visible on the other side of the street. The chime of a grandfather clock in the café rang three o'clock, but the darkness of the sky made her feel as if it might be later. She checked her watch once more, for certainty. The light had dissipated a little with the coming of the rain. Robert appeared again and absent-mindedly placed a cloth napkin on Qian's lap and set down the coffee.

"Here you are, Qian . . ." he announced, moving in flourishes.

"Oh, thank you. That's very nice of you," she smiled at him gaily.

"Can I get you anything else, while you're waiting?" She had already prepared herself with a question to ask him, hoping to gauge him in conversation.

"Yes, can I ask you a question?" she began.

"Of course, what can I do for you?"

"I'm trying to find the St. Francis Hotel. I'm staying there. I was supposed to be picked up at the airport, but my friend didn't make it. My bags have gone ahead without me and I desperately need to get there." Her story was an out and out lie. She was now just reeling him in. She'd stayed at the St. Francis Hotel several times through the years.

"I know exactly where the St. Francis is. How long are you staying in the city?"

"Oh … just for three days maybe five. I'm undecided. It depends."

"On business or fun?" he asked, smiling and crossing his arms. He slowly moved closer to personalize himself.

"Hopefully a little of both," she answered amused. "I've been here only a few times and I'm just awful about getting around." The words left her glossed lips like some polished cosmopolitan dinner toast.

"Well," Robert began, "If I'm not being forward, I'm off in about a half hour, I could show you around, help you get done with whatever I can," he spoke, providing like a typical groveling man, in his own special way.

"I wouldn't want to put you out, but that's awfully nice of you to offer," she said, sprinkled innocence over her remarks to attempt the most disarming approach possible.

Robert looked out the window at the weather. The rain had already thickened. The drops had begun to bounce off the cars and sidewalks like glass beads. "If you want, I can drive you down after you eat. The St. Francis isn't too far from here. I'd hate to see you get soaked. Catching a cab on a day like this might just prove to be impossible."

Qian was leaning forward in her chair absolutely enraptured by Robert's forwardness. "Would you? That would be very nice."

"Sure, after you're done, just let me know. I'll take you. Sound good?" he asked.

"Yes, thank you again, Robert."

"My pleasure. Your soup's coming right up." Robert turned and walked back across the restaurant and brought back her soup and then disappeared again, allowing her to eat in peace. The soup was good and the fettuccine was even better. She felt things must always taste better when your expectations have been raised dramatically. She sipped her coffee after she finished eating. The rain hadn't ceased any. The weather was at least true to form as San Francisco has always warned. Residents shuffled along the sidewalks, crossed the gutters, and hazarded the crosswalks with well-formed ability built from years of habit. She read the name of the Café in large gold letters that were arched across the front window, *Café de la Presse*. The place was known by the locals as an incredible place to eat and for its large international newsstand against the inside wall. Out of the corner of her eye she started watching a young Chinese girl in a flowery blue dress who had been standing across the street in the rain, for what she thought had been a long time. She was trying desperately to stay dry under a very large dark-blue golf umbrella. Qian thought she was pretty, but everything about her denoted that she might've been something else, something more familiar. The girl was a wolf in sheep's clothing, and probably on the hunt. The girl smiled at a young man with brownish hair who was passing by thoughtlessly. She grabbed him by the arm gently as he stood next to her, waiting at the signal to cross over. She began pointing at something up the hill, on the next block, maybe a house, maybe a cheap room. She was talking rapidly, as if delivering a sales pitch. Qian knew it all too well. Then they both left together. The girl clutched at his arm and he took her umbrella from her and let down the Wall Street Journal that had been shielding him from the rain. He followed her instructions. They crossed over and passed by the window of the restaurant, within a few feet of Qian, separated only by glass and rain. When Qian got a closer look, she realized that the girl was a prostitute, working the streets. The two girls made eye contact for only a brief moment. The girl smiled, she wasn't more than sixteen, Qian hid her smile behind her bitter tasting espresso cup. The man looked in his mid-twenties. Qian thought he was cute, just as the girl did. She relaxed, crossed her legs and finished her coffee. The whole city moaned, sighed and began to cry. She felt like it was reaching out to her. It was really coming down in buckets. Robert soon appeared with brown suede coat and car keys. He qualified once more in the recess of her mind as handsome.

"How was dinner?" he asked, somewhat nervous but obviously trying to play it cool. She was being taken in quickly.

"Fabulous, really," she burst, wondering when she spoke if it sounded too rehearsed, or Rive Gauche. Her words echoed off the wooden walls and surfaces of the restaurant.

She put some cash into the bill sleeve and left it on the table. She was hoping that he wouldn't insist on offering to pay or even having her not pay at all. She walked away from the table and in three quick steps, they were standing in the doorway, being pushed into each other by another couple running in from the rain.

"Whoa!" Robert exclaimed, connecting with Qian's shoulder and the seven hundred dollar raincoat.

"Oops, sorry …" Qian remarked, reaching her hand up against his lapel.

Outside the rain fell harder. Torrents and small waves eased up along the edge of the gutter. It was coming up over the side drowning out the painted red stripe, designating the area in front of the restaurant for valet service only. The Bellhop from the adjoining Hotel was in the street, blowing a cab whistle for an elderly couple probably on vacation. The down sloping sidewalk of Bush and Grant, brought a continuous blanket of water spilling down into the streets below, like some mad homeless rush of ideas on love and what it's like to be in San Francisco on a rainy afternoon. Qian watched a bum, muttering, in a brown beat suit, standing on the rainy corner with no umbrella. He was truly lost but she wanted to take him home, too.

Qian and Robert stood stoically and well placed under the large nylon black shield that Robert was holding above her. "C'mon my car's over here, by the back," he shouted to her.

Something from somewhere else had caught Qian in a moment. She just felt like standing there in the rain with the bum smoking cigarettes. Robert's sexual sheen had begun to tarnish, but she finally blinked and followed along anyway. Bum: one – Robert: zero.

He unlocked the passenger door of his severely driven and road scarred 1993 brown Honda Civic. Qian giggled to herself wondering how many times she'd be finding herself getting into a brown Honda Civic. He opened the door for her. She got in slowly, being extra careful of her seven hundred dollar raincoat. The little car was being used for delivery, Qianqian realized this once she got a good woof of the interior. Her eyes latched on to a small pipe setting in the ashtray. Smells were emanating from every crevice. Robert popped in from the other side, his fleshy face with his gargantuan smile seemed monstrous and disproportionate to the atmosphere around her. All of the sudden, he seemed surreal and out of place. The car was actually smaller on the inside than it appeared on the outside.

"St. Francis, then?" he exclaimed, as he turned the ignition over and began a small man's checklist of his worn and beaten moneymaker.

"Show me the way . . ." she spoke encouragingly, making herself comfortable amidst the trash. Robert seemed a little embarrassed by his transportation.

"Please forgive the state of this car, my uncle lets Rayal, our bus boy, use it to make deliveries."

"How nice of your Uncle," Qian stated, making yet another judgment of him.

"True . . ," he sighed, "but family business is business. We have a reputation to live up to," he added lightheartedly, making Qian laugh and gaining points in the process. Qian was keeping score on him in her head to see who would be ahead by the time they both got to the St. Francis. So far, he was neck and neck with the homeless man.

In the game of chess, Robert would've been considered an 'Isolated Pawn', and in order to hold on to him, he would have to be defended. It was the first thing Qian contemplated. The second was, if he was worth it. She realized that he probably wouldn't last the day, let alone the course of her visit. Even though she still found him to be attractive, she partially regretted having him 'advance the board' so to speak. But as with all passed and isolated Pawns, the lust to advance is everything. She could feel the sexual tension building in the closed cabin of the brown car by the moment.

"Do you smoke?" Qian asked bluntly, pointing to the pipe in the ashtray. Her tone was aloof, Robert couldn't decipher how to play to her, he hesitated. She looked over at him from the corner of her eye. He laughed.

"I do smoke. Do you want some?" he offered, "Go ahead," he motioned to the pipe with his eyes, handing her the lighter.

"Well ..." now, she was the one hesitating. He adjusted the windshield wipers, turned on the lights and pulled out into traffic with only a casual glance behind the vehicle. She thought about her rules again. One of them was *'never get high with strangers'* and another was *'never get arrested'*. While she didn't feel in any immediate danger, she didn't see anything wrong with letting go.

"Who knows 'what' Rayal puts into his pipe when he's out on his deliveries?" she put forward, mysteriously. She investigated the bowl with the small blade from her fingernail clippers. It looked and smelled like nothing more than harmless and cooked Mexican crapweed. Looking for the tainted addiction in Rayal, she pressed forward finding none.

She took a large and prolonged hit while poised at the red-light. Next to her, a man in a blue Volvo was looking at her with a shocked expression. Qian rolled down her window, and surprisingly, the man in the Volvo did the same. When he did, she leaned out the window and blew the smoke at him. She smiled at him like a five-year-old child when she was finally out of breath. He grunted at her without responding and she felt the buzz come on smooth and light. She sat back down and Robert drove on. She left the window open, letting the rain come in and find its way across her face and on to the arm of her seven hundred dollar raincoat. She slowly ran her hand across her sleeve.

"Dooode! I cannot believe I'm fucking high in San Francisco!" Robert gave her a strange look and took the pipe from her hand and hit it hard, three solid times in row until it was played.

"You sure are a strange girl, Qian," he spoke his words un-thoughtfully as he exhaled his hits all over the interior of the car. It would've been a 'hot-box' had her window been up. Qian laid back in her seat and felt the parts of her hands and feet come back to life, the parts that you can only seem to feel when you're high. The thought that her limbs just laid there dormant, as if they were dead her whole life, or rather, most of it, left her with an uncomfortable feeling. She thought that she was just feeling less and less the older she got.

Every inch of her lower extremities seemed to be vibrating. Feeling something beneath her on the cushion of the seat, she lifted herself up and pulled out whatever it was. Upon examination, she discovered a Peter Gabriel cassette tape. She looked over at Robert and popped it in. He didn't seem to mind. She listened intently.

> *Is that a dagger or a crucifix I see,*
> *You hold so tightly in your hand?*
> *And all the while the distance grows between*
> *you and me.*
> *I do not understand.*

She'd never heard the song before but she thought the lyrics were beautiful.

"Where are you from, you never got around to telling me?" This question made her feel too far from home and a little sad. It took her a few seconds to answer.

"Los Angeles," she answered, almost under her breath. She slid behind her two hundred dollar shades. Donna Karan by defacto. She crept back inside herself, defensively, in her patented state of grace and quiet panic. She didn't stop to ask herself why though. It was all too much stimulation for her mediocre senses to take in.

"L.A.? That's cool. I went to school there . . ." He was now losing more points. "Indian Springs High School," he said. She spun surprised in her seat, giving him a confused look.

"You've got to be fucking bullshitting me, man? So did I. What year?" She was now completely stoned.

"I graduated in 1994. Do you always curse like a sailor, or just when you're high? I didn't expect to hear you talk like that."

"Ohh . . . sorry. I graduated in 1996."

"But here we are in sunny old San Francisco," he stated.

"I grew up in Palms," Qian confided.

"Brentwood" Robert stated, sheepishly.

"Uugghhhh!" she punched him on the arm. They both laughed, it was a territorial thing. She was thirsty now and needed a drink. The unseen line of division made by money. The students that had earned their way in usually came from South of Wilshire Boulevard, while the ones whose parents paid for admission lived North of Wilshire. It was a distasteful classist rivalry that permeated her school and enforced a notion in many about never really having to produce. Here she was in San Francisco, now with Robert, and they were both, metaphorically now living South of Wilshire. However, Qian believed that she had the material advantage.

"I'm thirsty. Can we stop for some apple juice or something?" Qian asked looking around at the old buildings, hoping that a 7-11 would appear from some crevice.

"Well, we're almost there now, however I do have several bottles of wine in the back. Rayal keeps it in here for deliveries, just in case someone asks for it after the fact."

"Wow, you've thought of just about everything," Qianqian answered, sarcastically.

Robert pulled the tinker toy around back of the hotel and parked in what seemed to have been allotted spaces for delivery drivers. No one seemed to think anything out of place as he killed the engine. The security guard in the booth waved Robert in immediately without hesitation. This made Qianqian realize that if the security guard recognized him as a delivery driver. Then by default was he the delivery driver, or was Rayal? She became more suspicious as Robert waved back. Her chemically affected brain tumbled out of control on absurd thoughts that just kept coming in waves. Maybe Rayal didn't exist at all. Maybe she had hallucinated the whole thing.

"What kind of name is Rayal, anyways?" she asked.

"Huh?" he blurted.

He turned off the car and got out. Qianqian watched him come around to her side of the car through the hazy windshield glass. The third possibility existed that he often accompanied vacationing girls back to the hotel for flings and kicks, making him out to be more of a sleaze. She had a desire to leave him in the parking lot, then and there.

Valet-style, he opened the door, positioned the umbrella and offered his hand to help her out of the car. This gesture re-instated his allure, gaining him a much-needed point. She had now confirmed within herself that Robert was playing an 'all-pawn' game.

"Let me walk you inside," he announced as they huddled together up the stairs. Inside the back door, which was of highly polished brass and gilted glass, the golden red ambient glow of the St. Francis with its tall cream-white walls comforted them both as it had intended to. Once on the carpet, they stopped and looked at each other smiling.

"What are you going to do with that wine, Sailor?" Qianqian asked him, unbashfully.

"Please accept it as my present to you for allowing me your company."

"Past or present?" Qianqian replied. Robert looked at her confused. Qian did what she was most afraid of, but most natural at – "Would you like to come up?"

"Love to . . ," he quietly responded, smiling.

Trailing off towards the front of the hotel and to the elevators, Qian was having a moment of Déjà vu, but definitely not second thoughts.

"What room are you staying in?" he asked.

"Ninety seven, it's on the corner and has a good view."

"Y'know ... I never asked you what business it is that you do? What brings you to San Francisco?" Qian searched through her arsenal of collaged lies of what answer to give him.

"I'm a documentary filmmaker; I work for Syndicated Press ... National Geographic at times." The second whopper almost stopped Robert in his tracks upon the carpet as they headed out of the elevator.

"Did you say National Geographic? That really must be cool," he was dumbfounded.

She turned her head and smiled at him, "Yup, it is, pays well." She swiped the card through the magnetic locking device that released the latch with a click. The door opened to an overly decorated, plush two bedroom suite with full kitchen and front-room. Robert was impressed but his demeanor suggested he'd done this before, yet he still appeared curious.

"I'm curious about something . . ." he asked, scratching his head with one hand while the other was in his pocket seemingly scratching something else or looking for something that wasn't there.

"What, what is it?"

"Well . . ."

"Yes . . ." Qian prodded.

"Don't you have any filming equipment? I've never seen photographers travel so bare. The only thing you have is that little tan bag."

"It's a contracts only trip," she bluffed out. "I'm just coming back from China for the billionth time." She was playing an advanced game, and he was grossly outmatched.

"I'm a photographer myself, I've done a lot of work for the Christian Science Monitor, AP, Sports Illy, a few Hollywood things here and there. Nothing lately though."

"Wow, that's cool," Qian replied, edifying him the best way she could to get the heat off of her.

"Are you planning a shoot here?" he continued. Qianqian was beginning to get agitated. She crossed the room and opened the drapes and sheers to watch the fog and rain swirl across the edges of the old buildings. So far, she felt as if she'd boxed herself in.

"No . . . Morocco," she sidestepped, trying again to deflect, feeling stupid for her lies.

"Have you worked NG for a long time?" he kept going. She was getting the feeling that he was starting to utilize her as a future contact and less of a fling. Qian marked him down for a few less points, street-bum had amassed the high score and was now Lancelot.

"Why don't you just open that wine, Robert?" she asked bluntly. Qian sat down into the plush grasp of the velvet peach sofa that seemed not just hideous, but gaudy. Comfort though couldn't be slighted, not at the Saint Francis. She began to feel at ease, sinking into what would soon shape up to be a full afternoon for her. She lounged on the sofa looking at Robert like a lioness ready to eat the neighbor's cubs for a quick snack. He found himself sitting down next to her, bringing two rocks glasses.

"Strangely, it's all I could find," he admitted rather boyishly. "Should I call down for some wine glasses?"

"No, that'll do, pig ... that'll do," she smiled again, brushing her hair out of her face as he poured the wine. Her eyes lit up as the smell hit her nose. It approached her better than she first assumed. She sipped, he sipped. He brought his leg up closer on to the couch near hers, touching her leg. She leaned back into the sofa and closed her eyes. Giving herself over, she knew that she only had so much time to have her fun and be done with him, or make plans for the next day. Layden wouldn't arrive back at the Hotel until after nine p.m., absolutely no sooner.

Robert moved over and kissed her on her neck. She felt his warm breath moving in closer. He smelled like the soup du jour. Almost immediately he was laying on top of her. For Qian, it seemed more mechanical than anything else. He came across as sloppy and impatient, he worked at her like a rank amateur, a dullard. She had advanced her Queen and he was still fondling his rooks. She giggled, gave in and kissed him back politely. He had no idea as to what was really going through her mind. She grabbed his head and pushed him back off of her, all while pushing her tongue as far down his throat as she could possibly manage. Suddenly, or at least to Robert, he was on his back, Qian was straddling his waist and undoing his belt. It was the moment of truth once more. Robert tried to get up and become part of it, but Qian wasn't ready for him yet. He was still an observer as far as she was concerned, and needing some mentoring.

Quickly she had it out, and in her mouth. Robert wasn't all that well endowed and Qian's interest waned even further and her thoughts returned once again to how much fun the homeless guy would have been.

In the act, she tried to forget everything. It was more for her than it ever was for him. His penis was like the universal language inside her mouth. He realized he was beginning to be swallowed not just by Qian, but by the couch as well. He fell into the category of men that all they could seem to muster during a sex act was the old internal gasping and sighing and a few twitching kicks of the left leg. Qian was hoping for something a bit rougher from him, but wasn't going to volunteer the information. For her, it was a perfunctory collegiate performance. She was inundating him and all he could do was help her off with her clothes. Her dark skin shocked him into another one of his light, feminine gasps. Qian disrobed him as if he was a peasant on a farm and slammed his belongings down as if it was all trash. She was advancing a Pawn into promotion, utilizing one of the three special rules. The first being to castle, thus moving yourself out of danger by employing somebody more willing to fight and possibly take a bullet, and the second being en passant. A strange rule where Pawns 'politely' exterminate each other. For the moment though, she would just prefer to temporarily promote Robert from a Pawn to a Knight but the rest was up to him.

Qianqian didn't want to laugh at the size of the boy's penis, so she took another hit from the pipe before fully engaging him, hoping that if she did start laughing, she could say that it was the pot. As she eased herself down onto his thin shaft, she hoped that he would at least find the experience pleasurable, and not feel as if he was falling into a black hole. Which of course would have been because of his size, and not because she was a black hole. She played up the moaning, as usual, and fussed around as if she was plugged into a power outlet.

She detected his flaccid cock a few moments later and suspected that he had come.

"Damn, you came!" she bitched, pounding on his chest.

"I can't believe it ..." he said. "Sorry," he felt embarrassed, but was still smiling. He was high and began floundering around inside of her, figuring out what to do next. She stared down at him and thought that he looked like a retard having a fit.

"Well, can you get hard again?" she demanded, incredulously. It was a command more than a question. She had a steely determined look upon her face and she waited only a few moments for an answer. He said nothing.

"Okay then, leave. Take your shit and go." She got up from the couch and went for the bathroom. She left the door open and watched him carefully, and stupidly collect his things and dress. She washed her hands and face, but all she really wanted to do was masturbate. She sat down on the toilet with her legs open, letting his stuff ooze out of her. He hadn't worn a condom. Yet again, she failed to mention it before hand, but it didn't seem to bother her much. She pushed and contracted her inner muscles to work to get his stuff out of her. She shook her head in disgust hoping that he'd been better. The white tiles of the cold bathroom floor absorbed all the air-conditioning that it possibly could. Her foot pad felt it creeping into her, making her long for her slippers left bedside at home. She sat on the toilet listening to Robert heading across the carpet and leaving. He didn't even say thank you, or goodbye. He'd been taken out of play for making a bad move. It was supposed to be check-mate, but instead she just dumped the whole game in the trash can. But she had brought along her vibrator for all those unsatisfactory and lonely moments and knew that it wasn't a total loss. She had it tucked away deep inside her travel bag. Airport security always gave her quite a look when she was passing through the metal detector.

She thought hastily about douching, to lessen the chance of Robert getting her pregnant. She quietly cursed him for coming inside of her as she jumped onto the large king-size bed. The television was on but the volume wasn't. It was that movie again. *Buttercup was demanding a pitcher from the young farm-boy, who was now leering at her suggestively.* She closed her eyes and spread her legs between the sheets. She hummed away with her rubberized friend that she kept calling 'oh god' until her eyeballs rolled into the back of her head several times, and the room went black from sheer exhaustion.

From the Bradbury ...

I sat at my desk catching up on almost three weeks worth of surveillance reports that had been sorely neglected. A grand-total of thirty-four different files with audio attachments. Most of the material was telephone transcripts concerning gang activities, drug trafficking, blackmail, white-collar crime, two cases of B & E and an art theft case that needed to be tagged and copied. Also unattended were several cases involving the District Attorney's Office that were under investigation, a few run-of-the-mill Home Invasion Robberies, which were cases that actually belonged to Kim, and various other wire-tap investigations that the tax-payers were paying for dearly. I had little stomach to confront Kim on dumping his workload on my desk under my own reports, and elected to let it go. I knew that I could find a better way to get back at him later. I always figured him to be a state-employed slacker on the payroll just punching-in.

Three days a week, I was forced off my mountaintop, so to speak, to fulfill my duty by taking up residence in the Administration Headquarters. In the last several years, Administration had taken over what was known as the 'The Bradbury Building', located on the corner of South Broadway and East Third. As with every day, I would have preferred to wear plain clothes, but having to come to my regular police-issue office Downtown, I was forced to be in uniform. The dark blue attire of the Los Angeles gun-slinging elite.

I was surrounded in similar fashion, like the office I kept at the L.A. Weekly, by the cubicle heads and their decorative accoutrement. I was supposed to be working diligently in a sea of Statisticians and Academics that would probably only ever fire their pistols on the range for practice and annual qualification or if the world was ending and they had to fight their way out of downtown, like Charlton Heston in *The Omega Man*. The latter would probably never take place barring a riot, but by their own statistics a good twenty percent would use their service weapon to end the life of a family member or their spouse. Police officers have an uncanny ability to not just brutalize the general public at large but self-destructing in their own homes has become the new scenario behind '*officer involved shooting*'.

My office in the Bradbury Building was sparsely decorated and devoid of clutter or anything sentimental or personal. No degrees on the wall, no academy graduation records or anything that essentially had my name on it. Although I had occupied the fifteen by fifteen foot office that was situated on the corner of the building on the Eastern side, third floor for almost two years, no one would have ever known. Not even the door bore a plaque to label its occupant. However, the department had routinely placed one when the office was put into my care, but the plaque had fallen off during a minor earthquake and was never re-affixed. Several pictures had hung on the walls back in the days when my personal level of enthusiasm for the force was a lot higher. A picture of my younger self shaking hands with then-President George H.W. Bush, thanksgiving 1991, during Desert Storm. We were both holding a paper plate with canned cranberries and turkey. Another picture of me shaking hands with Willie Williams, the previous chief of the LAPD about a year after graduation, and a picture next to President Clinton in plain clothes on an escort detail. The last was a picture of my ex-wife in wedding garb surrounded by The Flying Elvis's in Las Vegas. These pictures now sat in a box at the foot of my desk with several hardbound police reference manuals which had been serving time as a footrest. By sight, anyone would believe me to be a determined and career-driven officer who was trying to get ahead. In reality, I personally couldn't give a damn anymore about advancing or finding favor with the higher-ranks. I now wavered between apathy and nose diving off the roof any given Tuesday.

I had always considered myself lucky. It always got me into places and opportunities that I would've never have chosen for myself. I could no longer handle being a lackey or a subordinate to anyone who was less of a leader than myself. It was that notion, and that notion alone, which made my decision easy regarding not re-enlisting in the Marines after getting back, stateside, in 1994. I had plateaued in the chain of command and didn't care what was coming next.

I sat quietly at the desk with my feet up going over the personal audio archive of notes that I had made specifically for the reports. Department policy for any *extraneous material of the classified nature was to be destroyed in the incinerator directly or shredded - following report.*

Every now and again, I had to stop the tape and make notes into the computer, matching dates and times where necessary, adding in names and basic events. As interesting as everything seemed, my mind wouldn't focus on the task at hand. I had gotten through roughly four days of reports, but my mind kept drifting over to Qianqian. I kept wondering what she was doing. I wanted to pick up the phone every few minutes and call, but resisted.

"Damn you, woman," I muttered, getting up and heading down the hall for another cup of coffee. I straightened my shirt, pants, duty-belt and badge, all in that order. She had been gone for almost two weeks and I hadn't heard from her since she left. But I could tell what the silence meant. When she had finally returned, she acted strange and indifferent upon meeting me at the airport. Her clothes smelled musty, like stale dope and cheap incense. It was raining heavily that day, and I spotted her wandering around the American terminal talking fixatedly into her cell-phone. When she saw me, she startled, as if she hadn't expected me or rather forgotten that she'd asked to be picked up.

"Ohh … hey … Sebastian, I totally forgot that we made plans," she uttered. Her hand was covering the mouthpiece of her phone, blocking whoever was on the other side from our conversation.

"Never mind, let me call you back," she continued into the phone. A voice of protestation came over the line from the other side, but she clicked it shut and turned off the phone. I raised an eyebrow at her antics.

"That's pretty drastic," I replied

"The battery is about to die anyway, it was beeping the whole time."

"Flight alright?" I asked.

She hugged me, kissed me on the cheek, acted coy and smiled. I was immediately beginning to feel like myself again when she wrapped her arms around me. People had started to gawk because all they could see was this young woman hugging a cop. I was holstered but the radio was off.

"Sucker for a man in uniform, huh?" I quipped.

"Only you, Sebastian," she responded, smiling and pressing her flesh against me.

"Someone forgot I was coming to pick them up," I replied, whispering into her ear. I could almost sense my words and breath bouncing off of her delicate earlobes as I spoke.

"Nu-uh" she denied, smirking, grinning like a guilty cat that just ate a plate of mackerel from the table.

"Carry on only, no checked baggage?" I asked.

"You know me well," she answered.

"Your carriage awaits." I had brought a cruiser, it was Wednesday, and I had taken the rest of the day off to be with her. I had parked in the *Police Lane* by the American terminal. Law enforcement has its rewards, the airport stooges didn't seem to mind a bit when I pulled in. Most of them wave, some are even part-timers. moonlighting for the money, or retired cops.

While I was waiting for Qian's plane to land, two day-shift rent-a-cops had approached me about the Chief. They recognized the numerical markings on the squad-car that denoted its ownership to the Chief's Office or Special Operations. Most ask how the Chief is to feel out the waters, letting you know that they can read number codes. I always say the same damn thing. "He's just fine, but up to his ass in Internal Affairs." That was the million-dollar-line that always put them off-guard and at-ease. The rest is just more bullshit stories, laughter and anecdotes. I usually have to cut the conversation short, shake hands and disappear. Everyone of them end up staring at my name plate, squinting, as if they've never seen or read the name 'Raines' before. It was all too much watching their faces ball up and grimace as they tried to memorize it for later use, if they ever got called over. Most believed they were somehow better off for talking or knowing someone from Administration. It is the fallacy that's created by big bureaucracies and the name for it is '*Bureaucratic-Hallucination*'. Unfortunately, being on the job, the camaraderie follows one everywhere. The truth of the matter is that I wouldn't help any one of them.

After we got to her house, we spent the next twenty hours in bed, making love, watching television, and trying to find another condom. She behaved as if she hadn't been with anyone in months, but I knew it was all an act. It was then, reminiscing about that day, drinking coffee in my office that I remembered that she told me that she loved me. It was something that hadn't happened before. She believed that I was clueless about her affairs with Layden, so I let her continue believing it. She thought I was obtuse, but I had no reason at all to adjust her, or her feelings about me. Even if they were malformed or misguided.

Thinking hard, I thought I probably should've ended it with her after I had gone home that night. It was like leaving Las Vegas with your pockets full of winnings and never going back. I remember the moment when the idea crossed through my numbed brain and how I roundly rejected the notion outright, because I 'thought' I was in love with her, too. It was comical now, over a cup of coffee, but really just too damn sad to go around repeating to anyone. There were memories of her that I wished I could exorcise from my brain, but I knew better.

A knock on my office door brought me back from my thoughts. I knew that I had better things to do than day-dream.

"Raines!"

A young administrative officer was standing in my doorway. The Captain's Secretary, Gershwin.

"Officer Gershwin, I believe my rank and time in service warrants you to address me correctly. Detective is more appropriate. Don't make that mistake again."

He stood dumbfounded, but unfazed. I was often the target of open criticism by all my superiors and peers. Gershwin, by default had little respect for me but had nothing personally tangible to support his feelings. Loyalty to the Captain, pawn captures Kings Bishop.

"Uh … yeah, whatever you say, Raines!" he answered annunciating the 'R' syllables of my surname. As I got up to cross the room and give him what for, Gershwin pivoted through the exit and quickly began heading for his desk, not believing that I would catch up with him. A few feet outside my office, I called out and tapped the boy on the shoulder.

"Freeze, Gershwin. That's an order." The young man stopped, a little shocked at my agility and tone and became immediately uncomfortable standing before me.

"You better get your attitude in check, young man. You've never worked a day in the field yet. Neither with me, nor anyone else for that matter. Everything you know about me is second-hand information, given to you after the fact. You don't own any of it. Am I clear about that?" I asked.

"Sure, Detective."

"Let me ask you one thing Officer, you're not going to fly a desk your whole career, so you might be best served not openly alienating yourself with misplaced loyalties amongst your fellow officers. I've known Captain Okana since the Iraq War. He's entitled to his opinions, you're just a runt. How long have you been on the force?"

"Fourteen months" Gershwin answered.

"Just over a year, huh ..." I repeated, confirming the young man's doubt.

"Do you know what he wants to see me about?" I asked, advancing my King pawn into the classical pawn center. A crucial move for maximum piece deployment.

"Something to do with your reports, and Detective Kim. He's in the office with the Captain."

Hmm. I thought about it for a moment as we walked down the open-aired hallway to the staircase. The Captains office was located on the second-floor. Kim was sitting with an agitated look on his face with his hands folded across his stomach and his legs extended. Okana was going over some audio notes on his desk.

"Detective, come in." Okana got up to shake my hand, but Kim stayed put. I looked over at him and he was staring at the floor, dejected. He had the look of a dog who just had his nose rubbed into a pile of shit.

"What gives, Captain?" I asked, very casually. Queens knight pawn to B three. Fianchetto. Okana suggested I have a seat. A chair was vacant a few feet from the center of his desk, positioned a handful of degrees to the right. Okana sat and continued going over Kim's audio notes one more time.

"Disturbing," he stated. It gave me nothing. Sometimes it's just best to sit quietly and let the game unfold around you. I did exactly that. I crossed my right leg over my left and smoothed my trousers over my knee with the palm of my hand. I was being deliberate, even if I was the only one in the room who was aware of it. But I didn't want to close my body language off to Officer Kim.

Finally, Kim sighed. It was more of an exhalation of stress than anything, but both Okana and myself looked him over.

"It seems that there exists a conflict at the listening station, and I'm unsure about what I should do about it." He put the paperwork down and sat back in his chair.

"I thought that it would be best if we all sat in on this together and discussed it, before I'm moved to take action." I felt as if I was being drawn out to make a sloppy or deliberate play. I could feel the atmosphere in the office constricting around me. The thought of the newspaper job being addressed surfaced in my mind. I would have been check-mated early if that was the case.

"Well, fill me in ... I seem to behind the rook here, so to speak." A mention to the Fianchetto, signaling that I wasn't taking the bait. I moved my King's knight to its rightful place on the board. Textbook. In a brief moment of analysis, I realized that they weren't playing that strong of a game, even at two-against-one. Three if you wanted to count Gershwin as a threat. Something was wrong.

"I'm considering taking Kim off of the Surveillance detail and assigning him back to Metro."

Something was definitely wrong. I chose to be aggressive for the moment and go on a discovery.

"What's the real problem? Can't stand working nights anymore, or do you miss jacking up innocent kids in Brentwood, Kim?" I had swiveled in my chair to face him.

"I've got several pages of notes that detail the activities of Officer Kim, here," the Captain was motioning to my colleague. "Informing two known members of a Korean Drug cell of on-going surveillance and an impending arrest. All of course translated into English." Okana was clearly rocked by this and visibly let down by Officer Kim. I was too paranoid to even see it coming. I thought I was the one up on the block the whole time.

"If this information goes any farther, Kim will go up for review, maybe put on administrative leave, who knows, possibly even let go from duty," Okana stated.

"What the hell were you thinking, Glenn?"

"The man I told was my brother. I told him to stop what he was doing and go back to Seoul, immediately, or he would be headed for prison within days."

"Just curious, but how long ago was the information compromised and what happened?" I was hungry and the curiosity would've exploded outward foolishly had I not tried to control myself to stop from laughing out loud at Kim.

"Glenns' brother, Wan-Sook, was killed trying to warn some of his partners. They took him as a snitch, or a liability. Narcotics decided to bust everyone early, just after Wan-Sook was killed. Months of surveillance were compromised. Wan-Sook's body was found in a burned out stolen Astro-van in Palms this morning. Capt. Billingsley, in Vice, gave me this 'unofficial report' this morning with these audio transcripts from the surveillance. He said they weren't going to pursue action against Kim, unless he was instructed to later."

"So now, it just comes down to the three of us and trust," I answered. I got up and walked over to the window, contemplating my long relationship with Glenn Kim. In the Academy, he came off as arrogant and overbearing, constantly pitting himself against me. Hoping to curry favor or show me up in front of the trainers. Later we had served in the same unit in Beverly Hills for almost two years, but not as partners. He always felt cheated when he was assigned to a bicycle unit and I had been given a better assignment in command. He had filed several complaints against me, which had all been investigated and later dismissed. It was a simple matter to say that he despised me.

"Look, Kim," I addressed him directly. "Ever since the Academy you've always seemed to have 'a distaste' for me, that's always been pretty clear. Now, almost five years later, here we are." I scratched my head and sat back down. He shrugged hopelessly, ashamed that he was even in this situation, at a loss against me, one more time. Poor bastard, should've been an Optometrist.

"Well?" Okana asked, staring at me for a direct response.

"I think we should be merciful and keep this between us, in-house, so to speak," I spoke slowly. "But what would you do, I wonder?" I asked, looking carefully at Kim. Both of them knew what I was driving at, either of them would've been ecstatic to see me fry.

He didn't answer. He sat speechless, watching the floor, clearly struggling with his bruised ego, feeling useless.

"However, watching 'you' fry, just aint my style, Kim. It's not very hospitable if you ask me."

I got up to leave, making eye-contact with Okana.

"It's your decision, Captain." I left feeling slightly disgusted concerning Officer Kim, but relieved in the realization that my ass was in the clear. Mercy is always a better route, they might be more inclined to show some in return if the tables were turned.

"I've got two-weeks worth of reports to finish, I'll see you tonight, Kim. If not ..." I nodded and left the office heading back upstairs with a ridiculously smug look on my face that I was happy enough to catch in the reflection of the elevator door. I had seen the same look on Kim's face a handful of times.

I buried myself for the rest of the afternoon. I thought more about Qianqian than I thought about gang-reports, statistics tracking and audio logs. My mind drifted momentarily back to Kim. I was surprised that Okana had even brought me into the room. I knew deep down if I had fucked up, there would have been no discussion or group meeting. Vice would have filed an official complaint of Obstruction of Justice, tampering with an Official Police Investigation. Okana would've taken my badge and gun before I even got out of bed and Kim would've found out my fate while being promoted. I didn't expect things to be fair at all, if it was ever supposed to be in the first place. If it ever was, I would've been immediately suspicious.

My desk was covered in thick manila folders, full of typed transcripts and a silver compact disk taped to the inside cover of each. I was supposed to be journaling the entries, building case logs and dossiers against individuals who would later be damned in the court of law when my handi-work was trotted out before them. Every detail sifted and considered. Time and place, motive, associations, contacts, assets, spending, aliases, nick-names, children, arrest records, crimes committed while under surveillance that were not ready for prosecution. I was the department's secret weapon against gang-activity. I was the first silent cop trying to chain link probable cause from one person to the next. But, in the overwhelming nature of it, I was better off letting it go. I was asleep at the wheel, and as far as I knew, I was the only one aware of it.

I was still fuming, internally, about Kim and could sense my blood beginning to boil. His actions had got someone killed. Just because it was his brother, the department had an extra dose of sympathy for him. Personally, I would've been pleased to see him drummed out and made to forfeit his shield. Most of the officers that I knew were like Kim. He was another example in the long line of officers that were a detriment to themselves and a hazard to everyone else. Every day was about them and their ego. And they always believed they were cop-of-the-year. For them it was an exercise posturing, making lewd announcements of *pre-homo-habilis* body language to every passing female in the department and on the street. A constant art gallery of unseemly displays of awkward manliness, walking in-between the water-cooler and their desk, yawning, belching, farting, grunting, barking, loud laughs and the ridiculous desire to overwork their bodies at the gym so they could appear to be the Nitzchean supermen with a cleft-jaw. The saddest part of all was that they all had been given carte-blanche with a firearm even though most had failed to successfully master the Olduwan era (Early Paleolithic) tool case, or even identify it. It all made me want to puke, and everyday it seemed being a cop only attracted more of the same. I was glad my office had a smoked glass window and that the door had a lock.

The phone rang at four-thirty. It was Qianqian, and not Okana letting me know that out of sympathy, he'd 'nominated Kim as cop-of-the-year and was sending me to Bicycles'.

"Thank god, it's you," I said into the phone that was pushed against my face as I reached out to toss a few files into the 'done' box.

"Everything alright?" she asked.

"You wouldn't believe it, even if I told you. But everything is still in one piece, thankfully. You?" I asked, sinking into the depths of my chair, putting my feet back up on the desk.

"That's good, because abusing you is supposed to be my job," she responded. I could hear the sound of her smiling as the words drifted through the electricity. I was imagining her large grin like a 'sharks mouth', ready to take a chunk from my flanks.

"You know, you're the only person that can get me off over the phone. Keep talking like that and I'll probably spend the next twenty minutes by myself in the bathroom."

"I thought this was a secured line, you can't recieve 900 hundred numbers can you?" she joked.

"Ohh, don't worry about that, I've got plenty of illicit conversations to choose from over here. So how was San Francisco?"

"Rainy, of course and Tosca's just isn't the same without you."

"I'd place money that you've already had quite a few mad-cap adventures in the short time you've been gone."

"You didn't hire a private-dick, did you?" she asked, emphasizing the word *dick*.

"I thought that was my line?"

"Huh …?" I'd stumped the band.

"Can you come up tonight, and spend the rest of the weekend with me?"

"I don't know," I answered fidgeting with the phone cord.

"So, are you coming or aren't you?" she pleaded, slightly annoyed.

"Kim is suffering a personal meltdown over here. I shouldn't really leave right now, and Okana is getting ready to pull my badge as well."

"What makes you say that?"

After a few seconds of silence, I answered … *"Lucas Powder"*.

She went silent for a few moments , Lucas Powder was our code-word for my moon-lighting job at the paper.

"I see …" She finally spoke. "Don't worry about all that, just come up tonight. It's not too late to catch a flight from Burbank. We can be at dinner at Luisa's on Union before seven-thirty."

"Hold the line for a sec, okay?" I put the poor girl on hold to listen to some Burt Bacharach or Beatles or Roy Orbison.

It clicked over and the line blinked quietly.

I headed back down to Okana's office, surprisingly he was talking with Chief Parks. My eyes widened and my stomach fell into my small intestine. When Chief Parks saw me at the door, his face puckered like a pit-bulls asshole getting ready to crap all over me. I had to be 'unflinching'.

"Raines, what can I do for you?" Okana asked.

"Chief, how are you, sir?" I was being polite, but he didn't respond. I thought he was going to draw his weapon by the amount of hate he was sending at me in waves. Something told me he already knew about '*Lucas Powder*'.

"Captain, I've got some business to attend to in San Francisco for a few days. You don't need me to tomorrow, how does Monday sound?" Well executed, I thought, no begging - purely suggestive.

"Take the time, Raines, not a problem. When you come back though," he rose from his chair and handed me a form, "have your uniforms adjusted, you're in charge on the Hill from this moment, orders of the Chief."

I was in shock, I had just been promoted and it was the last thing I saw coming. The Chief finally floated over, and shook my hand and cracked a smile.

"You don't scare easily do you, Raines?" he asked. "You always play everything so cool?"

"The only thing that scares me, Chief, is my hairline," I answered.

"I got my eye on you. You fail to get the Hill dialed-in up there and I'll personally take that slide from your glide. Is that clear enough for you, son?"

"Crystal, Chief."

"I bet. We've been taking a lot of heat regarding that assignment. It's probably only got another six months at best. If I was you, I'd start bringing whatever cases you got open to a head."

"I can do that. No problem, Chief."

"You've got testicles the size of baseballs, you know that?"

"It's been brought up before," I answered.

"I'll crush 'em like dust if you fuck this up, Raines. Monday, be ready." The Chief was now only inches away from my face. Okana waved me out, nervously trying to avoid a catastrophe that seemed imminent. I headed for the door, but the nagging thought of one last pertinent thing.

"One thing, Captain?" I asked, addressing Okana.

"Yes?"

"Kim?" I asked.

"Who?" he replied. That was that.

"Monday, then." I went back to the office and picked up the receiver, surprisingly, she was still holding.

"Qian?" I spoke into the receiver. She fumbled with the phone and a groggy voice came on. She'd snapped out of it. "Yeah?"

"See you in a few hours, better chase your boyfriends away."

"Thank god, I thought you were going to leave me stranded for the umpteenth time."

"When have I ever let you down?"

"Uhh … you want an itemized list on that?"

"No, not yet, but I'm leaving right now." I hung up and headed for the door.

From the Cliffs of Insanity ...

The knock at the door signaled the arrival of a late dinner via room-service. I had been momentarily unconscious as I had physically collapsed inside of Qian after a long journey in sexual exertion. The last thing I wanted to do at that moment was to disengage my body from hers. It had felt like an eternity since I had been that comfortable, that physically exhausted and drifting off into a relaxed embrace. She had already passed-out beside me. When the maitre-de knocked the second time, she stirred beneath me. I pulled myself slowly from her and she opened her eyes but didn't move.

"I'm starved," she said slowly, and smiling. She was still wearing her glasses, as she looked at me blinking trying to focus. I grabbed the sheet from the bed, exposing her naked frame and wrapped it around my mid-section to open the door for food.

"Good evening, sir. Your dinner," the maitre-de answered. I opened the door and greeted him with a smile and my half-nude torso.

"Excellent. Do I need to sign?" I asked. He handed me the cheque staring at the bullet-hole in my chest that had been a gift of the Iraq war. I was also aware that he could also see Qian's bare ass and long legs across the bed directly behind me. He tried not to look, but clearly couldn't help feeling compelled. I could also feel Qianqian's eyes watching the whole thing in the reflection of the large bay windows. I signed, wheeled in the cart and gave the man a twenty. It was the smallest bill I had.

"Please tell me you ordered some type of shell-fish?" she asked excitedly.

"Cracked crab do?" I replied.

"Absolutely, I could eat raw horse meat."

"As I have just been promoted and can easily afford the bill, I don't believe that we'll be reduced to that, but being a Police Officer, and you having a fetish for horse-heads ... well, something could be arranged," she laughed and looked at me as if I was crazy.

"I think I finally got one of your jokes," she said. "But it still wasn't all that funny." Reaching over for the remote, she flipped on the television. She propped herself up on the pillows and the headboard and grabbed a bath robe that was on the chair.

"What is it about men that always find it necessary to reference *The Godfather*?" she asked. Their was a palpable taste of sarcasm invading her tone. I fixed her a plate of cracked-crab, spiral pasta, three sprigs of asparagus and a half-slice of baked cheese toast.

"Butter?" she asked. Her face was gleaming with satisfaction. I handed over a small metal dish with matching saucer full of melted butter.

"Where would you like it, darling?"

"Hopefully no place that would cause chaffing."

I hadn't even noticed but *The Princess Bride* was on the television. Andre was climbing the sheer rock face of 'The Cliffs of Insanity'. The volume was muted.

"I'm very surprised that you didn't change the channel," I suggested, knowing what little she enthusiasm she had for the film.

"Well, I just wanted to make sure that you're not deprived of anything."

"Oh, not me," I asserted, fixing my own plate. I handed her a glass of Gingerale. She stared at me as she drank the entire glass and then handed it back with a belch that caused her to squint and pucker.

"Refill?"

"Mmmm-mmm," she responded, positively.

I joined her on the bed and ate the dinner, which had billed-out at seventy-five dollars plus change. My body felt as if it had been melting after such a long period of neglect of all the things that any man needs to survive. Sex being one, seafood being another.

She was staring at the TV, slurping up butter with the aid of a meaty crab leg.

"I'll never understand your fascination with this movie."

"This is the best part," I remarked, pointing at the screen, it was the scene where Mandy Patinkin helped Cary Elwes up to the top of the cliff and then tells the story of his father. She unmuted it, knowing it would keep me happy.

"Maybe I'll explain it sometime."

"Have you always felt this way about this movie?" she whispered into my ear. I could smell the warm butter on her face, coating her lips and chin.

"Probably from the first," I speculated. I had a brief memory flash to 1988, watching the movie playing in the background at band practice, asking my friend, Scot Blick, *'What the hell are we watching'?*

The television continued:

Inigo Montoya:
"When the Six-fingered man appear and request
a special sword, my father took the job."

I sat transfixed, watching the camaraderie between two
would-be villains and who might've ended-up killing each
other had the writing gone any other direction. I smacked my
lips in satisfaction, and was glad that I had ordered beer.

"So, are we going to catalog any more secrets this
evening?" I queried, seeing if we'd cover evening traditions
and new ground all in one fell-swoop.

"Well, that depends on you? Doesn't it, Sebastian? It's
your turn to pick the year and you have to have something
exceedingly good," she stated.

The rules were simple, but explicit, we had made a
pact a year earlier and we started the practice trying to search
each other for something new and unknown about ourselves
that we would have to share. Maybe it was something that we
had thought about a thousand times but never had uttered
aloud, something shameful or boisterous or completely
forgotten.

"How about 1990?" I suggested. "Shouldn't be too
invasive."

She looked at me strangely.

"You've never gone that far back before," she
responded, looking at me with furtive brow.

"Sorry, I sometimes forget about our difference in age.
You must've been what … fourteen then?" I asked, looking
her over.

"I was twenty-one," I continued. "I celebrated my
twenty-first birthday in Iraq. I remember thinking about it only
once that day, and that one time is actually my secret."

"Okay, I'm in, sounds juicy enough," she answered,
signaling me to continue. Her tone of voice changed and I
suspected that ninety-two probably wasn't a good year for her.

"I was at the Kuwaiti Hilton with the Second Marine Division Head-Quarters. It was pretty awful ... late April through May. It wasn't a pretty time of year there. Lots of shelled out buildings, burnt cars in the street, sun blotted out by the oil-fires. Not a holiday in the sun, as I remember," I spoke very matter-of-factly.

"I'm kind of uncomfortable with 1990," she interrupted.

"Really?" I replied. "I've actually got a doozey, it's very heavy and very revealing, you'd probably want to hear it."

"That good?" she asked, piqued.

"Actually, Military secrets classified: 'Confidential'."

"Alright, alright ... all in," she began to do some yoga stretches in the bed while sitting cross-legged. She leaned forward with her arms outstretched above her head. Her back folded forward.

"October of '90 ... Kuwaiti Hilton. A few things happened that obviously didn't get reported by the media, despite the fact people with camera's were everywhere. In those days, there seemed to be more camera's than guns. From the word on the ground, they had already knew 'what was where', so to speak, because of information gained from 'forward-observers'.

"Forward Observers?" she asked, chewing her last bites of food. "What's that?"

"Scouts, you could say, Marine Recon, Army Rangers. Special Forces usually gather intelligence long before the foot soldiers arrive. Just in case there's a need for confinement or cleanup."

"What like hiding stuff? Destroying evidence?" she said, perplexed at military atrocity.

"Sometimes, but not quite."

"Sounds shady."

"Of course it does, why would it not?" I fed her imagination a little. "It's all pretty basic. The embedded media usually float with certain regiments within the Army that are in areas that are clear of anything that would be thought of as 'provocative'." She wanted to say something, but chose to remain silent instead. I could hear the wheels turning.

"When we got to the Hilton, I was probably the third person in the building. I had been sent forward acting upon reports from the forward-observers. There were dead bodies everywhere in the Hotel lobby. Corpses were about two to three feet high in some places. It really was like the end of the world inside that building. The stink was awful."

"Is this a story about dead bodies in a war?" Qian looked over at me and asked, seemingly unamused.

"It could be, but not quite," I answered.

"If it is, you might just want to stop right there. 1990 was pretty significant to me, and this, so far, doesn't seem to equal."

"Just hold on, it's back story. I assure you that you won't feel let down."

"Okay," she answered, with a sense of resolve. She had turned down the volume on the television, and had leaned into the pillows to hear me unwind my tale of obvious woe.

"My job was to photograph and document with a few Naval medical personnel of 'what was' the Kuwaiti Hilton. The place was the typical grand hotel with endless rooms. It was built to eclipse all the other Hilton Hotels anywhere in the world. It had marble for as far as the eye could see. Roman pillars that looked modeled from the Smithsonian or Rome. It was lavish. However, there was some three-hundred and fifty to four-hundred dead bodies on all seven floors of the place. Unfortunately, there were people from all over the world, too. Every tourist or business-person was killed, beaten or tortured and then either dumped at the hotel as a symbol or taken to new horrific lows in the unoccupied rooms upstairs. There was an abundance of woman and children to give you a thought of what really happened. The upper floors were sickening" I finished my food and set the plates on the trolley and pushed it away from the bed. I set the ice-bucket with two last beers on the floor beside me. Qian yawned.

"I'm sure that most of the people were just listed as missing and the families were notified later. It was a War and the government could claim ignorance anytime it wished if it wanted. Military reporting then, was vastly different then than it is today."

"So, I was with six others. I was the youngest on the ground. If I hadn't been assigned as the battalion photographer earlier during the tour, I would've been asked to leave. There were also two senior Naval Corpsmen and a Marine Lieutenant, who spent most of his time on the radio, outside. He seemed the most bothered and could only stomach a few minutes of what he saw."

"Didn't have a stomach for atrocity and the dead, huh?" she asked.

"Most people don't," I answered. "The smell was pretty fucking horrible, I wanted to puke every few minutes but slowly found myself getting used to it. It was hot everyday and the corpses were rotting in the heat. There was no Air-Conditioning. We had to shoot wild dogs all the time, but they had pretty much given up on the place as well. I had to go through almost every room that was accessible. The person in charge was a forty-year old Chief Petty Officer. Back home she said she was a Mortician. She normally worked with the Naval Reserve on weekends and had joined out of boredom. She said it was a family business and had worked alongside her father since she was in High School.

"Was she hot?" Qianqian asked, bluntly.

"She wasn't bad, nice figure, looked good in a uniform, red-hair," I responded laughing.

"I see," she reacted, unconcerned.

"We had two days to go from room to room and photograph, document and catalog the whole damn thing. She wanted to be done in one day, and I didn't blame her, and neither did our Lieutenant. I'm sure orders came directly from the Pentagon to burn the place to the ground the next day, but in the meantime, I was searching for ranking dead, intelligence info and anything that stood out. Everyone else was still outside eating chow or on extended break."

Qian immediately burst out laughing, "You've got to be kidding me, you didn't," she hooted, seeing the inevitable left turn. "Oh my God, Sebastian!"

"We had found a portion of the Hotel that was on the other side of the massive laundry facility. It had gone unnoticed and had been left untouched. It included a total of two large conference rooms and a couple of large suites. The power was out and you could only access these rooms with the elevator off of the restaurant or through an obscured corridor from the laundry room. Well ..." I hesitated, clearing my throat. "Chief Petty Officer Lewellen, who was very shapely, had long red hair that was braided into a bun, and pink cheeks. She was a nicely manufactured female, a bit homely, but married. Tough as nails and straight faced every moment."

"So, what happened?" Qian asked looking for what she was expecting the whole time.

"I was surprised when she closed and locked the door behind us in one of the bedrooms. I was caught off guard and didn't have a way out. Before I knew it, she had dropped her gear and began to unbutton her shirt. I was a little confused, and it was the last thing I was thinking about amidst all that putrescent and fetid atrocity on the other side of the laundry facility. We both stunk or rotting flesh and human stench, but she ordered me to hurry up and get undressed because we'd only have a good thirty minutes before anyone would began to wonder what the hell we were doing.

"She ordered you?" Qian laughed.

"I had been in Iraq for over six months, hadn't had any sex the whole time. So it was strange, but magnetic. I pulled my clothes off as fast as I could, fumbling badly with combat boots. And we had sex on that dusty Hotel bed on my twenty-first birthday. Of course, I didn't tell her until later on about that, too. Maybe it was all the death surrounding us, but it excited us both and made it almost unstoppable. I just couldn't stop myself. I thought I was possessed, but she was the same way. I couldn't get her off of me. She was going for it.

After that, I remember going back downstairs and no one had even noticed that we had gone. The Lieutenant had asked her when we had both walked back to the Hum-vee what was on the schedule for tomorrow, she responded: 'We're done here, we got everything we need. Give it to the Army and let them do whatever they've got planned. And that was that."

"Did you ever see her after that?" Qian was completely fixated on the story. I knew I had succeeded unearthing some part of me that had been forgotten, and now made whole.

"I did actually, in October after coming home I was back in Washington D.C. and we had arranged to meet up and go out. I remember it being an equally spectacular evening that lasted through the weekend. Sunday morning came, she got dressed, packed and caught her flight back to San Diego. We had made plans to meet up before the holidays on the West Coast. I flew out the night of the Marine Corps ball in dress uniform and when I got to San Diego, I ended up sitting alone at the bar of the Doubletree in Downtown, drinking Old Bushmills Irish Whiskey. She never showed, and being that I was young and naive, I took it pretty hard. I got drunk, almost got arrested, but the cop, was an ex-Marine and was shocked at the cabbage on my chest and stuck me into a cab and told me to take it easy. The next day, I went home." I raised my hands in frustration, shaking my head, clearly signaling the end of my secret.

"Never heard from her again, huh?"

"Nope," I answered, realizing my momentary sorrow from an experience that I had never examined sober, or aloud.

"I never told anybody about that story, and I certainly never told anybody about her. Tragedy, strange elation, disjointed emotions, sexual desire, loss. That seems to cover the full spectrum."

"Not quite, but almost. My story should fill in any missing gaps." Qian lit a cigarette and handed me one. I got up, still naked and walked to the window, the curtains still open and stared out at the city filtering through the fog, rain and red traffic lights.

She was watching me carefully, adjusting her glasses with one hand and smoking with the other. The television was still going. The man in black was on his back screaming with the volume down as the machine sucked away a century. Chris Sarandon was giving Cary a lecture on true love and his misfortune.

"Well, make yourself comfortable. 1992 undoubtedly was not a good year, and before I begin, you're going to have to promise me that you'll never repeat this to anyone ever. If you do, I'll never speak to you again and I will vehemently deny the whole thing."

"I promise to never repeat what you're going to tell me." I gave her my word without having to be asked for the second time.

"Sebastian …" she became concerned, serious and almost overwrought. "I mean it, I'll never speak to you again. Imagine a world without me."

"That's not a world I'd wish to know, I certainly wouldn't thrive there. I give you my word."

"Well …" she exhaled and quickly lit another cigarette. "Nineteen-ninety-two was strange. I was fourteen. I was dating this Korean guy named Song. We were both going to that Magnate school in Culver City together. It was my first year and it was his third. He had a car and his parents were pretty wealthy. He was sixteen and had his independence. They didn't seem to care where he was, because they had several restaurants to run. Simply put, I lost my virginity to him on Valentine's day."

"I believe you told me this before," I interjected.

"Stop interrupting, I know, it's just background, and it's not the story I'm going to tell you. What I didn't tell you, comes after. So hush." She was serious. I poured another glass of beer from the service tray. I had one more bottle on ice. I began to feel it was going to be needed.

"Well after a few months of having sex, which was new to me and very addictive, I was absorbed in puppy love with Song, who had had sex before. I wasn't his first, and I thought he was pretty good. By May, I was pregnant and terrified. I couldn't believe it and I began to worry about what I was going to say to my parents. I just couldn't it. I called Song, told him about it, of course he acted aloof and distant, I didn't quite get it at the time. He told me not to worry that it would be taken care of. At the time I had no idea about abortions, unprotected sex or even the thought that he was just playing me. I knew he had probably done it before. He stopped calling me, he wouldn't come by anymore. I had no car and no way of going to see him. It was awful. I couldn't ask my mother to take me over to his house where I'd have to confront him in front of her. I just couldn't do it. I finally had my girlfriend Anna, whom you've met, the girl who you said 'looks Japanese.'"

"Oh, yeah, I remember her, you've known her that long?" I was surprised. She was Chinese, very plain, wide chest, no boobs, dressed like a 1950's sock-hop girl.

"She took me over to him and we confronted him. Of course, I melted and broke down into tears. I was so stupid back then. It was Anna who yelled at him when she realized I was being useless. She threatened him that if he didn't pay for my abortion, that she was going to go into his house and tell his parents." She sipped her ginger ale and stared absently at the television.

"The next day, he showed up at my house with a thousand dollars and told me if I needed a ride to the doctor's office, he'd take me. I made the appointment a few days later and he showed up as promised to take me to the private clinic where I had my first abortion. It was really awful. I wish I had gone with someone else because when I came out, Oh was already gone. I had to call Anna who was mad at me for not calling her in the first place. The doctor was rough and I bled a lot. I didn't know what from, but later when I healed, I

realized that he had cut me. I didn't know if he had done that
on purpose or not but it was not a good experience.

"I recall some of this, we had …"

"I know, just please be quiet."

I held up my hands, indicating that I was backing off
from interrupting. I drank my beer, and stayed silent.

"After that, obviously I never heard from Oh again. It
seemed like Anna was my only friend that summer. I was so
ashamed by what had happened and I could never tell my
parents. I really just decided to sink into the background. I
took my photography more seriously and decided to take a
few classes at Santa Monica College. I believe it was Drawing
class 108, Photo 101 and Photo Lab 102. My parents signed
the underage consent form because of my age.

"It's odd that you had no problem getting an abortion
but needed a permission slip for higher education."

"My thoughts exactly, welcome to California.
Anyways, In my parent's eyes, everything was going great for
me, they didn't know I had an abortion and had no idea I was
severely depressed and was trying to get out of the house so
they wouldn't catch on. My dad had even bought me car to get
back me and forth to school. If there was a God that was
watching after me, or over me, he or it or whatever would've
and should've stopped me, then and there."

"I was actually forgetting what had happened with
Song, and happily focusing on my summer classes. I had also
told my parents that I didn't think the Magnate school was the
place for me so they enrolled me at Indian Springs High
School. They were silently thankful because they didn't have
the burden of paying for the tuition, and it was closer, which
strangely, to this day even, leads to me meeting you, so …"

"Of course …" I replied, smiling.

"I'd also met some people who were very much into
photography. Mark for one, he was the instructor. Obviously
much older, a Vietnam Vet, a black guy who had lived most of
his life in Venice Beach and often told stories about surfing
and traveling. I know it sounds really cliché, but … he was

also one of first black men that I had spent anytime around. What did I have to worry about? I was learning and enjoying the summer, going to school, driving around with Anna and was completely over Song. Anna was happy because I had enrolled in her school, so we'd have some of the same classes at Indian Springs. Summer was ending and the last week of class came, Mark had told the entire class that there was a photo trip planned to go out to the Angeles Crest Forest and take some day shots, some waning light shots and some night-time time-lapse. It would go from three o'clock to almost nine pm, depending on how many students showed up. It was also suggested that it would be a good opportunity to get a lot of photos or at least a few, to help start a portfolio."

"I had told my dad that I was going out with Anna to take pictures and wouldn't be back until the next day because I was staying at her house. Why I said that to this day, I have no idea."

"I drove out to the spot on the flyer and when I got there Mark was already there waiting, he had a friend with him named 'Sydney' who was supposed to be out helping him assist. At first, I was a little bit strange about it, but after we started talking about photography and cameras and setting up shots all the negative ideas I had about being outdoors with two semi-unfamiliar black men vanished. Of course, no other students showed up, so it was just the three of us. As planned we took daylight shots, many with different films, lenses and filters. We walked down the trail some distance to a small brook or a stream, whatever it was, to get some shots with light on water, the same in waning light, some of those that you've actually seen and thought were pretty good."

"You still have those, oh my God, I've seen them," I responded, feeling the impending horror.

"We followed the trail further out until we got to high ground and we took several rolls of the setting sun, in disappearing light which weren't very good. I didn't really care how those turned out. We decided to take a break and have a small bite to eat. Mark had brought a bunch of granola bars and some sodas. I don't know if the whole thing was planned or not or if it was spontaneous but we set up our third spot on a grass field off the trail a short distance from where we had taken the previous set of pictures." Qian exhaled deeply, it seemed as though in telling me this, her heart had sped-up and started to race and she was nervously trying to calm herself. She lit another cigarette. I took one as well.

"I had some problems setting up my shot and both Mark and Sydney had both come to help, it was already dark. Sydney was adjusting the tripod and Mark was behind me looking over my shoulder at the aperture settings telling me what to do. Before I knew what was happening Mark had quickly grabbed my arms and pulled them behind me and dragged me backwards away from the camera. I remember my heart sinking into the pit of my stomach. Sydney had grabbed my feet out from under me and was immediately between my legs and was quickly on top of me on the ground. Before I could inhale enough air and relax the constriction that had gathered in my throat, even enough to audibly yell out, Sydney had put a long piece of black gaffer tape across my face. I was unable to open my mouth and I was unable to scream. Every sound I made was muffled. Mark bound and held my hands back while Sydney pulled down my pants and began to take off my clothes. I tried to kick and move around, hoping to get away, but I was completely over-powered."

"He took his time, knowing that there was no one out there to stop them or interfere. I started crying and was terrified but that wouldn't stop them."

I shook my head in acknowledgment, trying to understand.

"I hadn't ever had an orgasm with Song and was shocked that I couldn't stop any of it. To make matters worse it just seemed that I kept getting wetter. They both kept telling me what to do and when to hold still. My stomach was starting to hurt. I just didn't think being raped and having an orgasm was possible. I thought it would never stop. I felt Sydney underneath me. Even though they had removed the tape and the rag some time ago, I couldn't scream anymore, I was past that. My whole lower body was beginning to throb in pain from all the contracting."

When they finished, they just got up, packed up their gear and left without saying a word. I was shaking, I was too numb and shocked, and scared and whatever to move at all. I was literally frozen for over a good ten minutes. I stumbled around dazed after I heard their car pull away and some time had passed. They had taken off with my pants, my underwear and my socks, so I was stumbling around, cut up, oozing and bleeding in nothing but my Doc martins and a thin t-shirt. I grabbed my camera and tried to find my way back to the car, but I had gotten lost on the way and ended up wandering around in the dark for hours. I came out to the road several miles south of where the car was parked and had to walk back. That was when the real fear had begun to set in. My knees, my back and my hands were all scraped up and bloody. Paranoid, I hid in the bushes every time a car went by. I think I even missed a cop. I thought they would come back and within a good fifty feet of the car, they did. I hid in the bushes until almost dawn waiting for them to leave, hiding for my life. It was the most horrible thing I think I ever went through."

Qian was streaming with tears. I was so transfixed and visually into her story that I was really elsewhere. I was with her on the road and in the woods on the side of the deserted freeway. I had never seen her cry about anything. She had never shown much emotion at all in the four years that I had known her and I had inadvertently found out why. It was that candid retelling of an absolute catastrophe of trust that made me realize why all the questions I had ever asked myself about her. The stripping, the father-figure, the lack of trust in things and people, the desire for money, which was nothing more than a supplanted need of power, the aloof demeanor. Between sobs, she was trying hard to speak.

"I love … you …" I heard the words but didn't know how to take them. I didn't know where they were originating from and what their real meanings were. I kept thinking it was a cry for help, but didn't know how to process it.

I kept quiet and hugged her close. It was all just a horrible fucking tragedy. Men with dicks being reckless and uncaring. The testosterone in me wanted to go find that cock-sucker and his friend and kill them both. I was slowly filling with rage, but realized that I needed to just quietly digest it because it wasn't the time or the place for losing control.

"I love you too, Sweetheart. That must've taken quite a lot to tell me that."

She sobbed, sometimes heaving and wiping at the tears falling across her face. "I've never told anybody until just now. I don't know why I told you."

"1990," I said, simply. She laughed a little in response and then punched me daintily in the chest. She hugged me and pulled me closer to her. Kissing me, she begged me again not to ever tell anyone. It was in that moment that I believe my heart broke and something within me changed and was gone for ever. I felt hopeless about the rest of the sickened world. I felt more hopeless than I had ever felt before. Qianqian wrapped her legs and arms around me and pushed her bare hips against mine and began to kiss me madly, slobberly, crying, and thrusting her tongue into my mouth. She was trying to quell her feelings once more with sex and I couldn't deny her. I would've been a bastard had I been so callous. Now was not the time for direct therapy. I could taste her salty tears across my lips and across my tongue, inside my mouth. She was pushing at me wildly with her hips and her feet slaving to get me hard.

We had both silently decided to make love until the sun came out, and it seemed to be a moral imperative, hoping to erase away the reality of our confessions. We would pass out and twice I had awoken to find her riding me. She awoke later to find me on top of her pushing for dear life, the bed sheets were soaked and the room smelled of sweat, sex, the dinner tray and stale cigarettes. Buttercup had long since ridden away bare-back and side-saddle into the sunset with the man-in-black. The morning darkness filled the room, extinguishing us both.

From the Yukon Mining Company ...

I felt as if I had been swallowed a thousand feet down into the deep realms of my king-size poster bed. Alone, tucked in, trapped in the general malaise and unable to escape for no more than a few moments to eat or get a cup of tea, sit on the toilet or uselessly change the channel. It had been weeks since I had seen her and it felt almost as if I was having withdrawals. I was only pacified by the news of the Presidential elections that were slowly beginning to rip away the para-cutical membrane from the surface of the country. After several hours of considering the claims of ill-cast votes, voter irregularity, gerrymandering, equipment tampering, recidivism, nepotism, political hacking and everything that would inject the proper amount of apathy into any viewer, I came to feel that I was far beyond effect, redemption or any point of political motivation. I couldn't stand another face barking across the airwaves at me from the Fox News network or even CNN.

I switched the television off and went back to reading Henry James' *'The Ambassadors'*. The thought of page one-hundred and eighty-five was already making me sleepy. My thumbs had traveled past the same spot in the same volume for years. I could almost hear the words in my head with my eyes closed. They played over and over until I was, again, elsewhere.

Chapter 4.
*"I've come, you know, to make you break with everything,
neither more nor less, and take you straight home."*

I was asleep before I had time to consider whether I had read the words or once again imagined them transforming my attention into a post-hypnotic suggestion. When I opened my eyes, Fuzzbody was sprawled out on my chest, purring, staring at me contemptuously.

"Hello, darling ..." I mocked, but she had nothing in retort.

I looked over at the clock and found it to be fifteen after four in the morning. I awoke in a sweat and felt as if I was beginning to come down with the flu or at least a fever. I was hungry but felt depressed, a combination that's usually counter-productive. In the next moment, I became cold and stared at the ceiling. I knew that I was in the clutches of something awful, something unexplainable, something that was literally turning the seconds of my days and the muscle-mass of my form into a worthless and abandoned ash that would find itself shoveled deep into the earth and quickly forgotten. If only the damn phone would ring, everything would be fine again. If she could find a brief second, enough to just dial the numbers, wait and whisper my name lightly into the receiver and hang-up. I would barter a large piece of my soul to find a moments relief. The last words she had breathed to me, were simple and now I was as dark as the lyrics from a Phil Collins ballad.

"I'll be back in a few days, don't worry," she lied.

"Is there any need?" I was a shell.

"Qian nettle and Raines root ... why would you need to?" She had alluded to an interesting and true piece of botanical information that I had discovered in an Audubon Journal one wintry Saturday afternoon over coffee after researching my own name. Qian nettle was listed as a lethal poison that could quickly bring about death to a full grown adult upon breaking the dermis. The first time I had read that, I laughed out loud which raised a stir. While there were several direct antidotes listed, the third one on the list was Raines root. I had found this tid-bit of scholarly information both fascinating and amusing. Qian was quite put off by the notion that she was lethal, and that I was the cure. She had rolled her eyes thinking that it seemed heavy handed. Raines root was also listed as a possible homeopathic cure for Yellow Fever, and although I knew that I wasn't suffering from any symptoms of malaria. I was sure that I had nothing within me that could cure me completely of her.

I watched her. She was slowly packing her bag without much thought or order. I knew what was happening but I was powerless to do anything about it. I had been in this place before.

"I'll be with Brittsy, you shouldn't worry at all."

"You're already reading my mind, aren't you? Brittsy is an excellent female influence on you," I replied. My tone was deeply sarcastic, I was desperately scrambling for something interesting to say that might make her change her mind and stay.

"I'll call you when I get to New York."

"By the time you get to New York ..." I stopped in mid-sentence, she was already out the door.

♞ ♛ ♞

When I finally stopped thinking about Qianqian and was able to pull myself outside for fresh air, it wasn't until I was several blocks away from the house and driving recklessly that I realized I was still wearing my striped green pajamas with my black bathrobe and slippers.

"Damn," I spat, out-loud, further realizing that once again I had left without my wallet. I had left a twenty in the ash tray with a bunch of coins for the sake of parking meters that were the blight of most Hollywood streets and used for emergencies only. Resolved, I drove on.

I found myself at the *Yukon Mining Company* on Santa Monica Boulevard in West Hollywood. I had driven to my destination automatically, consumed in thought. My brain was deeply engaged in trivial matters that seemed to be burning me down quicker than the Malibu fires. Not a soul looked at me strange as I strode across the dingy brown patterned carpet to a booth at the window on the far-side of the restaurant in a darkened corner. The *Yukon Mining Company* was one of a very few and very last establishments to observe the indoor smoking regulations imposed throughout the county of Los Angeles. The thick acrid air could've easily been an item on the menu. The night crowd that found its way in off the streets for a cup of mud, a patty melt, an enchilada or a slice of meatloaf at anytime between the hours of one and five am, would shock, horrify and almost send any unsuspecting mind over the edge if you weren't properly prepared.

The Yukon Mining Company was colloquially referred to as the You-can-mine-me-honey by the schools of Mexican transvestite queens, curb-dwelling black cock-suck burn-outs, Armenian Johns with their sixteen-year-old Mid-Western desperate boy-toys, some-in and some-out of make-up, mini-skirts, high heel transparent stripper pumps with peckers like axe-handles always ready for a long night out and the promise of making a few hundred dollars. The place was far too much like a turn-of-the-century burlesque or State-Fair for men, locals and tourists. You would never see anyone from the West Hollywood Sheriffs department casually stroll through the front door and order up some scrambled eggs and coffee. Knowing this, and having never been approached, accosted, or given a hard-time, I could find myself there on some of the most 'darkest' nights of the year on the register of my soul, tending to my on-going depression.

Most of the waiters were seasoned veterans of the fag-hag hustle and stood the test of time, impervious to clutches of a pro trying hard to strike 'pay-dirt' at the end of the night for either a place to stay, or a mad-dash at the tip-money. Several of the waiters had the stereotypic mustached, Police Motor-cycle-rider, YMCA wannabe, middle-aged salt going for them, replete with tattoo's, earrings and ring-around-the-collar.

Two tables down, was seated the Alpha Queen of the street corner, Jizella. As always, eyeing me cautiously, carefully and lustfully. She knew full well that I was a cop, but always wanted to make me a new conquest. I acknowledged him smiling at me, and it being a free country, smiled back and broke off to stir my thick, brown, mud. 'She' had dealt herself a strange hand of cards in life being one of the most convincing girl-wannabe's I'd ever seen. No tell-tale signs of rough, workman's hands, or hobbit-esque feet. Just a slightly protruding Adam's apple that would most-likely stay hidden behind a scarf, a collar or a well-manicured hand. It was enough to make anyone gag.

I felt myself from the torso down, slipping lower into the booth and mentally drifting further away as I stared aimlessly out the window across the Santa Monica Boulevard. The street lights were languidly camouflaging every chance of a shadow, making the scene all the more lonely and frustrating. Cars past in the night outside and I got the distinct impression that all of them were up to no good.

The waiter finally showed up with my chicken-fried steak and three eggs scrambled, wheat toast with marmalade and a side of cottage cheese. I did my best to cut through it all, navigating the clouds of the second hand smoke that were so desperately trying to occupy rooms in the corner-offices of my lungs. The food was good, but I felt like shit. Jizella was still eyeing me with a toying type of maneuvering, like some practiced cold-war genius. Thankfully YMCA came and blocked the view, refilling my coffee.

"How's the food, Honey? Everything alright?"

"Not bad," I answered, wiping my mouth with a cheap napkin.

"You know you left the house in your pajamas again?" he asked me, suggestively.

"Absolutely, trying to start a new trend," I responded, half-heartedly, with a smile leaking out from the side of my chipped porcelain mug. YMCA immediately slipped into a practiced routine of sachet, hip-leans, cocked-neck and limp-wrist mixed with disdain.

"Have you seen the get-ups in here, honey? Pajamas are cute, but the Felix Unger thing might not bring it home, if you know what I mean?"

"Good thing, I'm not trolling for royalty", making a nod in Jizella's direction, "or an Oscar Madison, huh?" I smiled.

"I know exactly what you mean, me neither," he laughed, refilling my coffee. He floated away at the sound of the small silver bell on the kitchen counter signaling more hot food ready for an ensemened belly.

I was trying not to fixate on my surroundings and ate the remainder of my breakfast quietly. I hadn't eaten a bite of food in over eighteen hours, so everything tasted good. No matter if it was, or not. Paging my way through the most-recent copy of the LA Weekly, I laughed a little to myself and a little out loud, especially when landing on the full-page spread that had been given to my article which was letter-set around a second-hand graphic of an Uncle Sam in a ratty beat suit with forefinger pointing directly out to the reader, accompanied by a stern gaze and a frown. The title read 'Uncle Tom's working for Uncle Sam', the sub-head directly below in a smaller font read 'and a few that just won't go away.' Before turning it in, I had wisely deleted a paragraph highlighting Uncle Tom number 5: Chief Bernard Parks. I felt it better to not overtly antagonize the Chief in such a provocative and lascivious manner, lest I find myself exposed, and dismissed. Going after easier targets seemed the softer option. I had hoped my readers hadn't noticed. Nationally Syndicated Black radio talk-show host, Larry Elder was a usual media whipping-boy. It was easy to demonize the local Angelino and accuse him of selling out on the local black communities by shouting down every non-white voice that called-in, whether he agreed with them, or not. Naming Kobe Bryant as an aloof, detached from reality, misogynist débutante and listing several snippets of conversation 'overheard' at a local restaurant seemed cheap but print worthy. Number 1, Clarence Thomas, Supreme Court Justice. A sub-head read: 'What ever happened to Anita Hill?' I had sunk to new lows of degeneracy. I guess I was reaching to the black audience the best I could as another sheltered white writer.

I flipped through the pages, moving from the articles, advertisements, music, film, art and then deep into the back-pages where scores of men, women and various 'other' genders advertised themselves for services to render for a small fee per hour, available at any time. I wondered how many of the girls were stock photos, and if I called, would the girl in the photo arrive or someone similar? The odds seemed to go against authenticity in advertising. The unsuspecting reader could, possibly call any one of the patrons of the *You-can-mine-me, honey* restaurant. On page seventy-two, in a large ad, the queen of the evening, Jizella stared out at me in a moment of frozen beauty. The only give away to knowing that an axe-handled man-woman would be beating down your tight-dime anus was the two very simple and large letters to the right of the ad, 'TS'. Transsexual. God forbid the unsuspecting seventy year-old man addicted to watching Howard Stern on cable, who finally musters the courage to call one of the many your-surprise-awaits ladies and seizes up like an epileptic having a coronary at midnight. I always half-expected to see Qian as I leafed through the call girl ads of the weekly. I wouldn't put it past her to work out new ways to expand her hustle. But she had a long way to fall first before that happened. But maybe she didn't. She was steadily becoming more pro as time passed.

I cast the paper aside, annoyed at the detail and depth of pandering that was palpable in the pages now resting beside me. Looking across the restaurant, Jizella, on the pay-phone with his/her back to me was methodically returning a page to a would be client. She would either make the scene, punch it ala legs akimbo, or end up back at his/her pre-paid room at the St. Moritz Hotel on Sunset, stuck watching Katie Couric wondering about her legs, her hair and how big her little bird breasts might be. If they're still soft or nice to hold in hand. Fleeting thoughts from a hetero-sexual reservoir of un-tapped emotion.

Grabbing the attention of my Harlequin-Romance waiter, I made the universal sign in the air for 'check' and dug a twenty from my robe pocket. Breakfast for one came to eleven-seventy-two. I quickly found my way back to the truck and onto the dark Hollywood streets. I had enough time to make it home, get eight more hours sleep and then head in for four more days of twelve hour shifts.

Forty-eight hours every week equaling ninety-six hours per pay period at Detective grade two, pay rate of thirty-seven dollars per-hour, which comes out to eighty-seven hundred a month, not including overtime, shift differential or week-end pay. I made more then enough money, had yet to purchase the burden of a mortgage, and had enough time and energy on days off, but sadly though, I was more miserable now than I had been when I was broke, surrounded by debt, student loans and no job. I realized that if I didn't find a distraction soon, I was probably going to destroy myself or at worst end up as a chronic-masturbator, breaking new worlds records, surpassing the fifteen hour mark, shamelessly. I needed a vacation. I needed to get my mind away from Qianqian. I had little desire for therapy or discussing the way I felt in detail. An exploration at this point seemed mostly self-indulgent, mis-directed and strategically unsound. The desired effect would be to cleanse myself of her face, her voice, the smell of her skin, the sound of her laughter, the mentally registered pattern of her footsteps, the pauses, up to tip-toes – and back; the shifting and un-still pattern of her distracted focus via phone calls, both planned and unplanned, five minutes in a book and then another cigarette, a sigh; the shape of her hips while lost in deep peaceful slumber, her turns and pulls on the blankets; the vast collection of eyeglasses, both worn and unworn, cleaned and un-clean; the piles of new shopping left in unopened bags set carefully in different corners of the house and uncollected as to not feel the guilt of the cost, mostly which contained high heeled boots size seven in nude, beige and sometimes, but rarely, black.

If this was the way things were going I knew that I was in for some rough times ahead without her. I felt almost delirious. I was already aware of the fact that she was traveling around with Layden almost every chance he had to jump on a plane. I knew in my heart that she was also having sex with him and I had turned a blind eye to the whole subject of her promiscuity. We never said that we were going to be exclusive with each other and it was far too late to try to set new ground rules. She lied to me when she knew that I needed to hear something from her that made our relationship seem normal. Unfortunately, normal was something it would never be. I ignored the phone calls from the steady stream of male callers that always seemed to be waiting just on the periphery. Layden usually called in the daytime or when he knew that she'd be alone. Andrew usually called every Thursday to make plans for the next day. I could have, with almost no effort, listened to all of her calls from work. I could've made audio logs of everything she said and made a list of every one that she spoke to, but that would've been a breakdown of the relationship I had with myself and her. I didn't want to become a voyeur like the rest of the men that she met at work. I had always saw myself as a little better off then sleazy middle-aged burn-outs who were looking for new ways to fulfill themselves. I knew I was above the fray of degenerates that wandered in off the street with a handful of one-dollar bills. Then again, maybe I wasn't.

From a coffee stand in Central Park ...

The first thing she realized when she got out of the cab in mid-town Manhattan, was how cold it was, how rainy it was and how different the energy felt on the street, as opposed to back home in Los Angeles. Qian had been to New York many times, but usually in the summer or later in the year, when traditionally, the weather is at its zenith. Most of the tourists find their way to New York in October, November and December for the absolute luster and brilliance that the city takes on during the waning of the year. April, seasonally, is rainy and gray, devoid of most of the white-plastic bag toting tourists and usually much less distracting and much more enjoyable. March and April are the wettest months on the calendar and it's also when most of the super-models, artists and elite yuppie businessmen overdose by the gaggle-load on heroin, staying inside their cushy, over-decorated fourteenth-floor apartments trying to avoid the bad weather, desperate panhandlers, and every-other-john-doe-trying-to-bum-a-smoke, curb-side.

Qian wandered into the Westin, slowly, dazed, trying to take in the difference of the experience all at once. She felt for a brief instant as if she had found the secret to the city, like a magical lottery that only hits once out of the 365 days in the drawing. The prize being 'the best day to be standing curbside in the city is today'. It was late April, and she felt she'd secretly broken through to someone else's version of New York, something more pure and tangible. She could feel it beginning to surge through her like a flow of low-amperage current escaping from an exposed wire below the concrete. Brittsy was already in the city. She had caught a different flight a few days previous, wanting to spend time with her brother on Long Island. Layden wasn't due in to town until Tuesday, so she knew she had the next two days to tool around the city with Brittsy, unencumbered.

The Maitre-de took her bag, asked her name and escorted inside. "Staying long, Miss?" A tall African man, who loomed almost to the seven foot mark smiled at her with a mouth full of teeth and diamonds for eyes.

"Four days," she answered.

"You couldn't have picked a better place to stay then." He held open the door for her as she ducked inside, escaping the downpour and shaking herself off. In just a few minutes traveling from curb to counter, she had taken on the look of a drowned kitten. The African escorted her forward to a smiling young Indian girl in a dark blue vest, white shirt and calm expression. "Miss Mao to check in," he finalized, smiled and headed back outside to stand under the awning holding his umbrella.

"One moment Miss Mao, let me find you here … ah yes, room 4510. Suite, 4 days. Do you have any other bags?"

"No, just the one," she replied. It was the first time that she had wished she had packed more. She needed more clothes to be able to adjust to the change in climate, but it was as good excuse as any to have to spend a small ransom on shopping. She took the key and headed across the multi-colored lobby to the banks of elevators. It was only when she stepped inside the elevator car and saw the looming rows of buttons, that she realized that she was staying on the top floor of the hotel. It wasn't that she minded heights, as heights didn't bother her so much, but riding up 45 floors in a small box gave her a distinct feeling of claustrophobia. No amount of xylophone jazz would make it any better either.

When she turned the door handle, she half-expected to hear the television on, or Brittsy talking loudly into the phone, but the lights were off, which cast a gray shadow across the carpet. The atmosphere was silent, if you weren't counting the loud tapping of the rain on the large square windows on the far side of the room. She was alone. Britts was probably out meandering through the city by herself, with a strange man she'd just met or had sex with, or still spending time with her brother. Either way, Qian resigned herself to have a shower, change into dry clothes and settle down. She knew that she would later call her, hoping to find out what the hell she was up to.

She flicked on the television to break the thick silence of the room and began undressing by the bed. The room was a two-tone taupe train wreck that seemed as if it was trying to over-compensate for its unusually cramped feel. Minimalist was fine, if done with enough space. Otherwise it was just a well decorated closet. Her eyes scanned the room for an ashtray, but alighted on nothing that would even double as a stand-in. While the television was clamoring on softly in the background about the usual inane things that wind-up being covered on slow news days, she got undressed, towel dried herself, sat down on the toilet, lit a smoke and listened from a distance about the relevance of it being national High-Five day. She couldn't have cared less and would've killed anyone on the forty-fifth floor for a ginger-ale. The weather report said that it was also raining in Los Angeles, which made her feel better, but not by much. A fleeting thought of Sebastian passed through her soft nicotine massaged brain, but she forgot it as instantly as it had surfaced, reassuring herself that she wasn't going to spend a minute of thought on him while away. Maybe it was because she was going to be with Layden, maybe it was because she felt guilty. She didn't really settle on it, but either way, she wasn't going to loose sleep over him. It took her exactly six and half minutes to smoke her cigarette, the majority of the time she spent staring at her tanned toes contrasting against the beige tile floor of the bathroom. She had always felt that her feet had a sort of squareness to them, her toes seemed to stop abruptly on both appendages and looked as though at times, that they might all be the same length. Her left foot was adorned with a thin white gold toe ring that hadn't left her foot since high school. A few times it had come off, but not by her, usually by the curious at heart during an afternoon nap.

She smoked another cigarette after her shower and vaguely took note off the *no-smoking* sign that was clearly glued to the back of the hotel room door. Settling in, she called her only true friend who picked up on the second ring, almost as if she was waiting for the call.

"Hey! Where are you?"

"I'm in the lobby, bitch, on my way up to the room. Are you here yet?'

"Yeah I got in a couple of hours ago. I'm already upstairs. And I'm completely naked."

"You know how to turn a girl on, or is this just foreplay? Should I ask if you have a customer?"

Qian laughed at the thought of it. "Absolutely not, you know I don't work as fast as you do. Well … unless you consider yourself."

"How much do you charge for the night, baby?" Britts teased.

"Don't call me baby – Ho! And too much for you to afford!" she laughed and then hung up the phone, giggling in satisfaction.

146

♘ ♛ ♘

Qian stared at herself closely in the bathroom mirror, slowly applying black eyeliner and lightly brushing the fine hairs with an eyebrow pencil. She wondered if the mole on her right cheek was getting bigger as she was getting older, hoping that one day it wouldn't sprout hairs, become cancerous or grow into something the size of a birth mark. Brittsy was on the phone and affixed to *CNN* all at the same time. Her mother, somewhere on the other end of the phone line, was distraught over two boys dressed like Keanu Reeves in Colorado shooting up their classmates during an otherwise slow news day.

"I don't know what to tell you, Mom. Yes, it is tragic, without a doubt," she sighed, threw up her hands, and searched for a cigarette in her jacket pocket. Qian continued putting on lip-gloss via the hotel room mirror, smiling at her girlfriend and her mother in-absentia.

"Alright, mom, I know. Sure … gotta go … I know, I know. Yes. I love you to. Okay, bye." The cigarette was lit with the closing of the phone. Brittsy sat down on the toilet, beside her, shaking her head.

"God damn, who the hell cares about some spoiled rich kids who are obsessed with violent movies. This country is going to hell." Brittsy's bored face, uninterested with headline news, tanned, and lined with time, inhaled her cigarette, crossed her legs, and straightened her long, chestnut brown hair into three sections and slowly began braiding. She had bleached several blonde-streaks into her long bangs, which Qian noticed and wondered about. The more time past, she began to realize that Brittsy was becoming the white-version of herself, except much older. She was forty-four, making her almost twenty years older.

"I'm sure they'll say it had nothing to do with them watching that movie," Qian responded coldly. "Spoiled rich boys aren't my cup of tea either."

"Really," Brittsy exclaimed, "I would've thought otherwise. How do you explain Sebastian? Even the name sounds like he's some fag from Philadelphia."

Qian turned around and looked at her friend directly, "Wow, you really don't like him, do you?"

"Don't like cops, hate security guards and I don't care for lovesick puppies that have that endangered species look in their eyes." Her tone was mocking.

"Damn, and I was going to invite you to the Policeman's Ball."

"Yeah, right, ho. If I showed my face at a 'pork-chop hop', I'd probably embarrass half the bitches there because I'd slept with the most of their husbands and smoked glass with the rest," she spat from the side of her face in a rant, defamingly through billows of cigarette smoke. "I wouldn't last long," she chuckled.

"Don't worry, I'll never make you suffer his company again. The last time he picked us up at the airport, you talked about owls, Carlos Castaneda and witches all the way back to Sunland. He asked me later if you were high or just overly-concerned with your arrest record."

"That son-of-bitch said that? What a mother-fucker!" Brittsy stood up, unbuttoned her jeans and sat back down on the toilet to pee. "Did he run my record?"

"Quite some time ago," Qian answered, smiling, zipping her make-up purse shut and leaning against the door frame.

"Did you see it?" her eyes widened.

"Yeah ... jealous?" Brittsy just laughed, wiped herself, stood back up adjusted the twig of a butt hanging from her lips, half covered in lipstick. She buttoned up and closed in on Qianqian, with a light grasp of her hand on her backside,

"Honey, I lived that damn story, he aint got a damn thing on me, not even a hand on my ass."

"You're so riled, I love it," Qian laughed.

"Cops suck, Qiannyqianqian. He's depressing as shit as well."

"Do you feel the same way about Layden?" Qian added.

"Layden is another fool. It's a good thing that he's not here yet, either."

"What exactly are you planning now?" Qian sat on the bed and began inspecting her camera, the two lenses and her pack of glass filters.

"I don't mind putting out, for sure. I've had plenty of sex and been well paid for it, sweetheart. But if you haven't noticed … not only is Layden a bit of a freak, he's also a chicken-shit living off his wife's money. It's kind of sad. I 'sometimes' draw the line with cripples."

"Layden's not a cripple."

"No …" Brittsy guffawed, "but his wife is, and after watching the two of you together for the last several months, it makes my mind feel retarded watching you two commingle like sweaty fetuses in a glass. And besides, he's always suggesting that we have a threesome."

"I know, what's up with that? I noticed that in San Francisco. He said something about it twice, on the last night."

"Qian, listen … I wouldn't bat an eye if I had to eat your pussy. It's quality buffet and I've never turned down good trim yet."

"Britt!" Qian slapped her on her ass as Brittsy lit up another smoke.

"Baby, you wouldn't be a bad lay, but if he wants to try out the both of us, he should just come right out and say so and name the figure. Beating around the bush to beat around our bush … that's just childish, especially at his age." Brittsy smiled, winked and teased her just a little further.

"Britt, you can be so gross sometimes."

"Don't be such a prude, Qiannyqianqian. I eat pussy just as good, if not better than anyone. It would be a lie if I told you that bumping cunts with you was totally out of the question as well." Brittsy was being forward, but having several hours to kill and being bored, she didn't mind pushing the issue.

"Besides we got the next five days together, girlfriend, and I don't want to be dragging strange men back here every night. In-house pussy is so much more convenient. But don't worry," Brittsy sat on her lap and played with her, toyfully, "I don't bite, baby."

"You better not, you dirty little bitch!" Qian teased.

"Just think of it like jail. Tastes like chicken!" Brittsy laughed, and flashed Qian her ass before running off into the bathroom to shower and change into her pajamas. The last thing on Qian's mind was having an awkward love affair. Qian scooted herself up against the headboard, grabbed the remote and turned the channel. *The Princess Bride* was playing once more on Home Box Office, it had just started and it seemed like it was getting a heavy run this month regardless of the channel. It was a nightmare that she was unable to escape. The next channel up was *Breakfast at Tiffany's*. It seemed appropriate, and she had never watched the ending, either.

"You hungry, Britt? I can call out for food. What are you in the mood for?"

After a brief pause, Brittsy answered sheepishly, "Chinese."

"You're funny."

"You've got a dirty mind, little girl. I would love some fried rice with extra egg, pork chow mein maybe, pot-stickers?"

Qian picked up her phone to order-out and noticed that at some point in the afternoon her mother had called. She was probably wondering if she was going to show up at the house and stay over. 'One Message' read across the LCD display. She searched through the stack of menus stuffed into the bedside table drawer and began looking for something other than high-priced shellfish or pizza. The problem with staying at a hotel in Times Square is that every restaurant and eatery is ready to cater and deliver goods and services at the tourist rate, plus tax, plus tip. She settled on How's Deli, an order of pork chow mein, spinach pot-stickers and egg-drop soup with tofu.

Brittsy had finished showering and found her way back to the bed with a brush, wearing a set of purple 'Barney' pajamas.

"Barney ... are you fucking kidding me, chick?"

"You know how much I love great phallic Neanderthals."

"You're a sucker for a man in a purple felt suit, huh?"

"Barney's got a pretty sweet two-wheeler, you know. He rides to Sturgis every year."

"Yeah, but probably on a Metric Cruiser," Qian added.

"Nothing like a Yamaha, cockroaches and shrimp. The three things that will probably survive a nuclear winter.

"My first motorcycle was a Yamaha," Qian confided, naively.

"That so?" Brittsy clarified, smiling like a hungry prairie lion. "Almost every organism that ever inhaled oxygen cut their teeth on a Yamaha, retards included. Join the club, honey."

"And you, what did you start on?" Qian lit a Marlboro, inhaled and tossed one at her rustic partner.

"A red Schwinn three-wheeler. Had tassels, too!" The lighter sparked four or fives times in vain, before Britts could suck down her momentary dose of nicotine. Her dark tan was a duplicate of Qian's, and on almost every occasion, they would find themselves staring at each other because one had dressed very much like the other. Brittsy had a hard look in her eyes that would've only come from heartbreak, saddled with disappointment and cemented by a lot of personal disapproval. Qianqian and Britts both worked at the club on the same schedule and Britts had taken her in, almost from the first. Whether it was from sexual attraction or not, was questionable, but Britts had spent a lot of time and effort grafting her personality, her choices and her life-experiences into the young only-child, mostly through subtle direction, peer-pressure and Qian's strongest desire to be accepted. Brittsy had discovered early on that Qian had a hard time resisting and desperately sought role models. Brittsy had been stripping for almost eight years when they had met. Her life had been privileged before, but had turned south after several bad relationships that were pretty much repetitions of each other. Uninteresting and uninspiring. Wealthy, young, mal-adjusted trust-funders picking up the tab, spending years abroad, supping on extravagance until the cash evaporates and the relationship inevitably fails. A lifetime depending on men to stick a teet in one's mouth, only to have it yanked out every time prematurely leaves one a tad jaded and wary of the opposite sex. People flounder uselessly for a whole lifetime, unable to find a true and constructive purpose, going from one person to the next to feed on for money, youth, sex or security. Brittsy had long ago sworn off men, or at least relationships with men. Qian considered Brittsy's place in her life and the on-going relationship itself. She was just thankful that she wasn't alone.

The television carried on in the background. Audrey Hepburn was throwing her orange cat out into the rainy New York Streets. A day, much like the one outside, and Greenwich village not far away at all. George Peppard sat by, ready to set everything right with his brotherly love and intense devotion. Brittsy pulled a small journal from her bag and quietly made some reflective thoughts regarding the early events of her day out.

"How was your brother?"

"I hadn't seen him in a few years. He's always critical about my life and how I am. I found it annoying, but it was good overall."

"Isn't that what family is for? It's natural for them to care about you."

"Is it natural," she asked, "do they care, are you really sure about that, Qiannyqianqian? The girl that goes home every weekend to mommy and daddy?" There was a detectable amount of bitterness and sarcasm in her voice, but it didn't penetrate her polished armor. Being emotionally numb causes one to disregard the true target of a snide comment, personal attack or even petty jealousy. Useful at times, but mostly isolating.

"What the hell are you gonna do, Britts?" Qian added, coldly, "Go through life alone?"

"No, my little China girl. I'll always have you."

"You sound so confident," she smiled in retort.

"You'd never leave me, would you?" Britts asked, fishing her for a comic response.

"Ohh, just you wait till the money runs out, Chic. I'll drop you quicker than a sack of rotten apples."

"You wouldn't dare!" Britts pummeled her with her bed pillow and jumped on her, tickling her underarms.

"Say you'll never leave me, you little tramp. Say it!" Qian laughed and tried to wriggle free, caught in a wave of hysterics and Brittsy's smiling face and fingers. She straddled Qian from above and held both her arms with one hand and began blowing air-kisses against her underarm.

"Agghhhh! … Stop! … Please!" Qian couldn't stop laughing, and struggled impossibly to get out from under Brittsy, who was quickly mastering her. Qian felt her breasts pressing against her chest and realized their closeness, and quieted to only a girlish, almost uncomfortable giggle.

Brittsy had her left hand softly holding down Qian's arms above her head, and slowly moved her right hand in between her legs and into her pajama bottoms, massaging her. In that instant both of their hearts began beating in their chest like an oversized circus drum. Qian's eyes glassed over and her body relaxed as Brittsy closed her eyes, leaned against her cheek and kissed her. Qian's mouth magnetically found hers and pulled her in close with her legs until their hips met. It happened that quickly. She had often wondered if

153

she was ever going to go this far with her, and now the moment was literally on top of her. Brittsy pushed her hand down into her underwear, pulling off Qian's pajama bottoms in the process. Qian opened her bare legs wider as Brittsy massaged her, accepting the moment for what it was. She held her close to her, pulled her downward against her and somehow, instinctively managed to undress her completely, piece by piece. Her warm flesh against hers felt comforting, more so than what she thought it would be like. Brittsy's scrawny browned arms encircled Qian's torso and head, framing her face and hair, stretching out across the pillow. She was watching her eyes, as if in a trance as she pushed herself rhythmically against her.

"Oh, Qian ..." was the only words that left her mouth. Moments passed, and Brittsy was between her legs with her tongue. Her lips locked onto her in a fluid motion causing Qian to pull back and buck around sideways on the bed-sheets in ecstasy. She stayed on her for an eternity, bringing her to climax several times. Qian, heated, found herself moving down Brittsy's body, kissing her breasts and moving down past her navel. She pushed her legs against her belly and chest and kissed at her gently. She was pushing inside of her, sometimes using her fingers, methodically, like a soft pulsing of a strobe-light, or the humm of a radio, warm from being left on all night. Brittsy continued moaning and melted under Qianqian's touch. The room sighed at the dropping of pretense and dissolved the awkward defense at the sight of would-be love.

They held each other close, Brittsy was holding firmly to Qian's left foot, clutching at her small toes and slowly fading into sleep and quiet dreams while her attention drifted from her eyes, her nose and her soft pursed lips until blackness overtook them both and night put time itself beneath the sheets and covers. They slept like carved stone, held fast in each other's grip until the early call of house-keeping.

♘ ♕ ♘

The next morning was spent slinking around Chinatown, through stores, café's and hovering selectively above plates of dim-sum in small and dimly lit doorways and restaurants that had been operated by some of the same families for over a century. Qian watched Brittsy, seeing her the same now, but different. She sat closer to her than before, stood nearer while walking or paying for trinkets in line, and felt more attached to her and less alone. Britts took it in calmly. She was cautious not to distance herself from Qian's transformation, which would've caused a rift.

The rain was steady all afternoon from a café on Catherine Street. Qian sat inches from the window, watching the people rushing by, huddling close under black, red and beige umbrellas. For a moment, she sat thinking of San Francisco, the unchanging weather that was following her from one coast to another. Britts sat quietly plugging numbers into a Japanese math puzzle in the funny section. Qian had pulled out her camera and snapped several pictures. A series of passer-by's through the rain-dropped covered glass, and a few throw away shots of her white porcelain tea-cup, now half full. Qian focused on Britts for several moments before taking a bracketed shot, without flash of her face half-concealed by the New York Times. The camera returned focus outside on a Police cruiser that was parking in front of the café, in the red-zone, with lights ablaze. Sebastian would be at home now, she thought, either in bed, or getting up and making the coffee. Qian wondered briefly how he was doing, and for an instant she had wished she was with him, if not to do anything other than play a few games of chess. The rain picked up and obscured the view through the glass like a shower curtain. Her thoughts turned to the routines that

Sebastian would recite regarding the opening three moves and the following twelve counters. She was able to remember as far as the eighth progression into the game. Visualizing chess being the real key to serious playing and surprising moves.

"Thinking of your uniformed Prince Charming, my young darling?" Britts smiled with a playful tone through the crease of the paper.

"Absolutely not, fancy a game of chess though?" she lied. Qian took several more pictures of people in line. The travel chess was secured in her camera bag as usual.

"I never learned how to play," Brittsy admitted.

"You're kidding, right?" Qian was dumbfounded.

"Not at all, but I'd whup you in horseshoes any day."

"Never played."

"You're kidding, right?" Britts repeated Qian's statement, mockingly. The two police officers came through the front-door after having a cigarette and shook off the rain, kicking their feet against the rubber mat, they both began lustfully gazing over at them brazenly and overt. Qian decided to take several shots of them in the act.

"Take an effing picture, cop!" Britts barked out at them, with a snakelike quality, contemptuous of authority. They were thrown off by the post-modern moment that they had been subjected to. They both turned away and stood at the counter looking for a coffee.

Qian smiled at Britts, trying not to laugh out loud. "I cannot believe you!" she whispered. Britts blew her a kiss, sipped her tea and disappeared back into the newspaper.

Later, Qian spent close to eight-thousand dollars on clothes at Barney's. Brittsy bought a men's wrist-watch while acting disassociated for almost an hour while traversing through clothes racks. Qian thought the watch was for her brother and a token of her guilt, her love or some way to tell him that everything was fine.

Britts wandered around through the accessories, then into the men's department and later followed Qian into the lingerie department. Muzak played Frank Sinatra like a sad, overwrought cliché from above. Qian yawned and would've killed to have someone turn it off. To her it sounded like music for people with oxygen tanks who play bingo, eat Jello and complain about not having enough fiber.

The afternoon passed at a snail's pace. The rain kept the immoral-majority off the streets and huddled around coffee bars, café's, bookstores and shopping malls. Feeling cramped, Qian decided to purchase two over-size umbrellas and get some fresh air elsewhere.

"Had enough of this place yet?" Qian asked, unamused.

"This place is killing me, where are we going?"

"Outside. Maybe across the park."

"Are you mad? It's pouring out."

"It never rains in L.A., consider it an adventure."

"I guess."

The walk through Central Park during a mid-afternoon shower was breathtaking. A *'Tibetan Prayer Flag'* art exhibit was in full swing. Red, white, yellow, blue and orange linen prayer flags were strung along both sides of the road. American artists obsessed with freeing Tibet and putting on an ostentatious display about it, which according to news reports, cost several million dollars to plan and maintain.

The ruffled flags were soaked and sagging in the breeze, dripping their wishes on the stone and grass below. In several places workers were re-adjusting sections of flags that had either been blown down, or pulled down due to cracked tree limbs splintered by lightning. With both hands full of bags and umbrellas, Qian and Britts continued through the park slowly, arm in arm.

After a steady ten minutes of puddle-jumping, huddling together and skirting around obstacles, Brittsy wandered over to an outdoor coffee vendor to stand under the awning, put down her bags and to take a break. "This weather's amazing, I just hope we don't get an ass full of electricity."

"The odds are against us getting hit by lightning, unless of course, you've been hit before ..." Qianqian quipped.

"Beinvenue, Mademoiselles, ecoulair?" an elderly gentleman inside the coffee truck called out from the tranquility of his warm and dry kitchen.

"Hello, can I have a cup of coffee, please?" Brittsy asked.

"Two, please?" Qian corrected.

"Tres bien, duex café." The man poured the coffee from a stainless steel coffee urn into white Styrofoam cups.

"Lids, sugar, milk, honey is there on the side. Help yourself," he suggested in a thick accent. Qian stood under the awning, sipping black coffee, watching the rain fall. Britts was engrossed in opening a multitude of flavored coffee creamers and creating a digestive concoction that seemed to take an eternity.

"Oh, I'm sorry," Qian exclaimed, bumping into an older man standing next to her under the awning, wearing a long, dark beige raincoat and smoking a cigarette."

"No harm, Miss, it always seems a little crowded under this awning on rainy days," he remarked, through a pirate's grin and a glowing gaze. Qian momentarily registered that he had a false eye.

"You couldn't spare a cigarette could you? My girlfriend took my last one about ten minutes ago?"

"Sure."

"You seem familiar, do I know you?" Qian asked, smiling, slightly off guard and taken aback.

"Maybe, you from New York?" he asked.

"No, I live in Los Angeles."

"L.A.?" he retorted, with surprise.

"Flew in for the rain," Qian replied, smiling from behind her coffee cup, trying to light her smoke.

"Peter. Nice to meet you." he extended his lighter for her, assisting.

"Qian. Thank you."

"It's always better for me to share them, rather then smoke them all myself. My wife gets upset that I haven't quit yet. She doesn't let me smoke in the house or anywhere around her. You know, she says they smell awful."

"She's right."

"These days, I just say I'm going out for coffee."

"Oh my, good lord!" Britts exclaimed. Qian turned on foot to see what had happened with her girlfriend. The man put his hand on Brittsy's shoulder and smiled, telling her "It's not really that exciting, trust me."

"You're Peter Falk!"

"I'm told that … you'd probably like to have a cigarette as well?" he suggested, politely offering, subtly seeming to change the tone of the conversation.

"Thank you," Britts was dumbfounded and noticeably shaken.

"That's quite an antique of a rain slicker you're wearing, Peter," Qian dryly noted, observing his frayed and over-worn long jacket. She ran her finger down the soaked lapel. She noticed that it had the look of being stitched back up on many occasions. The jacket looked out of sorts, compared to the suit he was wearing.

"You two know each other?" Qian asked, not understanding.

"Sorry, she doesn't ever watch TV," Britts confided. "I'm Brittsy." The three of them were standing in direct proximity of each other, the space between them was no wider than a foot at most.

"Now I'm embarrassed. Didn't you play a grandfather to that little boy who looks like Jay Leno?" Qian admitted.

"That's one way to put it," he answered, with a sip of his coffee.

"Nice to meet such two lovely ladies over a cup of coffee. Very divine. It almost seems like we had a date. How long are you here for, Qian?" he pronounced her name like their was a pause between the two syllables.

"Just a few days, no longer."

"In a rush to get back?"

"Not really, I didn't think that New York was ever this beautiful."

"Don't let anyone ever hear you say that too loudly," he joked. The man behind the coffee stand raised an eyebrow and continued listening to the am radio that was garbling low in the background. It sounded like Italian mandolins. Peter inhaled the last draw on his cigarette, exhaled slowly through his silver facial grizzle and put the butt into a small red coffee can on the ground behind him that was slowly collecting rain water, drop by drop. It said Folgers on the outside of it.

"I'm always surprised about it too, every time."

"You don't live here either?" Britts queried.

He laughed. "No, I live in Los Angeles, most of my life actually. I'd probably never leave. Still, there's absolutely nothing so lovely, lonely and late-night as New York. No, ma'am."

Qian put her arm through Peter's holding on to him. "You're probably the sweetest man I think I've ever met. Has anyone ever told you that?"

"A few times, maybe, but I've been around for awhile. I try to tell my wife that but she rarely believes me."

"You remind me of someone," Qian added.

"He's a lucky fella," he assumed, winking at her, "Are you ladies going to stand around here all day drinking coffee, or have you got somewhere to go, perhaps?"

"We're staying at the Westin, we're headed back now," Britts replied.

"What a coincidence, wouldn't it be nice if we all walked there together? This way an old man doesn't have to feel so lonely, in weather like this."

"Sure. Why not?" Qian added.

"You know, I've had this raincoat almost forty years and it still keeps the rain out. Some people were under a belief that I had given it to a certain museum, but I just didn't have it within me to part with it. After all, we've been through quite a bit."

"That's quite an understatement," Brittsy remarked softly.

"Now, I'm the luckiest guy alive."

♘   ♕   ♘

When they got back to the hotel, the small Indian woman was waving at Qian from across the massive expanse of lobby.

"I think that small ugly child is trying to get your attention, Qiannyqianqian."

"Why me and not you? You hardly ever make sense, Britts."

"Ok, I'll go over with you," she added, as they strolled toward the mechanically polite desk clerkette.

"Miss Mao, … you have a package."

"See, told you," Brittsy snorted, rolling her eyes. "No one's going to leave me a message, honey."

Qian examined the package which was rather large and carefully eyed the handwriting. Immediately she recognized the script across the label as Sebastian's. Flourishing hand script with the signature letter Q trailing down the entire depth of the address.

"The cop sent you my arrest record, perhaps?"

"Perhaps, I just wanted to know if your eyes really were blue."

"Would they be anything else?" she asked, playing along. "Open the package, little girl, the suspense is killing me," Britts tried desperately to feign a demi-sense of uncaring and flippancy. Qian opened the box on the counter and lifted the lid revealing a neatly folded light beige DKNY raincoat. Qian knew it was hers.

"Uugh," Britts groaned. "What a thoughtful man," she exclaimed, putting a dour emphasis on the word 'man'. Her tone grated, like it was the last word that she could've ever wished to utter.

"Hmm." Qian handed the semi-empty box back across the counter, without removing the small envelope that was on the tissue.

"Could you take this and dispose of it, please?"

"There's a letter here for you," the clerkette responded.

"Throw it away, thank you."

"Poor Qian, all alone in New York, without a raincoat. How sickening."

"Have you always been such a man-hater or was it something that happened over time?"

"You cheeky whore, I'm going to wash your mouth out with soap." Britts stared at herself in the reflection of the elevator door, slowly applying lip-gloss.

"I never thought of myself as a man-hater," she spoke in a low, thoughtful tone.

"Please, Brittsy, you have it tattooed on your soul. No need to play coy."

Brittsy's gold reflection glowed under the soft orange light, her bright white toothy smile grew across her face like the high beams of a tractor-trailer on a freeway at night. The elevator dinged continuously past several floors.

"Ever going to fall in love again, or are we just going to rain on everyone else's parade?"

"Oh goodie, there's a parade tonight?"

"A-void-ing the quest-ion."

"Love is for mortals, Qian. Haven't you heard?"

Qian couldn't hold back the laughter. "Haah! Are you going to live forever now?"

"No, darling," She stared, backing out of the open elevator doors, "My heart's been dead for almost a decade. Comforting thought, huh?"

"Yes, meds might do you a lot of good."

"A lot of things might do me a world of good. A stiff cock and a dirty Martini, in that order, wouldn't be a bad start.

"You sure that you don't want a dirty cock and a stiff Martini, instead?"

Qian collapsed on her bed and picked up her book from the bedside table that she had been engrossed in. She was on page 54 of Haruki Murakami's *'Norwegian Wood'*. She wondered if she would ever end up feeling as love-sick as the older girl in the book. She didn't feel like she was in love with Sebastian or that she had ever been in love. It was a fact that she had pondered many times and found unsettling. The writer had stated that you didn't get a choice in whom you might fall in love with. It was as simple as 'you did' or 'you didn't'. She had felt only a shallow connection with Sebastian, even though she thought he was taking love-heroin on a daily basis during their relationship and was already lost.

Britts turned on the television and laid out on her bed in her bra and panties with an ashtray on her chest, sipping a cold Mexican beer.

"No cock ... no martini, huh?" Qian pointed out sarcastically. Brittsy just chuckled and turned the channel to a movie half-way in progress. It was *The Princess Bride* again. Qian glanced over at the screen and grunted, turning away in revolt.

"Qiannyqianqian no likey-likey?"

"I hate this fucking movie."

"You're kidding me, right? You detest one of the greatest films ever made?"

"I believe that I just said that," Qian continued reading her book.

"Ever read the book?" Brittsy quizzed her with an ominous look, thinking that she probably already knew the answer.

"You mean to tell me this thing was a book first?" she countered dryly.

"Jesus Christ, William Goldman is launching his fucking Imagination Ninja's to dispatch you as we speak."

"Just as long as they don't stick anything in my butt, I'm fine," Qian giggled in retort.

Brittsy cackled thunderously, exhaling a noxious death cloud of nicotine between every gust. "Baby, that's the first place they're laying waste to."

Mandy Patinkin was drunk and disorderly, leaning against a wall, yelling for Vezzini.

Inigo Montoya:
"I am waiting for you, Vizzini. You told me to go back to the beginning!"

"Well, anyways, it says a lot about your character, Qian. I would hate to make a diag-no-sis," Britts suggested.

"This stupid movie has something to say about my personality? I've got to hear this." Qian lit a cigarette and put Murakami back on the side table.

"Of course, it's simple."

"Simple?" Qian responded, perplexed, but smiling.

"*The Princess Bride* is a story about everything that you cannot have and about either chasing it or losing it. The fact that you would subconsciously reject it suggests that have some very deep-seated commitment issues, just for starters. "

"Really?"

"Absolutely," Britts answered, "you can even hear it in the tone of your voice." She was baiting her. They both smoked their cigarettes, watching the screen for a few moments. The air in the room was starting to look and smell like the wasted atmosphere from World War Terminus.

"You see, there are several different facets, just as our new friend that we met over coffee today states at the very beginning of the movie, true love, revenge, kidnapping, fighting, monsters, loss, you name it. Things like this usually trigger off something deep within the soul. That's why everyone likes it. Well, everyone … but you, that is."

"Maybe I don't have a soul."

"Well, other than that being blasphemous, the truth is that you've just never connected with it, that's all. You laugh at fortune-tellers, priests, ghost stories, anything that's not tangible, not quick to grasp. You have contempt for the unknown, but yet you'll eat taco's bought from a Mexican in a toilet stall. You must've been the one person that that retard Sting was singing that song to, back in the eighties … spirits in the material world."

"How dare you call Sting a retard! I love him!" she joked.

"Are you fucking kidding me, woman?" Britts exclaimed, dumbfounded. "That man is so full of himself, he gives me douche chills just looking at him."

"You think you know me that well, huh?" Qian asked.

"Actually, I don't know you at all, that's my point. You have this strange aversion for the one film that covers all bases, goes through all the archetypes. That says a lot about you. You don't see yourself in the one thing that most of humanity does."

"So, what am I then? A Mannequin? An Imposter? Not real?"

"That's probably the deepest, most introspective thing I've ever heard pass your lips." Britts blew smoke at her.

"What the fuck am I then on the inside, a rabbit?" Qian was trying to shed the conversation.

"*Watership Down*? I never finished it. Maybe a rabbit wearing a girl suit," Brittsy laughed. Qian stared at her incredulously for several long moments unable to control her thoughts properly while Brittsy's words washed over her, insulin-cold. It was hard to determine what Brittsy meant. She considered the fact that she didn't feel stationary within herself, she felt trapped. She had never mentioned this aloud.

"A girl wearing a what?"

"A fraud, Qiannyqianqian. It's pointless to get worked up over your shortcomings. Join the world, baby." Brittsy sipped her beer, fixated to the television.

Qian picked Murakami back up and found her way quietly onto the streets of Tokyo and the would-be advertising exec, turned story teller. Brittsy chuckled and made several phone calls to her mom, her brother and a few people back in Los Angeles. Layden finally called after she had gotten off the phone. He wanted to meet them over lunch tomorrow afternoon, but wanted to spend some time alone with Qian. Brittsy saw this coming and in typical fashion, rolled her eyes, yawned and made several more phone calls to make plans to leave the two hump-hounds alone in their greasy privacy.

"God, I hope the old statue gets you pregnant. What hideous children you'll have."

"Brittsy!" Qian guffawed, shocked. "Take it back," she demanded.

"Tell me, how does it feel to fuck such an antique, such a statue?"

"Well, like all statues, Ho, rock-hard."

Britts groaned. "Uugh, please, maybe with a little blue pill and some methamphetamines. He's a heart-attack away from having to do a lot of explaining. Fucking the stripper of the month is just the beginning, I'm sure."

"Is that the sound of bitterness, my love?" Qian asked, "Do you want some kisses from your favorite only-child?"

Britts moved over next to her on Qian's bed, kissed her and continued watching television, absently. "See, I told you this was better than dragging strange men back here." She leaned in close and nuzzled her face against Qian's neck, effectively distracting her from her book. Qian took off her glasses and connected herself wholly into Brittsy's embrace, kissing her passionately with her hand lightly resting on the outside-edge of her shoulder.

"I'm going to take a shower and then I'm going to come back to bed and make love to you, Ok?" Britts smiled, as Qian rose up, undressed and walked naked into the bathroom.

From an ugly booth in Bob's Big Boy ...

Days later, when Qian had returned to Los Angeles, she sat on her white chaise-longue couch listening to a litany of messages from the answering machine. Andrew had called several times again and she had no desire to talk to him. He had come in to the club when he was supposed to, and for her, that was enough.

She had only been home a day, and she felt different from the inside-out now. She sat with the lights off in the front room, watching the last of the sun fade away to darkness, smoking another cigarette. Sebastian had left only one message on the house phone from earlier in the afternoon. His voice sounded deeper, more baritone than she had remembered. It had seemed like a long time since they had talked, and she could hear the sadness well-engrained in his words.

"*Call me.*" She could hear the last two words of his message ringing in her ears, but she was more than hesitant to call. After spending the first few nights in New York with Britts and the last few with Layden, she was feeling diffused and diluted. She didn't have much emotion left over to share with somebody else, especially him. She had also begun to regret the affair she was having with him. He had just separated with his ex-wife and not yet divorced when she began seeing him. Abbey had stopped speaking to her outright and took her relationship with him as a betrayal. She had always planned in her mind, if there ever would be a moment of conversation between them, to just blame Sebastian. She would've gladly told Abbey that he pushed himself into her life, hoping that that would rectify the situation and mend the relationship. Somehow, she thought that Abbey would probably never listen to her long enough to buy it. Maybe her regret was Brittsy's severe protestations about who he was. She felt detached and overwhelmed having to participate and give something back to the relationship in order to keep it going, unlike the casual relationships that she maintained from the club that sustained themselves upon sex, lust or money. Those were a thousand times easier to deal with. Maybe if things were different, she thought, it might work. Sebastian was looking for something normal, and she knew that currently, she was far from it.

Her mother had also left several messages, all in Chinese. Most of them she didn't even need to listen to. What her mother had to say was predictable, and revolved around her desire to see Qian, and to call her back.

Qian wandered around the house, watering the plants, dusting shelves, listening to Sting on small clock radio. She had lit several candles and a few sticks of incense. When Sebastian had mailed out the rain-coat, he had also washed and changed the bed-sheets. Outside, the water-fountain in the back yard sat silent. The pump had been switched off and several oranges littered the cobblestones around the base of the tree. A single star just north-east of the crescent moon in the sky shone bright. Qian had looked out at the same star, same moon just days before from her room atop of the Westin, in New York. Now at home, she felt awkward, sad and agitated all at the same time. No amount of cigarettes, green tea or hot baths seemed to quell her. Brittsy had left as soon as she had come back. She had planned a road-trip with several other girls to ride up to Hollister in Northern California on motorcycles for a few days, going through Big Sur and Livermore. She had asked Qian to go with her, but she wanted some time off from seeing so much of Britts, Layden, and everyone else.

She needed to digest her new direction and re-align herself with something tangibly intrinsic and essential. While the newness of her relationship was satisfying and comfortable, she didn't understand every feeling she was experiencing; sadness being the chief force the last few days. Surely, she thought, the fantasy of a new relationship must be easier to deal with than the reality of an older one, by far.

By eleven, she was in bed and the music was off. She watched the entire '*Tonight Show with Jay Leno*', without laughing once. The monotony was only interrupted when the phone rang. The caller ID displayed RAINES S - 818-765-7739. She let it go to message and listened to it as it recorded.

"Hope you're well, call me."

Halfway through *Conan O'Brien*, she felt pressured, couldn't bear it any longer and felt an overwhelming, desperate need to get out of the house. She called Sebastian back without any further thought on the subject.

"Hello, are you still up?" Qian asked, breathing deeply into the receiver.

"I am. I was just watching *Conan*," I replied. "You have this Darth Vader quality to your voice right now."

"Really, my voice? It must be the weather. Somehow, I knew you'd be watching *Conan*."

"I was beginning to think that you had banished me. I haven't heard from you in some time. Did you get your package in New York?" I sipped my tea loudly. I knew she secretly liked it.

"Yes, I did. Thank you, that was thoughtful. It came in quite handy."

"It rained here as well."

"I know, I thought of you several times, too. Back here, watching *Casablanca* repeatedly, on your days off, your face stuck to a tea-cup next to a half-open window overlooking Sunset and Highland.

"You know me well," I laughed.

"*You always were a rank sentimentalist,*" she added. "*How touching.*"

"Look … we need to talk. Maybe we should meet?"

"Name the time, name the place. You know that I'm far from reluctant."

"Stop trying so hard," she growled into the phone. I didn't respond.

"Meet me in an hour at *Bob's Big Boy* in Burbank."

"I know the place, Qian. See you in bit." I hung up the phone, dismayed.

After I hung up the phone, I switched off *Conan*, went to the bathroom sink and washed my face. I'd been hibernating away from the world, struggling with several pieces of writing, and tape reports. Most of it was mental masturbation meant to keep me away from the physical act of self-indulgence. Too many days at home alone and routine patterns tend to repeat themselves in smaller and smaller cycles. Hence, the longer I stayed cooped-up, the more I ended up playing with myself.

I grabbed my work for the paper as a precaution, in case the evening took a turn toward the pedantic, mundane or pedestrian. Many nights I'd left the work unattended only to regret later that I hadn't saved, printed or brought it with me. After resurrecting myself from an entombed shell with a quick shower, I grabbed my leather coat, my wallet and car keys. Fuzzbody watched me make my slow exit without a concern or protest. A lightning storm outside kept him over-occupied, going from window to window batting at the flashes.

The world outside rumbled and shook the streets, the buildings, the people under flat card-board boxes sleeping in closed and darkened doorways. I walked a block and a half to my car through the downpour. I had parked across the street from Micelli's, the oldest Italian restaurant in Los Angeles. It wasn't due to a lack of parking but more out of a sheer dread at facing down the inside of my apartment for another three day shift, and really needing to walk. I definitely needed a break from watching television, cleaning the cat box and sitting in front of the computer in the kitchen drinking tea, and whiskey sours.

My mind seemed focused on the same thoughts, the same swirl of longing that would always end up with a circle of questions regarding Qianqian. Why was I in this? What the hell good would come out of being with a girl that took off her clothes for money, having sex with various other men, and who would happily pay her large amounts of cash so she could travel the world without care. My mood registered thoughts on modern prostitution taken to new heights and the sunken depths of old lows. She was toying with me, which was one thing and bad enough, but worst of all, she was toying with herself and that would never make for a happy ending.

I needed her for some deep reason that I couldn't understand. I needed to be next to her, to hear the sound of her voice, to not forget the words she chose or her laughter. I told myself that I should try to take as many mental photographs as possible for the days ahead when I wouldn't see her. I realized that my relationship with her was like small grains of sand, passing quickly through a blackened hourglass, I never knew when it would be over. My friendship would at best be a fleeting series of moments, memories and bad mistakes. The world was moving by me slowly as I drove past the Hollywood Bowl, up Cahuenga Blvd, making the right onto Barham and then sat stopped for what seemed like a lifetime at a red light on Olive and Pass Avenue. I was transfixed by a movie poster the size of an entire building, announcing another new movie.

I waited for the glow of the green arrow through the sheeting rain. I could have turned at any moment, but chose not to. It wasn't any sense of duty not turning against a red-light, but more from trying to calm myself. I drummed the steering-wheel nervously and shifted in my seat uncomfortably, listening to music and trying to cut through the cerebral invasion of the impending moment. Seconds later, something off in the distance made a loud noise, sparked and the street lights on the entire block went black, both in front and behind me. The thunder crashed directly overhead with a deafening crunch. I was the only vehicle anywhere to be seen and I didn't feel too bad turning against a dead light. I drove for several blocks in an eerie blackness. I could see streetlights and red stop lights up in the distance.

When I got to corner of Riverside drive, I could see the restaurant ahead, surrounded by pink neon. All the lights were on and Bob's was in full swing. The oversized, fiberglass and lead-painted eternal man-child on the patio, held aloft his mighty unspoiled burger welcoming all late niters and would-be suicidals to the half-heartedly cooked fare. Only a handful of regulars sat randomly placed, having low conversations over coffee or by themselves and their chosen choice of reading. A few employees sat near the cash register eating patty melts on rye and sipping ice-cold Arnold Palmer's.

Qian wasn't there yet, as far as I could tell. I felt that she was probably parked a block away watching to see if I would show; trying to be slick, unobvious and detached. If I had decided at the last minute to circle the block, I'd probably find her smoking cigarettes, listening to the Eagles and stuck in the driver's seat with a blank expression on her face. In a world of retards, beautiful people work overtime to be perfect, or at least perfect in their own minds. Los Angeles is the 'great magnet' for this type of personality, dialed in on *high*. Unfortunately, Qian was no exception and this probably explained why she felt like the city was her home. The world to her, from my own observations, seemed to be a singular universe constantly circling her consciousness, and I was just a bit player, a figment on the periphery of her imagination, unimportant.

I sat in the middle of the front lobby facing the double doors. From the outside it must've looked like a modern version of an Edward Hopper in pink and burgundy.

"Coffee?" I nodded, as Utai, my male waiter acknowledged and drifted back behind the counter for an inordinate period of time, to not only grow the bean, but harvest it, ship it in, roast, grind, brew and then finally serve it to me, but not before hitting everyone else in the place first. "Thanks." was all I could muster. By the time he returned to the table, it was just lukewarm at best. The bastard was probably a struggling actor, which explained why he was just a shadow of what I expected at one am. I was never a fan of 'Bob's Big Boy' due to the fact that after 10pm, they stopped taking their responsibility as a restaurant seriously. Los Angeles area dining in the twenty-four hour spectrum was made famous by Norms, The 101 Café on Franklin, Sitton's in North Hollywood and the Copper Penny. Bob's though, wasn't on that list of distinguished eats.

By the time Qian finally arrived, she was almost a half-hour late. I was actually only a few moments away from leaving. Or, at least this was what I was telling myself.

"Have a hard time finding the place?" I asked.

"No, just took the scenic route. Felt like driving, actually."

"Nice to see you, too." I made no attempt at intimacy, I could already feel the space between us. The look on her face was so cold, she could've been frozen. "You've been missed."

She had pulled a pack of Marlboro lights from her purse, had one about an inch away from her face when the waiter began with a 'Sorry, honey,' sashay. Annoyed, she stuffed them back into her purse. "Sometimes, I forget that you can't smoke in restaurants here."

"Obviously, we're here for a reason. Seems rather grave," I said. Her head was bowed. The waiter brought her a cup of coffee, refilled mine and took our order.

"I need to confess something to you, Sebastian. You deserve to hear what I have to say." I kept quiet, sipped my coffee and tried to blend into the vinyl bench.

She moved around, straightened herself, looked out the window, and cleared her throat. "I love you," she began. "I really want you to know that. We've been friends for a long time, and I don't regret becoming involved with you, but lately I've been feeling like Mickey Mouse."

"Whaddya mean by that?" I asked stupefied. "Do you mean the one on television, or the one at theme parks? I think there's probably a difference there." She didn't answer. "Bukowski always thought that Mickey Mouse was a four-fingered monster with no soul."

"Who's Bukowski?" she responded.

"Anyways, that's a rather ambiguous feeling, don't you think?"

"I'm not sure that the person on the outside is the same person that used to be on the inside. Maybe it's the other way around, but sometimes, I feel like I'm wearing some-type of suit."

"Oh, theme park Mickey. Sounds pretty drastic."

"The problem is, it's been getting worse. More so since I've gotten back from New York. I just don't feel right, and I need a cigarette."

"You'd probably be better off not having a cigarette, in all actuality, that's the first suggestion I should make," I spoke slowly, unable to look away from her face. She had a stoic expression, that made her appear not be moving at all. She was perfectly still. She was staring back at me unamused.

"Second, from my experience, when people start talking about feeling like they're wearing a giant felt mouse suit, they're well past the beginning stages of detachment and disassociation. It usually leads …"

"Disassociation … what exactly does that mean?" She had heard Brittsy use that word as well in the hotel room.

"Well, according to the DSM-IV …"

"The what?" she interrupted again.

"A manual on psychological disorders," I sighed, tapping my spoon around in my coffee cup. "It's basically a defense mechanism, or a separation of certain thoughts, feelings and emotions from the 'rest of you', so to speak. Usually due to stress, lack of sleep, other things," my voice wavered. The further I got into my explanation, the more uncomfortable I felt, and I didn't want to say that disassociation was a direct symptom of a unique trauma, like in her case, rape.

"I wouldn't be too concerned, eighty to ninety percent of people between eighteen and twenty-five go through this experience. Another facet of your oh-so interesting debacle you call a life."

"Worst case scenario?" she asked.

"Why did I know you were going to ask that question? You shouldn't be thinking about that."

"Because I've spent enough time with you, listening to you reading your department pysch evals over the phone. Quid pro quo, I guess."

"Hmm," I shook my head, concerned. The waiter finally brought the food. I wanted to ask if they had to butcher the cow for the chicken-fried steak.

"So … I'm waiting?"

"Well, the worst case scenarios are two different diagnoses, but sometimes they're both connected depending on the case. You understand, this is absolutely the last thing that I should be telling you, it could be seen as 'suggesting' or 'biasing input'. I also want to point out, that I'm not a doctor, and you're not a patient. You could get a false sense of discovery here."

"I don't give a rat's ass, Sebastian, just spit it out."

I exhaled, sipped my coffee and shook my head. "Well, number one, which I would probably rule out immediately, but I don't have enough information not to, would be to put 'dissociative fugue' on the list. I don't think that you've been experiencing any blackouts, lost-time, or sleep-walking, so like I said, I'd probably rule that out. If you have been going through that, then it's safe to say your problem is deep and advanced."

She didn't bat an eye, I felt like my head was on the chopping block. Having a conversation regarding her mental-health wasn't quite what I expected to be doing, but here I was.

"And second?"

"Second, is probably closer to the mark, but let me just state for the record …"

"Stop hemming and hawing, there is no damned record."

"Hemm-ing and haw-ing, I never thought that I'd hear you say that." The unconcerned waiter refilled my coffee again and vanished into his own shadow like a crystallized dog turd.

"Well, a less well-known condition called 'dissociative disorder'. It's misunderstood by a lot of people who have been practicing for say, more than twenty years or so."

"Well, a lot of people don't believe that the extreme cases exist, but they do."

"What are the extreme cases?" she continued.

"Jesus … you don't know when to quit. Do you?"

"I guess not. Tell me why people dismiss the extreme cases."

"Because the extreme cases are what used to be classified as *Multiple Personality Disorder.* Does that sound like you?"

Qian's eye's widened, she reclined away from me, sinking back into the red-vinyl booth. "That's not quite what I expected to hear you say."

"Understandably, but that is the worst case scenario, Qian. And you do have to take your job into account, it has a lot to do with what's going on."

"How does my job have anything to do with this?" she snapped. I knew that I had to tread lightly and not pound her over the head with a lecture.

"You're still doing your Geisha thing?" I asked.

"Ughh ..."

"It has to do with *moral flexibility.* Working as a stripper in Los Angeles, my dear, is probably the most morally flexible thing I think you could be doing, other than being a Russian mobster, maybe. It's a massive catalyst. You're over your head in broken social mores."

"Isn't that a fish?"

"No, Qian, stop being flippant. You know exactly what I'm saying to you."

"So, you think I'm headed for a breakdown?" she asked. I just wanted to change the subject.

"No ... that's probably what you're thinking," I didn't want to suggest anything, even though I felt that I had already said too much.

"I got the distinct impression that you didn't call me out here to have an impromptu counseling meeting. Besides, my days of working with runaway youth at the Hollywood Youth Shelter are long past."

"Be thankful that you're useful."

"I am. How about you?" I put my face into my coffee cup.

"Useful?" she laughed.

"No, thankful."

"Whaddya mean?"

"Being thankful for everything that you have, your life, your youth, beauty, your family. That would be a start to feeling better. Indulging into apathy is probably counter-productive."

"Should I take something then, to calm me?" she responded, nonplussed.

"Other than sarcasm, I would just start with eating your peas. They're good for you."

"I think I'll just get a nose ring and fatten up … that's my whole agenda."

"Thanks for sharing." I could see where this was going. She would spend the next few months experimenting with pop-psychology trying to find a comfortable way to self-medicate.

For the next ten minutes we ate in silence and people watched. A skinny Persian man with died blonde hair came in and sat two tables in front of me. He was with a girl that would've passed for Ivana Trump, but wasn't. I had never seen a white woman wearing that much yellow gold before, for any reason. She was covered in it from head to toe. It was gaudy and ostentatious, but it seemed to please the man she was with who seemed to believe somehow that every one was watching him judging from the look on his face. He was so thin, it looked as if he stood sideways, he'd disappear. He had to be most self-absorbed and self-obsessed person I'd ever seen out on the street past midnight.

"I think we should take a break from seeing each other," she blurted out.

"That's what I thought you were going to say."

"I know," she retorted.

"I don't want to say this but …" I began.

"It's beginning to fit the diagnosis?"

"Yes, but you shouldn't make rash judgments, either."

"It's been on my mind awhile. There's a lot of guilt that goes along with this relationship. Perhaps it was a bit premature?"

"I know … there is … it was."

"I don't think that I can do this anymore, Sebastian. I just can't."

"How about Layden, are you going to stop seeing him as well?"

"Stop it."

"Why? You really sound as if the guilt is over-whelming."

"Sebastian, you need to know that I've been sleeping with Layden for almost two months or so, and well …"

"What, you're pregnant?"

"God, no." She recoiled at the thought of it.

"I've actually been seeing other people as well. I just figured that it was about time to tell you. And Layden and I … he said that he was finally going to leave his wife."

"Think so, huh?" I was a little hurt, probably would be more hurt in time when the information had a chance to sink in. I was stunned about her naiveté regarding her sugar-daddy.

"Look I don't have much to say to you about that, I definitely don't have an apology for you." My heart sank. "I just needed to tell you that I think that I've gone as far with you as I wanted."

"Well, Qian," I began, "I'm glad that you got what you wanted." I was beside myself.

"You've just never been my type, Sebastian, and our lives are going in two opposite directions." She sunk the knife in deep and decided to twist it now.

"That so?" The pain in my voice was apparent. I offered no defense.

"I'm sorry my existence is not very noble or sublime," she finally said, more for her own feelings of discomfort, rather than mine. "Look …I've gotta go." It sounded like a command from above. She grabbed her purse, put a twenty on the table, gave me a disapproving look, got up and walked toward the double glass doors. I sat stunned and unable to move. It was the moment I knew would come.

"Qian," I called out, but she was already gone.

From behind the face paint of a Geisha ...

Sitting in the club ignoring her hunger, Qian shivered and huddled close to Britts to avoid the continuous blast of the air-conditioning, which it wasn't getting any warmer. As a creative endeavor, she had started wearing Kimono's around the club. Most days, Qianqian slinked around in her old black, frayed, antique wrap that she was so reluctant to part with. She also had a second hanging in her locker, which was adorned with flower patterns and had overlapping bright colors. The only solid colored cloth was the black collar and cuffs which were a stark contrast to the obscenely patterned robe. For a while, she had been increasingly toying with the idea of being a Geisha. She only had one Japanese girlfriend, a demure girl that worked the night-shift named Taeko.

Lately, she had been using a lot more make-up. She liberally, but carefully applied a brilliant white powder to her face, neck and shoulders. The powder alone gave her a haunted visage in the reflection of the mirror. She put a large appliqué of light blue eye shadow over her almond shaped eye lids, lightly patted her cheeks with bright pink blush, darkened her eyebrows with a pencil and then applied a bright red, waxy lipstick as a final touch. She had also purchased several sets of cotton sandals, a waist sash and a Japanese lute from a Downtown import store to accent her on-stage costume. She went out on stage with her hair wrapped up in a bun, and carrying a parasol and fan. She never stopped to ask herself if it was all too much or if she was slowly slipping farther from reality. To her, it probably wasn't. If anything, she was trying to perfect it. She had been slipping into the masquerade for weeks, but she felt more comfortable performing as something she wasn't rather than being on stage as herself. She stopped having the DJ play R&B and went for the electronic, Japanese, lush-voiced lounge singer, Namie Amuro, and a strange sounding, but equally trance like *'Do As Infinity'*. These were two bands she was sure no one in the club had ever heard of. Her stage-show became more compelling and she was less nervous. Playing the role as a Geisha, she only fell over once in three-and-a-half weeks, rather than going face-first, twice weekly.

Even though Qian was Asian, she didn't even look Japanese. Most white men would never really notice or care - but several of the customers who were Asian, told the other girls that she looked ridiculous and shouldn't be making such a spectacle. She felt like she was giving them what they wanted which was a small private piece of the unadulterated yellow fantasy, available for either a lap dance for twenty bucks or much more if you were willing to pay and weren't too shy to ask. The older white customers were obsessed with her and would go through hell to get her phone number, meet her outside of the club or take her somewhere on a vacation. Even Britts had told her to be careful and stay out of the clutches of club newcomers. It was only when the Johns' realized how much money they were actually spending, would they calm down and come in for visits less often. It was fine by her though, she was well-aware of the pattern.

Asian clients were few and far between, though. None that came in, ever showed any interest in her, or would even go as far as making eye contact. They were more interested in girls like Britts, or tall, tan blonde girls with oversize breasts with a trademark fake and untouchable quality. She had only ever taken one Asian customer into the booth, which she had later regretted. He was an elderly Korean man who worked in a mechanics garage and stunk of oil and sweat. Qian thought that he was dirty to the touch, and that he felt greasy. She tried her best to just hurry up and get through the song and out of the booth. He had groped her with his dirty hands all over and left her feeling nasty and gross. The next day she was covered from head to toe in small red bites all over her body that itched painfully. At first thought, she thought she had fleas and immediately suspected the old man, but couldn't believe how fast they had spread. Later when she couldn't stand the pain any longer, she made a trip to the Emergency Room where they had confirmed for her that she had contracted scabies. Frightened and not knowing what to do, she told the nurse that she was a dancer in a strip club and probably contracted the bugs from a customer. The nurse looked at her as if she was high on drugs, mentally deficient or partially retarded. Regret immediately surged through every pore of her body. She realized that she had made a mistake and felt the eyes of everyone boring into her, with raised eyebrows. She had also made a silent promise to never divulge her chosen career field to anyone ever again, no matter what the circumstances.

She had also regretted her one experience working the evening shift. She had given in to Taeko, who had been begging her to work a Saturday night with her for some time. She wasn't ready to make a new friend, but was curious to see how much money she could make on a weekend night and what types of customers walked through the door. Qian had always turned Taeko down as she was usually in San Diego with her parents. She was hoping to make an extra five or six hundred dollars, but mostly, she was curious to see two other things in particular; Taeko's stage show, and if she had any regulars.

Through the course of the night, she was repeatedly shocked and let down to see that most of the men coming through the front door were young, barely-legal teenage boys, and bald-headed Mexican thugs in white t-shirts and tattooed sleeves. They were all too rough on her. They squeezed her tits to the point of pain and kept trying to take advantage of her in the booth either by force or by repetition. It felt more like rape, or workplace harassment than it did work. She was disgusted with the bottom of the barrel that probably drove themselves to her in their lowered Honda's with custom rims and windshield decals.

Taeko, as Qian had suspected, had several regulars but spent a lot of time sitting quietly without any clients. She had turned down several of the Mexi-bangers flat-out and ignored most of them the whole evening. No one said anything to her about refusing customers as it was a girl's discretion whether she danced with someone or not. She had several interesting costumes. Qian watched her strut out for almost every dance in some different and elaborate outfit. She topped herself around ten o'clock with a Rio de' Janeiro peacock ensemble that was all feathers, sequence and rhinestones. How the chick had the strength to lug such stuff around was mind numbing. Qian watched her get naked on stage and realized that she didn't have that bad of a body. She moved well and kept several of the customers waiting in line for a lap dance after her stage performance. She could've very easily been a feature dancer and strip in a different club every night. Clubs usually pay feature dancers a flat salary for showing up and take none of their dance tips unlike the other girls.

The other surprising thing about working nights was that there must've been close to twenty to twenty-five girls working all at once. The majority of the girls didn't even bother taking the John's into booths as most of them stayed busy all night. Several girls were having sex blatantly on the couch set along the back wall and some even gave dances at the tables on the floor when all the booths were full. Getting an eye-full, gave her new perspective about ever sitting on any of the furniture again. Working nights was a depressing, competitive wasteland compared to her more-tolerable shift during the afternoon.

♘ ♕ ♘

The shift, so far, had been uneventful and she had already spent a good part of the morning trapped once again inside a booth with Layden. He was still pressing her hard about going off with him on another trip, this time to Africa for several weeks.

"I was surprised at your fee for returning to New York."

"Everything costs money, Layden, how much are you willing to pay for happiness? That's the real question."

"I guess we're just not communicating any more."

"What do you call this then, distance learning?" she guffawed, annoyed.

"I guess you're doing well enough financially to blow me off and you're only in it for the money."

Qian seemed annoyed by his last remark. "Is there anything else that I should be taking my clothes off in a strip-club for? Please, if you have a better answer, let me know."

"I thought that a trip to Africa might've been appealing to you. I really despise thinking that this is all driven by money, but …"

"Layden, look …" she cut him off, "If you want free sex, go home to your wife. I'm not paying my rent in bottle-caps."

"Can't we just get past this part and just let it see where it goes?" he pleaded.

"See where it goes? You could be my fucking grandfather, that's where it goes, Layden. You need to wake up. I'm really getting upset with your crap." Qian was getting more bitchy and in no mood for games. She stood up, grabbed her purse and held out her hand, looking to be paid.

"Pay me and get on with it." She grew silent and stared down at him in anger. He dipped into his wallet frustrated and burdened.

"I guess I'm nothing more to you than a cash machine," he blurted.

"I guess I'm nothing more to you than a sperm deposit," she mocked him, taking the money and making a quick exit heading towards the back-stage dressing-room. Walking across the room she counted three hundred in fifties.

"Listen, wait …" he'd caught up, and grabbed her arm.

She turned, surprised, looking down at his hand.

"Qian, please, look, I'm sorry," he protested.

A bouncer had quickly made his way towards him and was now grabbing him by the shoulder. Layden was caught off guard and stuttering.

"Ughh … umm."

"It's alright, George. He's fine," Qian assured. "Just confused."

"You'd be best to let go now," George suggested, still holding firmly onto Layden's arm. Qian walked away leaving the two men discussing Layden's exit strategy. She was pissed and 'unavailable' for clients. She knew she had to cut the relationship between them, or at least for a few months. She needed a break. When she collapsed on the couch and started digging through her purse for a cigarette, she hadn't noticed that Abbey was sitting at the mirror talking on the payphone.

"Oh, God, that stinky tramp just walked in. God, something smells like cum." Abbey spoke this under her breath to the person on the other end of the line, but Qian had definitely overheard it.

"Fuck you, you silly cunt. I'm sick of your smug fucking face always giving me some shitty look," she shot back, standing up. Her frustration was at a boiling point. Abbey immediately hung up the phone. Erykah was walking out of the shower stall wearing shower-shoes and a towel knowing that she was about to see a knock-down, drag-out brawl.

"I don't give a shit if you are David's favorite," Qian barked.

"How dare you speak to me, you venomous street ho!" The insults flew through the air like daggers. 'Fuck you' was the choice expression of the moment. Qian launched her plastic cup full of ice cubes and coke, exploding it across Abbey's chest and face.

"YOU WHORRRE!" Abbey screamed. Flying into a rage, she grabbed the trash can beside her and tried to lob it at her. It bounced off Qian, knocking her sideways. Within seconds they were locked in each other's grip like mid-eighties mud-wrestlers caught in a battle-extravaganza.

"You crazy yellow bitches done lost yo' goddamned minds." Erykah was stunned to see it all going on in front of her, but did nothing to intervene. She leaned up against the wall and lit up one of Abbey's cigarettes.

They were both thrashing around on the filthy carpet screaming, grabbing hair and punching each other in the face. Qian finally landed a deafening slap across Abbey's face which caused her to recoil. After the wave of initial shock passed, she pushed Qian back against the couch and then shoved her head into the rubber trash-can, leaving her with her legs in the air, kicking and screaming.

"This aint no goddamned cartoon! Beat that bitches ass!" Erykah was goading Abbey, reluctant to see the fight end so quickly.

Abbey quickly grabbed her bags and bolted for the back door, leaving hastily before Qian could recover. Abbey had left wearing only underwear and her ripped bra. Qian slowly began gathering her belongings and was readying to leave when David stormed in.

"What the hell is going on in here! No one is on stage, and all I can hear are bitches screaming their heads off. What happened to Abbey?"

"I'm leaving, don't stand in my way," Qian said sharply through her tears. She felt humiliated all over again. The last several weeks had been working up to a head first confrontation with Abbey and now it had engulfed her. Everything and everyone in the club had stopped.

"You better cash out, Qian!" he yelled at her.

"Just shut the fuck up and leave her alone." Brittsy dismissed him, she stood in front of David, blocking his way, putting Qian out of arms reach.

"Don't push me today, white trash."

"I'd be careful if I was you. Better choose your words carefully, you fucking terrorist."

"Are you threatening me, Brittsy, you Sunland burn-out!" He got up in her face.

"Just leave her alone. She's never stolen a penny from you, so just settle the fuck down." Brittsy was just being dramatic as a diversion for Qian.

The disheveled would-be geisha, with torn kimono, tears and shoeless, inhaled her cigarette. She was wavering in place staring off into the darkness of the room, blocking everything out, clutching her purse and crying. "I don't think I can take anymore of this," she said under breaking breath.

"C'mon, baby, let's just get your things together. Your day just ended." Brittsy started to gather up her clothes and make-up into her black travel bag, giving David a filthy look. Erykah left the dressing-room to head back out onto the floor as if nothing had happened at all.

Qian sat staring at the dressing-room mirror in a trance, unable to break away from the feeling of humiliation, the trauma, her anger and the physical trembling that was pulsing through her body. She knew that she never wanted to see the Industrial Strip Club again after today. Unfortunately, she realized that not only would she be back within a week, she would probably have to continue giving herself to Layden and all the other lunch-time desperado's that came in to take a small piece of her and leave, exchanging her body for money. It all seemed too depressing, anybody else would've considered suicide, but Qianqian was too in love with herself to even make the attempt.

In the struggle of yelling and brawling, no one had noticed that outside the dressing room someone had shut off the music inside the club. Then, without any warning, the overhead lights came on. The switches were only accessible from the cash-cage near the front door. Before Qian knew what was going on, several of the regular Johns tried hurriedly to high-tail it through the dressing room and slip out the back door, which only meant one thing. Police raid. The fleeing Johns were met at the precipice of the backdoor by the LAPD donned in dark blue windbreakers.

When the back door swung open, Qian got a quick glance out into the parking lot which was now wall to wall with a swarm of squad cars, swat vans and groups of uniformed Officers on foot.

Within minutes, Johns, girls and management were all being questioned, cuffed and taken outside to one of the many vans waiting to transport them across town and book them on misdemeanors of public indecency, performing a lewd act in a public place and serving alcohol in an all-nude premises. Girls were not allowed to touch themselves while dancing on stage, but often did. Girls were also not allowed to collect money while being fully disrobed, which meant not getting paid in the booth. This was probably the most obvious violation. Regulars were often served liquor at the bar, Management always turned a blind eye, observing the main rule in the club – Management doesn't know, Management doesn't care.

"Shit. Goddamnit. Not again," Qian blasted. Britts just shook her head at the sight of it. "Yep, nothing like getting cuffed and stuffed."

Qianqian and Britts were all taken in together along
with a handful of other girls that were caught performing a sex
act with a John. Abbey had been stopped on her way out and
herded into the van first. All the money earned was
confiscated and was now being held as evidence. The routine
was to plead guilty and be released within a few hours after
being booked. There was no getting around the reality of a
long day sitting on a steel bench in the basement of the North
Hollywood Jail. Qian had already decided that she wasn't
going to call anyone for help, bail her out or give her a ride. If
she had to stay overnight, post her bail and walk home on foot,
then so be it.

    ♞ ♛ ♞

"Have you ever sold narcotics in the club?" the officer
asked her, staring at the blank form field in the monitor.
"No," Qian responded, annoyed by the rookie cops
questions.
"Have you ever bought narcotics of any kind, in the
club from a customer or anyone else."
"No."
"Have you ever bought narcotics in the club from the
owner, David Sarkissian?" She could now see exactly where
this was going. Her mind flashed back to the large plastic
cases that David and Rullo had been hauling around for the
last several weeks. Surely, he couldn't be that stupid and
obvious, she thought.
"No," she answered. "Never."
"How about from George or Rullo?"
"No, I have never purchased any type of drugs or
alcohol from George, Rullo, David or any customer. I don't
drink as I am allergic to alcohol and I have never voluntarily

done drugs." She didn't know why she had chosen those exact words, but they had also caught the attention of the officer.

"Voluntarily? What does that mean."

"It means *'against one's wishes or consent'*. Look it up, asshole." The Officer grimaced and grunted at the response.

"Have you ever performed a sex act on the premises of the club? Please remember that this is an official report and filing a false Police report is considered a felony."

"No. Absolutely not. I'm not a whore."

"Are you sure? Let me ask you again," which he did, while casually holding up a Polaroid of Layden. "Oh yes, Layden Strausse. He's been picked up on several occasions. Has a very interesting arrest record."

"Well …" she hesitated. "I have dated Layden – outside of the club, but that was in the past."

"I see. Have you ever massaged yourself, specifically your breasts, your buttocks or your groin while dancing on stage?"

She laughed in his face, "No."

"Yes," he said, typing in the appropriate response onto her arrest record.

"I believe I just said no," she scowled.

"I saw the tape, Geisha girl, the answer is clearly yes. Like, I stated, filing a false Police report is a felony. Would you like to compound your mistakes, or are you just looking to cop a year in a women's correctional facility?" which stunned Qianqian outright. She had nothing to say and remained quiet.

"I want to see my lawyer," she finally uttered.

"Oh, interesting, you actually have a lawyer? What's his name? Sorry, what's *her* name? I forget all you strippers are just paying your way through Law School."

Eyeing the cop's cigarettes on his desk, she politely asked.

"May I have a cigarette, please?"

"No smoking in the station. State law," he responded, but then proceeded to light one up, inhaled and sat back in his chair, taking a minute away from the computer to assess his 'client'.

"This is your second arrest at the club, isn't it? You were arrested just nine months ago on the same charges."

"Why ask me when you seem to know all the answers." The Officer looked hard at her, slowly smoking the cigarette. Several other girls were sitting on a bench, just outside his office in the hallway against a wall. Having nothing else to do, they were all eavesdropping on everything they were saying and whispering. Brittsy was questioned first and was already out of sight.

"Qianqian Mao. Any relation to the infamous Chairman from back home?"

"What the fuck do you think?"

"Just want to make sure that you're not going to cry diplomatic immunity or something."

"Diplomatic Immunity!" Qian cried out loudly, while raising her hand in the air. Cigarette smoke billowed directly across her face as the Officer laughed, but found her humor irksome.

"Your moaning won't get you any tips in here."

"Douche-bag," she spat.

"Okay then, little Geisha girl, go sit over there against the wall and someone will take you downstairs to holding in a minute."

"Whaddya mean, last time I was released directly after questioning and some Polaroid's."

"Not this time, China. You're a repeat offender, like that haggard trash you run with, what's her name … Brittsy Buchanan. You'll be staying the night with us, maybe even a few days. Besides, your boss's lawyer has her hands full. He's in a lot of trouble, far beyond Alcohol Control Board violations and harboring prostitution."

"How long do I have to stay?" Qian was now on the edge of seat with curiosity.

"Just go sit against the wall. It's going to be a long night."

"Can I make a phone call?"
"Keep dreaming."

From the end of the world ...

When Saturday morning finally drifted its way through the cracks of the vertical blinds, Qianqian's dissatisfaction returned to her entirely, triggered by the nagging events of the last several weeks. It was palpable across the roof of her mouth, sinking her heart further inside of herself. She laid on her side, staring across the room at a small portable television that she had turned on several hours earlier and muted. Scooter was curled up next to her sleeping soundly, with paws extended. Qian had slept with her contacts in again, not that she cared.

The red numbers of the alarm clock changed again and would in another sixty seconds. Instead of just the last digit going one higher, they would all reset and it would be one in the afternoon. She was in San Diego sleeping in the bed that used to be in her old house in Santa Monica. A futon, beaten, stained and well-past its prime. She hated it. It was uncomfortable and needed replaced, but it never stopped her from coming back to it on weekends. For now, she didn't want to do anything that involved movement. The sky outside was overcast and drizzling, thunder was eluding through cloud banks above. The weather wasn't as committed as it was back in Los Angeles, but it was trying its best to be just as bleak. She had no desire to work on her wood sculpture, no desire to shop anymore or hit the beaches. Hibernating in bed seemed a better idea than even going downstairs and making bao with her mom in the kitchen. Her body felt like lead in a cotton sack. She was momentarily curious to get up and familiarize herself with the chessboard that continued to wait for its next move. She pushed the Knight into position, moved his Pawn, shifted her Rook, countered and slid the Bishop close to the center as she had envisioned, finally ending the game. She acknowledged to herself that she would probably never play chess with Sebastian again, and forfeited her chance to beat him. It seemed weird, thinking about in such competitive terms.

Trying to block the previous days fiasco of being arrested from her mind proved difficult. She felt sickened by the whole incident. She had waited to be let out of the North Hollywood jail for almost a full day. The city must've had to justify the cost of paying for the supper of seven girls being held on misdemeanor charges, so she was put out onto Burbank Boulevard at exactly three-thirty in the afternoon. The last possible minute before the dinner roster was to be prepared. She had felt dirty and hollow from being held captive. Her self-destructive behavior was making in-roads on her personality. Abbey didn't say a word the entire time in the basement jail and had gotten picked up by someone waiting, as if it had all been planned in advance. Qian had sworn to herself while standing on the curb watching Abbey pull away, that she never wanted to see her or the club again.

Depression was settling in, she could feel it. There was no doubt. It was surrounding her on all sides, beginning to push every molecule in the world downward by its mere presence alone. She had left Los Angeles immediately, having shared a cab with Britts back to the club, picked up her car and drove straight to her parents. She had gotten in just after dinner, showered and went to bed early. Her parents were going out for the evening and thus thought nothing about Qian's dark mood. They had slowly become oblivious to their daughter's life. It was probably a knee-jerk reaction made out of necessity.

She pulled the blankets back over her head and tried desperately to block out the world and fall back to sleep. Several hours passed, and very slowly, the light outside changed the shape of the sharp corners and large objects making everything appear dull the later it got. Shadows moved across the wall, but the same movie on the television seemed to continue all afternoon. She would turn over once in a while, see the screen, and watch the actor, William Hurt, and a curly headed women traveling endlessly, going somewhere. Going anywhere. This seemed to go on for hours. Every time Qian would drift off, sleep and then wake back up, William Hurt and Curly were somewhere new. Haruki Murakami sat neglected and half-read on a pile of her dirty clothes near the door.

She didn't have the money to travel, but wanted to now more than anything. Fleeing into oblivion seemed like the best idea. Even if it wasn't out of the country, it was fine. If she had to sit in the back seat of a Greyhound bus and take back roads, it was a better offer than going back to another day at the club.

Britts had told her that she was going to cruise up the coast on her bike and that she should come as well, getting out would do her a world of good, but she just wasn't engaged. Brittsy now, was another attachment to her, another relationship to deal with. She was beginning to worry, because it was the second time that she'd turned Britts down on an invitation to go for a road-trip. She had told her that she had plans with her family for the weekend, which was an outright lie.

Scooter stirred, stretched and jumped from the bed. After sniffing Qian's dirty clothes that were left in a nasty looking pile on the floor, the cat soft-footed his way downstairs to investigate the more alluring smells coming from the kitchen.

Hurt and Curly were somewhere in Australia now from the looks of it. Red clay desert, Aborigines and an airplane door, it all seemed absurd. Qian began meandering around her room, oblivious to her naked body once more - now on the hunt for cigarettes. She'd left the pack that she had bought on the way down from L.A. in the car, along with her purse, her phone and probably the keys. Her mother appeared in the doorway and gave her a what-for in Chinese.

"Qianqian, close your door if you're going to walk around naked all day. For god sakes, *Hi zhi*, put some clothes on … it's almost one in the afternoon." She had a firm grip on the doorknob with a worried and urgent expression on her face.

"Sorry, Mom, I don't think I have any clean clothes. My stuff needs washed."

"Ay ya! I'll get you a robe and something to wear. Why didn't you say you had dirty clothes, I would've washed them for you this morning." Su Ying picked up Qian's dirty things from the floor in one swoop of the arm and hurried off down the hall. A few minutes later she returned with a few things for Qian to wear. Qianqian was now sitting cross-legged on the bed, still naked with the door wide open.

"Close the door, you and your naked body. I thought I raised you better, this isn't a museum, dear." Qian looked away from the television and stared at her mother dumbfounded.

"Huh?"

"Get dressed and come downstairs, you need to eat. You went to bed so early and ate nothing at all."

"I raided the fridge in the middle of the night."

"Na, na, na," her mother spoke like a machine gun spitting out her words in three-round bursts, beckoning her attention. All Chinese, all the time. Su Ying wrapped a robe around her daughter, and disappeared back down to the kitchen to the cooking and laundry. She closed the door firmly behind her.

Within a few minutes, Qian found a pack of import cigarettes under the bed with an ashtray and a box of matches. By the time she lit up, she was once again naked and Curly was somehow floating in space celebrating a birthday. She had absolutely no idea what the hell she was watching, but with the sound off it seemed intriguing. She wasn't interested in any one else's drama. She laughed, inwardly, just happy that it wasn't that stupid movie that Sebastian was so obsessed with. Smoking her cigarette, she examined the clothes her mother had left for her. She slipped on the yellow shorts and the faded gray Mickey Mouse sweater that looked like it hadn't seen human skin in almost a decade. Looking at herself dressed like that in the mirror, she couldn't believe that her mother would have ever worn something like this in public. But the truth of the matter was, that she had probably worn these exact clothes to the store to buy groceries within the last week. Fashion sense wasn't a priority with her mother. Brushing off the idea, she put out the cigarette, turned off the television and went downstairs.

She still hadn't seen her dad yet. She knew that she was about to face an inevitable barrage of questions regarding her life one more time. Her mind delved backwards into the catalogue of previous questions to reacquaint herself with the lies and try to make an acceptable repeat performance for dear old mom and dad who were clueless about her real life. Which ever one that was.

She could already hear her father's voice asking about work.

"Oh yes, I'm still working in lay-out at the *Times* in the travel section. Everything's going great. I just got another raise."

"Sure, still working part-time in the evening at the developing lab."

"No, Sebastian's fine. He was working this weekend,. He wanted to come, but couldn't." She knew that this was a lie that she would be better off bringing to a close at some point, even though her relationship had provided her a certain amount of credibility. But it was all lies.

Qian stood at the kitchen counter side by side with her mother rolling dough for pork bao.

"You smell like cigarettes, just like your father."

"Isn't that comforting though, mom?"

"Your father keeps asking about you and what you're doing with your life, Qianqian. You're not in school, you're not married and you no longer live at home. He keeps saying that he's going to send you back to Beijing to live with your aunt and uncle."

"What!" Qian was shocked. "He would never!"

"No, no, no, *um say ken* ... he's just talking. Your father is frustrated with you, that's all. He thinks you should be in school working on a degree so you can make better money. You know how he is, so old fashioned."

"I know, mom," Qian sighed.

"What's he doing now? I haven't seen him at all. I thought I heard him talking on the phone earlier this morning."

"He's working on papers in the office. I'll call him."

"Chen!" she yelled out across the house. "*Kau lai*, Chen!"

"*Um say kap* ... no need to yell, I'm right here," he answered, floating his way slowly into the kitchen, obviously bothered, his face crinkled. Qian had her head down rolling dough but was still happy to see him.

"*Ni hao*, Papa, how are you?" Su Ying glanced over at him, aware of the tone in his voice, knowing that something was askew. Chen was sitting across the room at the table with his legs crossed getting ready to light a cigarette.

"*Jun bui cafe bi ngo*," he asked, staring silently, rubbing his eyes.

Su Ying immediately stopped making the boa and quickly prepared a cup of instant coffee in the microwave. Chen sat silently at the table staring at Qian from the side of his face. Scooter was making figure eights around his feet and chair legs.

"What's the matter with you, father? Did your computer shut down again? You look like you lost a whole week's work. You have such a long face, you could run a horse race with it." Qian finally turned around, and looked squarely at her father who was glaring at her. She was now as surprised and concerned as her mother was.

"No, I lost a lot more than that. A lot more!" he replied, emphatically, cryptically, and very upset. His voice had raised. Su Ying didn't know if Chen was yelling or not, she hadn't seen him emotional in over a lifetime. The quiet peace had been violently disturbed.

"Here's your coffee, what's the matter with you?" Chen sipped his coffee, shook his head and mumbled several words under his breath.

"This is what I lost …" He threw a few rolled up pieces of paper on the table. Qian recognized them immediately as her copy of the arrest report that she had left folded up in the pocket of her dirty clothes.

"Oh my god," Qian stated.

"A daughter … that's what I lost. I've lost everything." Su Ying made a strange noise in confusion reaching out to grasp the two pieces of paper. One pink, one white. Qian had an urge to try and stop her, but knew that it was a useless gesture. It was too late. She slowly read aloud the important details from the document.

"Qianqian Mao." Her fingers touched the area of the page where her daughter had signed in acknowledgement of the facts.

"Arrested. Indecent exposure. Prostitu …
Solicitation ... oh, good lord."

Qian didn't have it within her to protest, put up a defense or start telling more lies. Regardless, her heart sank.

Her hands covered in flour, she brought them up and covered her face. Embarrassed, she slid to the floor and wept.

Su Ying collapsed in the chair, next to the table, staring at the arrest records. "Second offense. What have you done, Qianqian?" her mother cried. Chen had already stood up, becoming further agitated and started pacing.

"How could you do something like this, not just to us, but to yourself? I cannot understand this at all!" His voice was harsh and shrill. He was thoroughly disappointed and devastated.

"Ohh nooo …" Su Ying began crying loudly for a few moments, Qian had never heard or seen her mother so blown apart like this, but as quickly as it had started it stopped. Su Ying stood up, physically having an immediate change of heart, wiped her eyes and stormed over to Qian and slapped her across the face with full force. Qian buckled over and was now crying for her to stop, trying to tell her that she was sorry. Su Ying was yelling at her, pulling her hair and slapping her repeatedly.

"*Le le le, moo ta she he la.*" Chen came over and pulled Su Ying away, equally distraught.

"How could you, how could you, how could you?" her face was flushed and pouring with tears. "I raised you up just so you could be a prostitute? I don't understand what I did?" she bellowed, blaming herself.

"I'm so sorry, Mom. I don't know what to say. It just happened."

"Your life just happened that way?" her father yelled, infuriated. He couldn't believe his ears. "Are you kidding me? You just happen to be stripping at a club, exposing yourself? I can barely repeat what I read on that paper, and you've been arrested not once but twice now? My daughter?"

"I don't have a daughter!" Su Ying yelled, and then ran from the room crying, slamming her bedroom door behind her completely destroyed. They could both still hear her screaming cries from the kitchen.

Chen was visibly upset and over-emotional, but he tried to pull himself together. He stood with his arms crossed, and leaned against the door frame to the patio and the kitchen door, numb.

"Look what you've done to your mother," he scolded her. "I hope everything that you have is worth it. This is the most self indulgent and selfish thing I could have ever imagined. You did this for clothes and a used luxury car?" he asked, dumbfounded.

Qian took one of her father's cigarettes and tried to find some point to escape from the moment. She just didn't know what to say to him.

"You really have no shame, do you?"

"Are you going to keep tearing me down, dad? What the hell do you expect me to say?" she shot back.

"Is this how you've been making your money? Is this how you pay your rent, pay for traveling? It's disgusting, that's what it is Qianqian."

"I can't change it, I can't change it, I can't change it. I don't know what to do," she cried out, collapsing on the kitchen floor against the stove bawling her eyes out.

Without warning, her mother ran downstairs and outside with a large handful of her wet clothes from the wash machine and threw them out into the street. "Look what you've done. Your mother is falling apart, and it's all your fault. We've given you everything that you've ever needed, and this is how you repay us?"

Su Ying was outside emptying the contents of Qian's car onto the street, screaming. Qian was too afraid to move and Chen was shaking and feeling emotionally murdered.

If it was possible that all three of them had ever broken from each other as a family, then in those few moments that passed, they were as far from each other as they would ever be. Qian had no idea that she was going to cause a catastrophic meltdown in the only place that she knew was safe. Now it was stained and imperfect too, just like everywhere else.

Su Ying had gotten control of herself as she had finally come to rest on the curb, rocking back and forth. After wiping away her continuous tears, she began collecting Qian's belongings from the street and throwing them into the giant plastic trashcans in front of the house. The only thing she held onto was her car keys. After she had picked up the last piece of Qian's stripping costume and transparent shoes, she started the engine and then very matter-of-factly walked inside.

"Get up, lets go," she commanded her daughter. Su Ying was still crying between her words. Chen sat on the patio speechless with his face in his hands.

"Get up now, you're leaving," Su Ying barked. She pulled Qian up by her arm forcibly. Qian could see what was happening and began resisting, wailing for her mother to please stop.

"You're leaving. I don't want to see you in my house again. You're not welcome here anymore. You are a disgrace and I don't want to see you again. All you've ever done is lie to us!" She dragged Qian out the front door with every ounce of strength that she had. Fueled by her anger, "Don't call, don't come back. As long as you are a prostitute, I don't have a daughter."

"I'm not a prostitute, Mom, I swear!"

"Enough, no more lies from your awful mouth."

"Dad!"

Chen didn't interfere, he knew better, even though Qian was now crying for him to help her. It was all too much. It was epic heartbreak and there was no escape from any of it.

Qian pulled away not realizing that her mother had thrown her purse, her outfits, make up and credit cards into the trash. She also didn't notice that she only had a quarter tank of gas left and that she wasn't going to make it home. She drove with tears streaming down her face, cursing herself for being so careless with the paperwork from the jail. She had never cried so much in her whole life.

From a red-light at midnight in the pouring rain ...

I eased into the deep cushions of my blood red sofa, tired but unable to sleep. I was watching television, but letting it slip past me rather than sink in. It was well past one in the morning. Fuzzbody was licking the inside of his paw, staring at me and caught in a deep and intense purr cycle all at once. The coffee table, and the floor in front of me was covered in text books, paperwork, cassette tapes and a half-full cup of tea.

Maybe it was working with the department that was burning me out, maybe it was the city, and maybe it was Qianqian. The harder I worked on it, the more I hated it. Academic life was holding only slight appeal, and in actuality, my life seemed to be responding to an unknown formula that I was barely aware of. The more time pressed on, the less I cared about things that used to be important in equal proportions.

Drifting away into the static of my ambivalent life, and almost dead to the world from the narcotic of television, I startled when the phone rang.

"Pronto."

"Hey, it's me." I hadn't heard from her in almost two months. A lot of time had passed and much in my life had changed.

"How are you? I thought I'd never hear from you again."

"Sorry to disappoint."

"It's pretty late, you always seem to catch me up watching television."

"You're one of the few insomniacs that I know."

"You mean, that you can count on."

"Well, that too."

"Are you okay?" I plied in curiosity.

"I'm in Hollywood. It's raining as if a tropical storm just hit the coast. I caught a flat, and I have no jack."

"Lemme guess, you chose to opt out of the triple-A service plan?"

"Something like that. It seemed like the thing to do at the time. I'm on the corner of Selma and Vine by the DMV. Can you come?"

"Yeah, I'll be there in about five minutes. I'm on my way."

"Thanks."

I put the receiver down, quickly got dressed and struggled to put on enough layers to stand the chilly and wet conditions. Fuzzbody was now engrossed by the rain, with his head out the half-open window, oblivious to my late-night business.

Leaving my apartment behind me, I reflected momentarily about not locking the door. I continued regardless, knowing that no one was that stupid enough to try and come in. I had an umbrella under my arm, but I didn't use it. I never had, it was an over-size black umbrella that had a Police shield emblazoned on the handle. You could buy them from the Coroner's Office gift shop, but of course, I had an unlimited supply. It was for her, just in case she was sans rain-shield. She would think it considerate of me, and of course, I would probably just smile and nod politely, just like the jackass I was, further enabling her behavior, for that was my way.

I had parked the car half-a-block up on McCadden Place, and walked slowly along the busted maze that was doubling for a sidewalk. The rain had filled the gutters and was coming almost to the edge of the curb. It fell strong, curving around me, slipping quickly down the sides and back of my leather jacket. It had me clenched tight within its grasp, as if I was in the middle of someone else's dream. Where she was parked wasn't more than eight small blocks away. I'd be there in no time at all.

I hurriedly got in, turned the key, pulled on the seat-belt, more out of habit than anything, and cranked up the heater. The radio rambled on in the background, Art Bell was still on. He was talking with Father Malachi Martin about his thirty years serving the Catholic Church as its Chief Exorcist. I wasn't interested in listening, but I chuckled under my breath, not because it was a re-broadcast and I had heard the interview before, but because every time I heard her voice or stood within five feet of Qianqian, I felt possessed myself. I wondered if Father Martin would take my call and possibly give me some advice. I realized that it must've been a matter of control and that some people are more susceptible to demons than others.

The police scanner was whispering quietly below the dash, I switched it off. Eight hours a day at work and constantly on in my other car was more than enough. I had the window on my side rolled down, despite the nature of the weather. Looking for a cigarette, finding none, I wiped my face as water droplets sped down my left cheek and crash landed on the surfaces around me. I pulled away from the curb, flipping-a-bitch on the spot and turned right onto Selma. I wasn't in a hurry, but I was aching to see her. Our last conversation together had fallen apart quickly and wasn't the way I had envisioned our relationship ending. She must've felt justified, and maybe I didn't understand. The way I felt about her much of the time was open-ended, and it hurt more sometimes to be friends than not to be. This was one of those times, at least for me, repeating itself again.

I sat at the red light on Selma and Vine for what seemed like an eternity. I saw the tail lights of her white BMW on the other side glowing at me like two seductive eyes, waiting, wanting me to get closer. In my mind, I could already see her face. Her pale off-white, almost yellow-beige skin. I imagined she smelled like flowers and shampoo. For all the reasons I could ever dream, to me she was an addictive substance. Maybe it was the continual shocked expression on her face, with wide Munch-esque eyes or her naïve belief in everything that she was ever told. Whatever it was, it was something that I couldn't pin-down.

Even though two am wasn't late, for a Sunday it was unusually quiet. Only a solitary car crossed the intersection as I waited. It was a police cruiser, passing slowly. He recognized me, waved, and then I waved back. I watched to see if he'd slow down, stop or come back, fortunately, he kept going. After crossing through Sunset and Vine, passing the bank, he turned on his roof lights and sped further away.

The signal finally turned green, but in the haze of the heavy downpour, I would've swore it was blue. Crossing the sea of intersection and flooding water, I eased up beside her, and waited as she rolled down her window. Even though we were both wedged between steel, it felt good to be beside her. From what I could tell, she was wearing the exact same thing that she had on the last time we had met. A gray watch cap, a white thermal top and a black REI fleece jacket.

"Hello, Qianqian."

"Sebastian ... thanks, I didn't have anyone else to call."

"It's fine, let me park," I said, now partially satiated. It was good to look at her again. In this instance, she probably felt nothing but a sense of urgency upon seeing me. It was awkward for her and maybe even humiliating to have called after so much time. She probably wanted to just get the tire fixed and go home.

I parked in front of her and walked back. She was smoking, I felt like asking for one, but didn't. I handed her the umbrella which she thoughtfully took.

"Thanks, that was very sweet of you to think of me," she said.

"I've missed you. I'm sorry if you thought that I just gave up on you without a fight. I just wanted to respect your decision to break it off." I let it out, trying to display an obvious amount of sincerity on my face so I wouldn't be misunderstood. All I could feel was the rain around me and complete foolishness. It splattered like small grains of rice against her windshield and bird-shot against the shoulders of my jacket. She didn't speak at first, but pursed her pink lips and gave me a serious look. It was if she was now trying equally hard to be sincere.

"It's okay, Sebastian. I understand." My bare hand was resting on her door frame covered in raindrops, she reached forward and touched me.

"Pop your trunk," I said, trying hard not to be over-dramatic or sappy. I pulled out the spare and began changing the tire. I glanced up at her several times and saw her watching me in the wing-mirror. Cigarette smoke wafted away into the night around me. The weather wasn't doing what it was supposed to anymore, and it seemed to have a mind of its own now. A dense fog layer had begun to settle in around us, which gave a brief slowdown in the rain even though it kept falling.

She got out of the car, opened the umbrella, and knelt down beside me and quietly watched as I unscrewed the lug-nuts. I looked back at her and smiled. She had a look of curiosity in her eyes. I quietly inhaled, and I could smell her mixed against the weather and the rain. I wondered if she knew what I was thinking. I wanted to make love to her, but knew I couldn't. I stared absent-mindedly at her black-soled boots connected firmly to the paved-road beside me, my hands wrenching the tire-iron.

"May I ask what you were doing out this late at night?"

"I was just out driving. I couldn't sleep. Things have been strange for me lately." I considered her words and tried hard not to imagine what she really meant. I set down each nut by the edge of her boot, out of the way, removed the flattened tire and continued.

"I couldn't sleep either. Too much work lately. I've been pushing myself day and night." The rain picked up and began coming down faster. It began to bounce off the pavement it was falling so hard. "You probably should go wait in the car. You're going to get drenched out here," I suggested.

"I'm okay," she replied, reluctant.

"Fine with me," I continued working the tire iron after putting on the spare tire.

"I missed you a great deal, you know?" her words were slow, chosen and sincere, or at least I believed them to be.

"I hoped that you had missed me, if that doesn't sound bad?" I wiped my hand across my face, rain was everywhere now.

"No … it's not." she replied sheepishly, shouting to be heard over the storm. She pushed her stringy wet hair away from her forehead. Endless beads of would-be tears ran down her face, reacting with her make-up.

"Actually," I corrected myself, "I missed you immensely," I sighed, it had felt good to get it off my chest. I began to feel whole again. "Can I ask you a personal question?"

"Isn't it always personal?" Her voice made me yearn for her, upon every word. I was longing for something, anything, even a cigarette in the rain, if that was possible. I replaced the bolts, tightened them and began letting down the jack.

"Why do we keep going through these long periods where we don't talk, we don't see each other? Are we really that different?" The traffic lights above started blinking red and then went black. The power had just failed.

"No. You're just so damn emotional, always so heavily invested," she answered. She could've said anything to appease me or shrug it off, but she didn't. "Our relationship has been hard for me too, whether you believe that or not. So many times I have needed you more than either of us could imagine, but I can't always give in to the way I feel. I have to live my life on my own terms."

"I see, so it's me that's the problem in this equation, not you." I wished I could've taken it back, because it just didn't sound right. It came out like an accusation. I was merely thinking aloud.

She chose to ignore it. "Too many things have gotten in the way, and I just couldn't keep going on like that. You're a fucking cop, I'm a goddamned outlaw, what am I supposed to say? You want to come home every day, hang your gun in the hallway and have me play Betty Crocker with you. That's just a fucking pipe-dream."

"That's kind of harsh," I rejoined. I put the jack and flat tire in her trunk and we sat for awhile in the front seat of her car quietly listening to the downpour flooding the streets around us. We sat quietly, smoking cigarettes getting warm and taking off our wet jackets and putting them in the back-seat.

"Still work for the paper?"

"I do. Still stripping?"

"I do, but I've been doing more traveling than working lately."

"I see." I did my best to make conversation, but felt lost. I wanted to touch her, but knew that I shouldn't. The voice inside my head was asking if she was struggling with her doubts about her morality, her job, her association with me, her disassociation with the world and Layden. I had to push myself to reach out and touch her face and lean in towards her.

"No …" she refused, but as I found myself within inches of her mouth, she closed her eyes and pressed her lips to mine. I was overwhelmed and felt on fire from every cell within me. My heart felt like a heavy boulder inside my chest which was unable to be supported. I worried that it could've dislodged, falling over on top of her at any moment. I listened to her breathing as we kissed and tasted what had been on the verge of my every desire. Her tongue passed across mine and the salty rain intermingled past our lips, wet hair and cold cheeks. It was the one moment that later became indelible in my mind and would later repeat itself over and over in dreams for several years on top of each other. The words 'you've just never been my type', would always ring in my ears directly after.

♘ ♕ ♘

When I woke up later that afternoon, the apartment was quiet, the rain had finally tapered off and it all seemed like a blur in my imagination. My body was tangled in the sheets, but I made no effort to adjust myself for several minutes. Fuzzbody had somehow detected my waking and had jumped up to be given some proper attention. I tried to push him away, but he wasn't having it.

"I know, I know, I know."

He looked at me stone-faced, and didn't say a word. He made a few sounds and circled around on the blanket. When I put my feet down on the floor, I noticed my wet clothes from the previous late-night adventure and realized that it *had happened* and I didn't imagine it at all. The curtains shifted in the breeze from the open windows. I shut the one directly across from me, got up, and slowly started closing the rest. I turned on the heater, put on a sweater and went into the kitchen hoping to find enough coffee to make a pot. Fuzzbody followed me across the house and swarmed on his empty food bowl, tapping the crumbs in the bottom, and pointing out the disparaging reality that he couldn't refill the damn thing on his own. I obeyed, absent-mindedly, and pulled the coffee beans from a can in the cupboard. I hated keeping them frozen, whoever had started that myth, I felt, needed to be beaten.

"You only seem to come around me when you want something, cat. Why is that?" He looked up at me with his dark eyes and launched a tirade of mewing as if I understood. He was probably telling me that 'it's a bitch to be needed, huh, asshole?'

I started the morning coffee and looked around for something to eat. The answering machine steadily blinked the number three. I hadn't heard the phone ring, but rarely ever did regardless. I slept heavy and I slept long, for that was the nature of things in my life. I cherished sleep more than anyone I'd ever known.

After making a sandwich, and pouring myself a cup, I sat down at the desk and put my feet up, cradling the small white porcelain cup in the center of my chest. I hit the button now ready to hear the litany of messages.

Message one: '*Raines – Officer Gershwin. Just getting back to you about your final list of case files. I know you're off right now, but call me anyway when you get this.*' I didn't care at all, it wasn't her.

Message two: '*This is Detective Lauren Lee, could you please call me regarding our conversation we had at the County Coroner's Office.*' I took down her number.

Message three: '*Sebastian ...*' It was Qianqian. '*I just wanted to say thanks for helping me last night. I treated you badly before and hope that you can forgive me. Please call me back. I want to see you.*' I stared at my hands holding the cup and then deeper into the dark liquid as I listened to the message. I stared until I could see the image of her from the night before, sitting in the driver's seat next to me, her face only inches away.

I sipped my coffee and let it go.

From the parking lot of a Burger King ...

I was awake and outside in the afternoon sun, exposing myself to the stark light of daytime in Los Angeles. My eyes felt as if they were swimming in pain with every step I took traversing the sidewalk from my apartment to my office at the Weekly a block away. The clouds had burned off by noon, and without sunglasses, the whole city looked opaque. The glare had complete reign of the sky above. I couldn't see a goddamned thing. I had to carefully navigate myself and my cup of coffee past a skinny girl walking a herd of wiener dogs and a stump legged panhandler posted up next to the front entrance.

"A bit late in the day for pajamas, don't you think?" I was now being judged by a legless, homeless man who had been stewing in his grime and sweat for months on end.

"Never too late start a trend," I answered, in a comical voice. He laughed as I disappeared inside. The young Mexican girl, who was supposed to be the front-desk reception, looked me over condescendingly without breaking cadence into the phone. I didn't even bother to flash her my press credentials. She was doing a marvelous job at eight dollars and hour. I could've been on the FBI's ten most wanted list.

More people than usual had been milling around in the wings and in the break-room. Crossing the main editing room, several people that had been previously engaged in other activities all started to interrupt themselves and slow to accident speed. A few people leaning against the far wall had murmured to each other and pointed at me with close-to-the-breast gestures. I was quickly becoming a spectacle. Feeling cornered, I halted in the middle of the room, almost twenty feet from my desk, raised my cup of coffee and said hello.

"Good morning everyone!" I shouted. "Everybody having a good day?" It elicited a few laughs, a few hellos' in return but, quite quickly, it broke the mesmer effect that had been holding the room together.

I sat down at my desk, noticed a thin layer of dust across the surface, and pulled a small key from the pocket of my blue-striped pajama bottoms. Unlocking the drawer, I produced a bottle of Windex, a rag and cleaned the entire surface before setting up the typewriter and going through the mail. My associates must've thought I was mad observing my antics. Several of the people in the room had never laid eyes on me, but had heard of me. For more than a handful, I must've been a myth. I was the mystery-writer without a name who was working the local-dignitary, slash-and-burn celebrity column. I guess I deserved it though. I'd been haunting the place after hours, over producing and writing articles under pseudonyms and aliases aplenty. Articles that had set the place on its ear since my first day almost six months previous. The readership may not have been aware of who I was, but every writer on staff or penny-a-page rogue-for-hire typist was fully alerted to my contributions. The junior ranks probably thought

I was taking bread from their tables and I imagine they hated me for it. Let the fuckers dangle.

I sipped my coffee and eyeballed the room looking to keep the angry and curious at bay. I started up my routine of reading the post-its, the mail and then without warning, would interrupt the electronic silence with the clink-clankety Underwood.

From my left, I sensed a female form approaching fast. Looking up, I noticed it was the young Mexican girl from the front desk downstairs.

"I have a few phone messages for you that came in yesterday and also a few hours ago." She handed me each one after re-reading them and announcing the time of the call.

"Eight p.m., Eight fifty p.m., Ten p.m., Nine forty-five this morning and Eleven a.m. this morning."

"Thanks," I muttered. I took them gently from her smooth brown hand. Her nails were French manicured and she wasn't wearing a ring. She smelled of fresh laundry and gardenias. She was young, semi-attractive and extremely well-chested.

"Ho kay, honey, she replied with a girlish smile, then turned and swished her lovely rump in the air and retreated with a faux runway grace. Several of the other writers had already begun to grab their gear and head out, realizing that I was either less than what they expected or the office was no place for a Saturday afternoon in the City of Angels. Somewhere else, possibly somewhere more interesting, follies were to be had for the taking.

Most of the letters I received, were just outright hateful. Several were from seemingly embittered readers who were outraged that their favorite celebrity's dirty laundry was being aired in public with no mercy or no regard for their right to privacy. A lot of the letters started out with: *'How dare you,'* and *'You fucking asshole'.* Some people definitely had no manners in the field of correspondence, but I surmised that the persons named in the article themselves, most-likely wrote some of the letters. The least interesting of the pieces would usually have a series of words and sentences in all *'caps'*, as the term goes. The first sign of an unbalanced mind is the unnecessary and unexplainable use of capitals. Like a lunatic's manifesto. Several of them would start well, but would quickly degenerate into two and three levels of deviation from the main subject. Segue ways upon segue ways, if you will. Yet another key to spotting craziness in written work and conversation. Schizophrenia is often detected by a set of social tools, that, being one of them.

After twenty minutes of gleaning the public's continued psychosis, I put the letters away, sipped the last of my coffee, and lit a cigarette. Someone in the back of the room who'd been observing me, started to cough and clear their throat in protest. Sending me signals of distaste, I looked over, took a drag, and then politely extinguished it into the ashtray next to the typewriter. After several people guffawed in shock, I had to make a decision to start blocking out the monkeys or I wouldn't get any work done.

The phone messages were all from Abbey, and several more had been attached to a single sheet of paper that had been left at my desk. She had been calling incessantly since Wednesday and I had chosen to ignore the calls and let them all slip into the voice mail. I'd failed to evince enough interest in my own affairs to listen to any of them. But I just didn't care anymore.

I wasn't ready to start banging away just yet. I was unable to focus and distracted by other the other homo-habili in close proximity, but after a brief exhalation of hot air, I gave in realizing that there was no time like the present. It was better to deal with it now, rather than later when I might've been on a literary roll. I picked up my cell phone, dialed her number, which was still tattooed on my brain, and waited patiently. What the hell.

The phone rang three times before it picked up.

"Helloooo?" Abbey answered. Her tone was incredulously optimistic. I wondered if she was the last person in America without caller ID on her cell phone.

"Hello, Abbey, it's yours truly. You called?"

There was a short silence over the line. She said something in the background, her hand was over the mouthpiece muffling what she was saying. All I caught was: 'Can you give me a minute, I got …' I waited a long moment before she came back on. I had just enough time to put my face deep into my coffee cup to seek salvation.

"It took you long enough to call me back. I was beginning to think that you finally got shot."

"Ouch, kind of harsh, don't you think? Nice to hear from you, too," I replied. I could easily detect something in her tone that wasn't right.

"Look, two things. One … I need you to sign the divorce documents that I sent you. Stop fucking stalling me. Two, I know about you sticking your cock in Qianqian, my so-called best-friend."

"Okay," I fumbled. The proverbial cat was now clearly out of the bag and my neck was on the chopping block with no prep-time. Christ.

"How could you betray me like that? With her … of all people, you son-of-a-bitch. You've been fucking that cow for months behind my back and I had to find it from some third party by mistake."

I didn't know what to say, but sorry was probably the most inappropriate thing at the moment. "Sorry."

"Do you know how humiliated it made me feel?"

"What did you want me to do send you an announcement or something? What was I supposed to say?"

"Don't yank me around, Sebastian. Jesus Christ, I hope to God you get her pregnant, you both deserve each other. You really know how to pick them, huh?"

"Take it easy Abbey, I didn't do anything with her until long after we broke up, so cut me some slack."

"Don't you dare tell me 'take it easy', you fucking ingrate! Do you know I pushed her stupid naked ass into a greasy trash can at the club and scalped a hunk of her hair?"

"I haven't seen her in some time, so no. I didn't know that."

"If I see her again, I'll fucking kill that stupid cunt!"

"Maybe making death threats over the phone isn't the most intelligent course of action."

"Why, what the hell are you going to do? Are you going to protect her? That's just the classiest fucking thing I've heard yet. Sign the paperwork, pay off the credit card and don't come looking for a free fuck on a slow day after the chancreous yellow ho dumps you, too."

"Christ sake, Abbey." She had already hung up.

I looked around the room, a tad shook up. The crowd had thinned during my ass-chewing and only one straggler was manning his station a few desks over. He had his back to me, but it sure looked like he was surfing Asian porn. Nasty son-of-bitch. If he started jerking it there at his desk, I'd lob my empty coffee cup at him.

I realized that Abbey was entitled to her feelings, because I did her wrong anyway it was cut. I had stuck my cock in her toxic best friend repeatedly, and had destroyed a sacred level of trust that is usually shared between people and nurtured. Actions like that typically have serious consequences. I couldn't deny the fact that I had somehow fallen in love with Qianqian though and couldn't explain it to save my life, but the thought did cross my mind about how anyone in their right mind, would fall for a train-wreck like Qian.

I rolled a piece of paper into the machine and lit another smoke. No one cared now, and the guy in the corner wasn't paying me any attention. It took a few sentences as usual to get in the mood. It took even longer, because Abbey's voice was still maneuvering through the guilt-lined corridors of my mind. Not much to do but press on. I felt poisoned and the only antidote was work. Writing made me feel invisible. It was the only comforting solution. I slowly and methodically began cranking out page after page, laying them flat next to me on the wood surface of the desk. I hand typed thirty-eight, double-spaced pages of secrets, gossip and historical facts that all seemed relevant and damning, none of them of any concern to me – on any level. That was the beauty of being invisible, I didn't have to look at myself in the mirror, and if I did, there'd be no one there to confront me. I'd reached another high-water mark of shallow behavior. Someone, somewhere would've been proud.

When I was done, and had re-read it, I considered removing the final eight pages. I had written an interesting article regarding my position on the hill and several seedy details concerning Fourth Amendment violations in the name of 'gang-violence'. I had incriminated the department in turning a blind eye on citizen's rights. I realized that I was turning up the heat directly underneath me and it seemed somewhat careless and destructive. I knew I would have to answer for writing something that direct. I was witnessing the end of my journalism career with an article whistle blowing the Los Angeles Police Department. It was suicide but I was done, whether I liked it, or not.

Checking my watch, I realized it was just after seven. I had been absorbed in work all day, turning what should've been an hour's worth of writing into an entire afternoon. Only a few lights were on now across the editing room. The neon glow outside was already pulsing and constant, pushing its way across the ceiling tiles and down the walls like an ooze or massive water leak from the floor above. Like a neighbor that had left the tap on, just to let you know, if you weren't paying attention, that you weren't alone. Regardless though, I felt like that anyway.

I packed up my crap and carried what I could back to my apartment, recognizing that I probably wouldn't be back in the building. I left what was necessary on the editor's desk with a note attached explaining my changing situation, where to send the check and the name to make it out to. I had usually deposited checks made out to other names into the ATM machine at night, thus avoiding the security measures and scrutiny the bank had in place. I could've gone an extra step and had someone else cash it for me, but I didn't really foresee the department launching an investigation over a newspaper article, no matter how damning it was. It was, however, in my best interest to walk away, because I had started a shit-storm and distance was good advice. A voice in my head told me that I should've removed the eight pages.

I was now comfortable with the idea that I had effectively vacated my office at the Weekly. I had no plan to go back for rewrites, clarifications or twenty questions. If they wanted me badly enough, they'd know where to find me. I felt restless after struggling over four to five thousand words. My brain was now moving at a fluid speed, thoughts coursed through my mind with absolutely no control. Staying locked inside with myself on a clear night, with no rain for a change, was out of the question.

I slipped on clean clothes, wearing something different than a pair of laundered pajamas or a dark blue uniform. It felt like it had been months since I had worn anything else. I grabbed the usual essentials and locked the door behind me. It was close to nine o'clock by the time I had pulled out onto Highland, turned right and headed for the Valley.

People were now on the sidewalks en-masse. The bad weather which had held them prisoner to their indoor hobbies, had now abated and freed them to wander aimlessly up the boulevard, staring at each other, eating falafel, hot dogs and packing out the clubs to maximum capacity. All the regulars were manning their usual posts on Hollywood and Highland. I spotted people that I had arrested before leaning against the glass edges of tattoo parlors, tee-shirt shops and at the curb by the Burger King parking lot. Several of the usual street performers that dressed up like movie characters, Disney creations and silver painted robots were posted up, drinking coffee and fraternizing at the Chinese Food & Donut joint just up off Yucca Street. I was sitting still in traffic taking it all in wondering if a narration by Paul Winfield or Harrison Ford would have made it any more redeemable and complete. Hollywood at night was a classically predictable scenario. In the decade that I'd been living in it, driving through and pushing a beat, not much had changed. New levels of urban gentrification came along slowly transforming the city, at least architecturally, into something that appeared on the outside, more marketable.

The same amount of run-a-way teenagers flocked to places like the Hollywood Café, the late night used bookstore and the parking lot of the Burger King, hoping to score, sell a piece of ass, get a ride the-hell-out-of-there and a place to stay for the night. A spot on the map that had seen the fates of so many crushed, melt-down or turn pornographic. On the streets, the Burger King parking lot was used by the Police as a favorite spot to arrest people on weekend nights. Bets were placed before heading out on shift as to who would pick up the strangest collar. I usually waited until after two-thirty when the bars let out and catch a homeless man getting a blow-job from a pristine blonde teenager for a really dry and short bag of weed. In the days of wearing a uniform, these places were important. Now I just drive by without giving any of it a second thought.

Yellow Fever

From a Francis Bacon painting ...

From one moment to the next, I couldn't guess what would be coming out of Qianqian's mouth. Nor could I ever pin down for sure when the next time we'd see each other was. I had often been tossed from the house for no reason, been ignored and sometimes flat-out stood-up. A smarter man wouldn't have much to do with someone who behaved so badly, but being so beautiful, certain girls get more leniency than others. Men will tolerate a lot at times when they're in love, even if they know she doesn't feel the same. I had often surmised that Qian was outwardly the most striking and gorgeous women that I had ever laid eyes on. Other men often thought the same thing too. Many times I was pushed aside when entering clubs and restaurants so they could have a closer conversation with her, ignoring me completely. I never got bent out of shape for two very distinct reasons. One, I would do the same to someone else if I was desperate and wanted to talk to her. Two, being such a low-key, forgettable person I could blend into a blank page. It did me little good to be a hater. Inwardly though, she had the ugliest and darkest soul of anyone that I had ever met. Murderous, kidnap frenzied Chechen Rebels in Bosnia didn't hold a candle to her. Given the same choices she probably would've killed more people, more often. So all in all, after all the abuse I suffered just to be in her presence, I had at least learned to have a little patience with everyone else and as far as I was concerned, the experience was helpful. Sometimes, you don't want to stand out, and sometimes you're better served not forcing yourself on certain types, I was one of them, and so was she.

I was catatonic when the phone rang. I was dazed but answered the phone regardless. I still had several hours to sleep and didn't have to report until four in the afternoon for my mid-shift, atop the Mt. Lee. And before I knew it, still half-asleep, I had showered, dressed and headed out the door. She had beckoned and I responded without hesitation.

When I pulled up to the house, I noticed she had left the front door of her small house-cum-cottage open. I thought I had made my last visit to the place, but I was wrong. Qian's house was the only real house on Scott Road. Every other building was a large, looming apartment building. The small house was protected on all sides by an ivy covered brick wall.

I was sitting on the foot stool in her front room, only stopping at 7-11 for coffee and a donut, but after hearing her litany of complaints, I realized it wasn't enough sustenance to endure it. But as always, I did. Her full agenda was obtaining my set of keys and getting me to promise to never contact her again. What I thought was going to be an opportunity to converse and set things right, turned out to be quite the opposite. She wanted to make a clean break. She was now conducting her life with a strange, detached sense of businesslike formality. It seemed as if management was being restructured.

"So can you give me one believable reason why we can't work this out?"

"You're not my type."

"I'm not your type?" I replied, flabbergasted. "Is that how it is in your world? Just a desperate attempt to marginalize me, because I'm a threat to all those defenses?" I sputtered. I was hurt by her words and begun to feel a constricting in my chest. All it was, was rejection, but it was powerful. She stared at me, annoyed.

I was rubbing my hand across my forehead, staring at the floor. "Is this another ritual that you've developed, or rather, repeated? Or is this just how you deal with someone when they become too close?" She flicked her cigarette directly at me, striking me on the left side of my face.

"Fuck you, Sebastian. You're nothing to me and you've always been a bore."

"How convincing ... words to remember."

Picking up her purse, she headed out the door, started her car and ignored me as she drove away. I laughed to myself as I stood in the doorway dumbfounded. She had decided to recess inside herself rather than engage me honestly about the sanity of her decisions. Escalating her dating behavior to encompass anything at all ... just for money, even if she already knew the men, seemed disastrous. It would only be a matter of time before things would go from bad to catastrophic. Now, she was asking me to stand on the side-lines and watch her just destroy herself. All that, I couldn't bear, but it made me laugh. I was hoping that I was wrong, but the tone in her voice made me realize just how serious she was.

She had driven away leaving me alone in her house, it was an awful substitution. Within minutes, I gathered what few things I had scattered between rooms, locked up for the last time, dropped my only key in the mailbox and meandered out to my black and white, tossing the junk of my relationship with Qian into the darkness of the trunk. As much as I would have loved to follow her, and give her a piece of my mind, I couldn't. Even though I knew I had to bite the bullet, I had no intention of swallowing the whole rifle.

I had to get back up to the station and start my four-day work week. Kim was now gone and for the next several weeks, I would be alone on the hill. I knew that Okana would be coming in more often, so I was better off not becoming a target.

The fallout from Kim had strangely led outside sources to start asking questions. Kim's name had come up, which raised more suspicions than normal, because at first glance, he was an Officer, with a badge number, a payroll file, an academy record, but unassigned to any unit since being attached to the Surveillance detail. I imagined that the same was probably true for me, and it was only a matter of time before my name would come up, raising the same questions. Several over-interested reporters had been turned away without information by the bureaucracy at the Bradbury Building. This action caused a backlash and an article in the *Los Angeles Times* speculating of the possible existence of the job function which I now preformed. Several parties within the city government were furious over the possible idea of invasion of privacy, but eavesdropping without a warrant was vehemently dismissed as absurd by the chief. From that moment, everything had changed, and it occurred overnight. I was told to wear blues and drive a cruiser full-time. I was officially assigned to metro, but would continue to work on the hill and report into my Bradbury office three times a week. In the end it just equated to more overtime, which barely covered the cost of dry-cleaning several new uniforms. I was now officially providing security for the building that was now under the scrutiny of the public eye, and to protect company property from break-ins. Try selling that to a member of the press. 'Let me get this straight', it would undoubtedly start out, successfully providing the readership across the city douche-chills.

When I finally locked myself into the control building atop Mount Lee above the Hollywood skyline, I had to spend an extra few minutes turning on all the equipment. A job that was normally attended to by Kim. Several new files scattered my desk, but thankfully I had been pulled off over half of the surveillance cases that were ongoing due to the lack of manpower and the fact that the Chief had decided the 'post on the hill', would now make a smaller contribution on the whole, for the sake of discretion.

I wasn't unhappy about any of the changes. I actually concluded two of the cases, providing more than enough information to plan and execute a sting operation on a Russian Burbank-Glendale auto-theft and counterfeiting operation. Another day not listening to Russian or Armenian was a good day.

I had boxed up the last handful of closed cases and burned the last audio disk from the hard-drive, when I stumbled across a forgotten folder that had been placed on my desk at the Bradbury Building. Written across the top was the name Qianqian Mao. It was standard department policy to flag the jacket of a spouse or family member in case of arrest. I had flagged Qian's after her first offense. I had forgotten about it in the chaos of packing the contents of Kim's desk and finishing his business, trying to sort through his cases and his personal documents. He wasn't allowed back from the way I was interpreting it.

I had read through the report and flipped past her booking records from the past two indecent exposure infractions. Her driving record was also attached and was littered with speeding tickets and moving violations of all kinds. She was on the verge of a suspension with one more ticket. She had already twice filed for traffic school in the past eighteen months, so there would be no leniency. Most of the information was pretty standard, and I wasn't surprised to see the current arrest listed. I had done several night-club raids in the Valley as part of training in the early days of being a rookie. Booking strippers was always good bureaucratic practice. Man handling scantily-clad women was also, much better than dealing with greasy, grubby, mentally ill living in big-screen boxes on the street. In both cases, I was more likely to go home with fleas than getting a lap dance.

I read through her file carefully, all of her known addresses were listed, as was all of her phone numbers. Layden Strausse's name appeared as well, clear as day, in an area on a form marked 'known associates or accomplices'. His jacket number was listed beside his name. For half a second, I was tempted to read up just out of curiosity. I knew that I would find the obvious and the predictable, as one jacket tends to look like another after enough time.

I was still angry for Qian's earlier outburst, she had showed absolutely no regard for my safety or well-being and had spoken so acidic that it felt criminally malicious. I shook my head, mumbled to myself and wandered over to the coffee pot to get some fresh mud cooking.

The room was low lit and had a soft buzz as the air-conditioner stayed on constantly to keep the equipment cool and as dust-free as possible. I turned on the CD player and made my way over to a bank of computers, I punched in her phone number into the phone surveillance software and turned up the speakers so I could hear any activity from across the room over *Miles Davis at the Blackhawk*. Violating department policy didn't seem to have the same sting as I had earlier imagined. I had officially crossed the line.

The control room had a regular size kitchen for the purposes of long shifts and a small bathroom near the door. I had become accustomed to filling out my paperwork at the kitchen counter as my desk was usually buried. Even though things were now, vastly different, I didn't feel like changing habits. I must've listened to Miles for almost a half hour before I heard the ring-tone come over the speakers. Activity. Qian was calling out. I could hear her clearing her throat and breathing. A female voice had answered on the forth ring. I had already put the file I was on down, grabbed my coffee and stood up. Unmistakably, it was Brittsy's raspy, whiskey-soaked voice.

"Hello?"

"Hey Chick, it's me."

"No shit, ever heard of caller ID?"

"Yeah, you busy?" Qian's voice sounded both relaxed and innocent. A sea of difference from her tone at the house.

"Kind of … if you call getting laid by a bearded redneck busy?"

Qian laughed. "You can't be serious, are you having sex right now?"

"Sure feels like it," Brittsy groaned. "Hang on a sec." The line went quiet, but I could hear a few voices in the background. If I was that interested in Brittsy's relationship, I could catch it on the playback. The silence was interrupted by the unmistakable series of noises that could've only been Britts lighting a cigarette.

"Ok, I told him to finish. What's going on, are you at home?"

"No, I came into Hollywood, eating pizza at Jones. I had to call you because some shit went down."

"Well, you can't be that fucked up if you're at Jones. Does that fine-ass brunette chick with the 'tig ol' biddies' still work there?"

"Yeah, she just waited on me."

"What the hell was her name, Jasmine …, Jenny …, Justine?"

"Justine. I know your bullshitting me because you asked for her phone number and she gave it to you."

"So, what the fuck happened that you decided to call … me, during the middle of the … afternoon?" Brittsy's voice broke on two occasions and there was muffling going on in the background, I would've bet money that she had just been turned over.

"Are you still having sex with that red-neck?" Qian was surprised.

"I told him to finish, not get off."

"Anyways, I just had a blow out with Sebastian."

Brittsy grunted at the hearing of my name. I raised an eyebrow and sipped my coffee.

"French Pig," she murmured into the receiver. "Please tell me that you finally broke it off with him. He's an asshole. God, how … can you stand him?"

"First, he's not French, but I don't really know what I ever saw in him. I just told him off and ended it." I felt a tad strange though, hearing her version of the story. The end result was the same, anyway you told it.

"I thought you two were already done? Did you mercy fuck him, or something?"

"No, he just had a bunch of shit at my house and a set of keys as well."

"Well, it's about time you gave him his crap back and got your fucking keys."

"I can't believe that I was with someone that stupid for that long," Qian remarked. I almost spat up my coffee all over the counter. The thought crossed my mind that I shouldn't be listening. There was something unsettling about her thoughts about me. I wanted to tell myself that it was out of context and she was venting.

"I told him to take his crap, leave and never call me again. I also said that I thought that he was a complete dickless joke."

"You said that?"

"Yeah."

"No," I interrupted, speaking only to myself.

"Ouch, … ahh," Britts gasped. The man's grunting was slightly audible in the background. He must've finally finished.

"God damn, Chick, you're such a tramp. I didn't call to hear you get your box worked over."

"It's not like you haven't heard it before in the booth next to me in the club, Ho."

"Well, you know what they say, the lap dance is always better when she's crying," Qian teased.

"You dirty little skank."

"Hey, I'm not the one getting boned."

"So, you never told Sebastian that you were pregnant again?" Brittsy blurted.

"No," Qian answered, feebly.

"Why not, you could've made him pay for the surgery."

"No, I'd rather pay for it myself. I'm rather particular about having abortions. I guess it's kind of a ritual, and besides, telling him would've just made things more complicated.

"You might want to consider getting neutered or sterilized if you have no plans for reproducing."

I was stunned hearing them casually banter on about something so tragic, I was realizing just how emotionally void the two of them were.

"I've already made my appointment to get it sucked out of me. It's tomorrow at eleven a.m. Besides, it's probably Layden's, but it's a bit hard to say.

"Did you want me to drive you down there?"

"Sure."

"I'm busy tomorrow, fuck you."

"Stop it."

"I'm just kidding, are you coming over later?" Brittsy asked.

"I don't want to come over while you're getting nailed by some random Hells Angel wannabe."

"Hey, that's not nice, he works for the city."

"Slaves. Just the way you like them, huh?"

After a moment of muffled silence, then laughter, Brittsy came back on. "He wanted to know, since you're having an abortion tomorrow if he could have a turn at fucking you, since it didn't matter anyway. He said he'd pay you a thousand bucks to not wear a condom and work-out that little Chinese ass-hole. What do you say? A good poon pounding might do you some good."

"Does he have a big dick?"

"It's about average."

"Sure, tell him I'll be right over, but I don't take checks, cash only."

"You serious?"

"No, I think I'll pass this time. Thanks anyway."

"Don't worry, I knew you'd refuse me. We could've had a fun three-some."

"Joy," Qian responded already bored.

"Come over around seven then, I'll be back from the store then, we can go out to eat."

"Ok, sounds good. I'll call if I'm not doing something. Bye."

They both clicked off. I couldn't fathom everything that I had just heard. My head was swimming. I was beside myself, horrified. I couldn't help but wonder what exactly I was in love with. I paced around the control room for over an hour. I had started packing files away again when the phone rang a second time. It rang for a long time before an answering machine picked up. It was her mother's voice in broken English.

"Hello, no one is home now. Kindly leave us a message ... and we'll get back to you soon. Thanks. Bye."

"Mom, it's me. Can you please call me? I know you're still mad at me and dad's upset, but I really need to talk with you. Can you please forgive what I did?" Then just like that, she said nothing further and hung up the phone.

I caught my reflection momentarily in the mirror hanging in the small bathroom. The cigarette burn had caused a small welt to rise at the top of my cheek just below my eye. I was lucky she didn't injure me more seriously. The best thing I could do was just clean the damn thing with rubbing alcohol, even though it was going to burn like hell. But judging by the redness, I didn't have a choice.

I began to realize the power I wielded in this particular situation, having all the information in my lap. She didn't want to see me, talk to me or hear about how I felt. That much was clear. I didn't want to intervene in her life and create misery, tension, or a blow-out. My first thought was to just wait her out, eventually she would call me as she always did, when she needed something and had no one else to turn to. But for now, the only link I had to her was my job and at some level, the idea made me nauseous because that would be gone soon.

I left the call monitor going for some time, but the line stayed silent for several hours. I had fixed a sandwich, packed the last box of cases and finally got a handle on the actual surface of my desk. I hadn't seen that much gray Formica since the first week of my assignment almost two years ago. Now it was just a flat panel monitor, a keyboard, a few pens in a small holder and an issue of the American Journal of Psychiatry.

I had my feet up on the desk relishing the newly liberated space. It was feeling less like work and more like a home away from home. It occurred to me that it wouldn't be bad idea to bring Fuzzbody up, as he probably wouldn't mind a change of scenery. Half-way through tossing a few files into the trash that I had re-read twice already, the phone rang for the third time. Looking at my monitor, I could see all the pertinent information on the caller by the second ring. It was Layden Strausse with a registered number in Granada Hills. His complete address, his jacket number, and his entire legal life laid out in on-screen-text. Good thing I hadn't gotten up for coffee.

"Hello, Layden," Qian answered, sounding trite.

"You don't sound very happy to hear me?"

"Why should I be happy to hear from you Layden? A man that cheats on his wife and who frivolously spends money on women for sex and a multitude of other indulgent whims? What about you is so appealing?"

"Oh, yes … you could do to reign in that high horse Miss Mao, let me remind you that you were well paid."

"Again, what can I do for you, Layden?"

"I want to see you," he pleaded, sluggishly.

"I don't think so. Now, is definitely not a good time."

"Well what's so bad about it? Let me come over and stay the night with you. I'll take you out, we can go to Santa Monica and have something to eat on the Promenade. You love that place."

"You must be fucking joking?"

"No, Qian, I'm completely serious. Why the hesitation, is your uniformed boyfriend with you?"

"Layden, I can't, and no, he's not here, for one. Two, I'm not a home at the moment. Three, I'm completely done with Sebastian as I should be with you, and four – no – you cannot come over."

"You sound pretty matter of fact about it. Maybe I should try you some other time?"

"Yeah, Layden, why don't you just call some other girl from your Friday night fall-back list. You're a complete whore." She clicked out on him and the line went dead. I had barely enough time to take in the information from the last call when the monitor showed that she was making another outgoing call. It was a number I didn't recognize, and it was a cell-phone.

"Hello," A man's voice answered.

"Andrew?"

"Hello Qian, I was wondering when I was going to hear from you. How are you?"

"Not bad. Just thought I'd call and see how you were. I did promise to come over and see you."

"Yes, you did. Did you want to have dinner or have you got plans?"

"No, I'm free. Where do you want to meet," she asked. My mind raced at the thought that this must be the secret answer to the eternal question as to how women can break up with men and move on so easily. They just never get fully involved in the first place and put up a lot of numbers, so to speak. But then I realized, I was now comparing all women to Qian, and knew that that wasn't fair. I knew about Andrew, but didn't know much. Qian had been infatuated with him. He was a photographer that wanted to have her for a nude shoot. She had turned him down on several previous occasions, but knew that she would eventually cave in with enough attention. I had sat through many lunches with her while she was on the phone talking about 'planning a shoot' with him.

They made plans to meet and then hung up. I ran his phone number and went over his personal information without any dispensation towards his privacy. I felt in the mood for a stake-out, grabbed my gear, shut everything down a couple hours early and headed out, knowing wholly, that I was now involving myself in out-and-out stalking. Madness. I was also engaging in this on department time, which could later be seen as insurance or just a gross misuse of resources. I didn't care, I was too curious and I was becoming feverish and obsessed.

By the time I was able to pick up an unmarked car from the Rampart Division on the East side of Hollywood and drive over to Qian's house in Burbank, Andrew's Range Rover was already parked in the driveway of the small two bedroom cottage. I was carrying portable equipment that would allow me to monitor both Qianqian's cell-phone and Andrew's as well. I turned off the main dashboard computer in the car as it was a pain in the ass having to take it through a complete reboot and log-in procedure every time you restarted the car. Within minutes of waiting, they had pulled out onto Scott Road and headed away from me, apparently going to dinner. I pulled out behind them and drove slowly, waiting for him to push through the light. The only other piece of equipment in the car was another surveillance device that's commonly used for eavesdropping physical conversations from a distance. In old movies, you would sometimes see detectives pointing microphoned dishes at people while trying to stay hidden in a bush, or some such nonsense. Sophistication being the benefit of elapsed time in concordance with technology, I was able to employ this device subtly without being obvious or having to physically manipulate anything. Button-based activities dictate that when one's hands are full, the user becomes inefficient and becomes restricted in the amount of buttons he or she is able to push. In this case I had only to swivel a directional mic that was unobtrusively mounted on the dash board and turn on the stereo.

I followed behind them carefully, looking to keep enough distance. Andrew drove above the speed limit into Glendale and parked outside of a Persian restaurant called 'Sham-shiri'. Thankfully, and conveniently, they took a booth seat near at the window. I parked conspicuously across the street with the car facing them.

Qian was unsurprisingly dressed very well, although I would've expected her to wear black and be covered head-to-toe in turquoise. Instead she decided on white, adorned with several pieces of amber jewelry. I laughed inwardly at the thought of her choice of jewel stone. Amber is typically sold with some 'once-living thing' encased in its center for all time, traditionally a scorpion or a scarab. No doubt Qian had at least one stone containing such a prisoner close to her skin at that moment. I watched them through magnified binoculars in the safety and comfort of my darkened sedan. The isolation was stifling, which reminded me of how much I hated stake-outs.

I adjusted the volume on the distance microphone and tried to listen in on what was being said.

"Thank you," Qian responded, looking up at the waiter as he brought over a glass of coke with ice. Andrew looked like what I expected a letch to look like. Much like arrest records, perverts too, tend to all look alike after enough time.

He was much older than he should've been, completely gray and overweight. He dressed as if all his clothes were combinations of different pieces of the same suit, bought in the same store, made by the same designer. There was an aura of cheapness to him that seemed comical. But this probably had more to do with my bent feelings than objective or empirical deduction.

"Why is it that I only ever hear from you when I least expect it? You didn't return several of my calls."

"I'm sorry Andrew, my life is always hectic. I'm never really sure where it's going."

"Sounds drastic. Has it been like this always or just recently?" he asked. He was choosing his words shrewdly. His tone of voice was very off-putting. I just didn't like the guy, it was that simple. The waiter interrupted the answer by taking their order. Qian had ordered chicken bahrg with saffron rice and Andrew had Eggplant stew and gor mahsahb si and another glass of white wine. He oozed trouble and I could smell it. Magnified, his face seemed to make my stomach turn.

"So?" he stated, indirectly repeating the question.

"Hard to say, things have always been questionable, I guess more so the older I get. I feel like I've been just drifting lately. But changing a lot, so I guess it can't be all that bad."

"Depends on what you're changing into, I guess, or which direction you're headed.

"*My thoughts exactly*," I said, under my breath as I watched alone.

The conversation turned to photography. He did his part to impress her by telling her that he had recently been published in several magazines and had done some film work for the Discovery Channel while continuing to produce a large volume of erotic still work.

I took a break from listening as the sound of Andrew's voice became unbearable, giving me a headache, chills and an upset stomach. I followed them back to his house in Encino where she had casually disappeared with him inside. I parked halfway down the block on the opposite side of the street. The sun had long set and little traffic passed, I was hidden well under the foliage of nightshade. I felt reluctant to wander outside and to try and get a better look through one of the back windows. It was the absolute last thing that I wanted to get caught doing. I relaxed and listened to AM radio for over two hours knowing full well what was going on inside. Obviously he was getting an opportunity to use Qian as a model, which wasn't a bad thing, considering her day job. I had to not let my mind get the better of me as I sat there quietly. All I could do now was wait. I eased the seat back into a recline position and stretched out inconspicuously.

♞ ♛ ♞

Andrew turned on the lights to his studio room that had been set up with a red background and a long red couch in the center. A thick red curtain hung down from the ceiling and was draped over the bottom end. It looked like a set directly pulled out of a renaissance masterpiece by Caravaggio.

Several lights were positioned around the room in a triangular array facing the set.

"The room was actually all black earlier, but I've already done several shoots with that set already. I had my assistant set this up earlier in the day, just after you called. I figured I probably wouldn't be able to get the chance to photograph you again seeing how often you call me."

"Yeah, I guess so. I'm sure I'd be old and married by the next time."

"Hasn't anyone ever told you Qian, that women like you never age, never marry and certainly never fade?"

"Sounds lonely, my nightmare and someone else's dream," she admitted. She relaxed, feeling relieved to be in new surroundings. She lit a cigarette as she reclined on the red sofa feeling the warm heat of the lights.

"This is actually a nice set."

"I just hope the pictures turn out. Sometimes you can never tell. I'm going to shoot you with a medium format.

Should be real nice." Andrew had repeated the mantra all photographers go through, hoping that 'everything turns out' and that it wouldn't be a waste of time and money.

"Have you done a lot of modeling?"

"No, not really, just once before."

"Did you like the way the shots turned out?"

"Not really," Qian announced, looking down.

"Why not?"

"I guess I always thought that I ended up looking fat and uninteresting."

"All women say that about being fat, without exception. What exactly did you believe looked fat?"

Qian laughed. Andrew busied himself setting up and adjusting the lights, the tripod and probably the shutter speed.

"My calves, I suppose. I guess I'd have to say my calves, thighs too."

"Hmm," he grunted. "Well maybe we can mentally use those pictures as sort of a dry run, what do you think?"

"A dry run, how so?"

"Well, we can recreate some of those poses, I can take some photographs like that and then we can try something new. That way we'll both know that we've broken new ground."

"Sounds intriguing," Qian answered, feeling secure that he knew what he was doing. She stretched out on her stomach and picked up a magazine from the floor and read while he was continuing to get ready. Andrew snapped a few pictures, adjusted the camera's position and then took a few more.

"Ok, ready now?" he announced. Qian stood up and began to lift her dress of over her bare frame. She wasn't wearing underwear.

"No. Wait on that, Qian. Why don't you leave it on for a few shots? Let me do a few standing then a few sitting."

She half expected him to immediately suggest that she undress. His patience made her feel even more at ease. She had wondered if she felt awkward about it all.

"Fine, whatever you say."

Andrew snapped several with her dress hiked up and her shoes still on. Then, after a whole series of suggestive poses holding various different things, from a rifle to a bunch of bananas she stood up and undressed. He suggested that he leave her jewelry on which would have a nice effect if he took a few of her close up. Qian was enjoying herself for a change and considerably relaxed.

Soon Andrew stopped and very casually took a few hits of something from a glass pipe. Qian laid still, quietly like a lioness in the grass, patiently waiting, looking on.

"Here," he said, handing her the pipe. She took it and the lighter, rolled over onto her back, splayed her legs and took several large hits. She had absolutely no idea what was in the pipe, and for all she knew, she could been smoking weed soaked in cyanide. Within moments she could feel the muscles in her body releasing large pieces of knotted tension as she exhaled smoke which billowed across the studio. Andrew took a picture of that as well. She blinked, smirked and looked down at her crotch in acknowledgement. Quickly though and unexpectedly, her mind went numb. Whatever it was that she was smoking, it was overtaking her rapidly.

Andrew had turned on some classical music while Qian indulged herself on the sofa. In flashes of the camera and the narcotic, everything slowed, but she was still responsive. A few times she phased in and out of consciousness on several occasions and stopped noticing the passage of time. Being loaded and naked in someone else's house usually requires a certain amount of moral flexibility that most people rarely harness. Qian had it in spades though and any feelings of discomfort faded in her like water off a duck's back. When she came around on the third or forth occasion, Andrew had his face and tongue buried in her crotch, her legs were still splayed akimbo and her head was back, pushing her chest forward. Her back had molded to the chaise-longue and even though she was completely out of it, she felt comfortable. She could feel his warm breath pulsing into her stomach. When she came around again, she opened her eyes and saw that he had mounted her, was nude and fucking her for dear life. Her whole body pulsed with warm vibration as she laid there taking it. She had known from the moment that she had agreed to go home and take pictures with him that she would end up having sex with him. It seemed inevitable. The apparent absent delicacies leading up to intercourse didn't bother her enough to stop him. Once, she came to and almost gagged upon finding that she had his cock buried in her mouth and her hands around his waist. The thought of continually phasing in and out started to become unsettling. Andrew worked himself up into a frenzy, pressing his fat stomach hard against her face as he ejaculated into her mouth, she relaxed her neck, swallowed and unplugged his penis from her face.

After a few minutes of falling spent, and worn out on the sofa, she picked the pipe up once more. Something in her was compelling her to keep going.

"Do you have any more of this shit to smoke?" she asked, realizing that the pipe was played. She wanted more. "I think it's wearing off."

"No, but I could get you more, if you feel like going out."

"Sure," she urged. She was in no condition to go anywhere but was fiending to continue chasing her high. Andrew re-mounted her and was now slapping against her bare ass with his corpulent flesh. She was swaggering back and forth like a small boat in a large body of water as he busied himself pushing his penis around in his momentary fantasy. Honestly, Qian couldn't give a shit, she just wanted him to finish so she could get something else to smoke and get properly dialed in.

It was just after eleven when they got into his Land Rover and headed over to Andrew's connection. Qian sat with her feet on the dashboard and her knees pressed up against her chest. Dreary-eyed, she monitored the lights of the passing traffic and the reflected ambient neon glow radiate against the buildings like phosphorous. The radio was slowly bleeding

Craig Armstrong like a requiem mass. The song made her think of Brittsy, who was probably wondering what happened to her. She knew that she had already written her off for the rest of the night.

"Where are we going?" her voice broke through the thick atmosphere in the cabin of the vehicle which had become like bong-water.

"My dealer lives in Studio City, we're almost there." Qian didn't know the deeper reaches of the valley, but she thought for sure that the sprawling ghetto that they were drifting through was Van Nuys or North Hollywood and going further from Studio City every moment. She ignored her instincts and lit a cigarette instead.

"You're oozing out of me., she mentioned. He just ignored her as he focused on trying to keep his awareness at peek performance in order to drive. He was still higher than a kite, drifting around in his lane and not fully aware of his poor performance. From out of the corner of her eye she knew the car approaching fast from Andrew's side wasn't going to stop. Andrew had blown through a red-light at the corner of Lankershim and Victory. She frowned as the surprised look of the driver momentarily registered in her mind as the two speeding cars collided.

The impact was deafening inside the steel and glass cabin of the Land Rover. All the windows on the drivers side shattered into thousands of pieces and filled the small space around her like a massive snowstorm. The airbags deployed at mach speed filling her nose with burnt talcum powder as the collision continued in slow motion. Andrew took the biggest brunt of the collision head on in his seat. It looked to Qian as if the Rover was crumpling around him, wrapping him in plastic, padded leather, roof felt and hard metal exterior. The Rover continued moving but now spiraled sideways out of control and sailed into a bank of newspaper machines on the North West corner.

Outside, Qian watched the newspapers exploding beside her like frightened pigeons that sailed away into the sky momentarily frightened, but quickly returning to their routine. She was dazed and closed her eyes and lost consciousness as the horn continued but the vehicle did not. It was only a few short seconds when she opened her eyes and felt the warm trickle of blood running down her cheek from her hairline. The inflating of the air bags had pushed her hand with all her rings, bracelets and protruding stones straight into her face at one-hundred and seventy miles-per-hour. She wasn't aware that it was the air-bag that had caused her injury, but the pain and the blood were real enough. She felt dazed, but strangely calmed, not really aware of what had just taken place. To her right, she turned and saw the silver Volvo in the middle of the intersection trying desperately to re-start their car and leave. She could smell gas now, transmission fluid and antifreeze, or at least that's what her brain was telling her it was.

"Andrew ..." her voice floated from her body as if it was detached and sounding like something broadcast over the radio. She didn't connect with the words she was speaking as her own.

"Andrew ... what just happened?" When she turned and saw Andrew slumped over the deflated air-bag and not moving, she noticed that the door had folded around his chest, contorting and mangling his body into something unrecognizable. Through her unfocused haze, he looked as if he was now apart of the car and as the fog parted, her thoughts cleared and the only thing that immediately came to mind was to get the hell out of there, and to do so quickly. As she stepped down from the truck, she had to squeeze through a small opening as the door wouldn't open all the way due to the front end being mated with the newspaper stands. When she looked over at the car in the intersection, she saw two middle-aged Mexican men finally starting the car and staring at her as if she were a ghost. It finally registered that she was bleeding pretty bad. As the car sped away leaving her in the middle of the road, she clutched at herself oddly, taking some type of instinctive inventory that her body was performing. She felt as if she had re-booted. The bright 7-11 sign that was glowing off in the distance a few blocks away was the only thing that seemed to make sense. She thought about getting help.

Being late, and deep within the valley, not a solitary car was out on the road and the streets were quiet. She looked down at her white dress and saw that blood was running down her chest and soaking her white Donna Karan sleeveless dress. Walking South down Lankershim, she knew that it was fucked up to leave Andrew dead in his car at the scene of an accident without calling for help. Maybe at the store, she considered.

When she finally got to the 7-11, she realized that it would be a very bad idea to be seen looking the way she did. Her only thought was to call someone. She hid behind the building in an abandoned dirt parking lot and called Layden. It was instinctual.

He picked up immediately, "Hello?"

"Layden, I've been in an accident and I need you to come and get me now." The words barely left her lips. He knew she sounded distant.

"What? Are you kidding me? Have you called the cops?" he stammered.

She became annoyed with him very quickly and started feeling light-headed. "Layden, listen to me very carefully. I've been in a fucking car accident. I'm bleeding pretty bad. I'm stranded, and I'm telling you to come and get me."

"Okay, okay. Where are you?"

"I'm behind a 7-11 on Lankershim about a block before Victory."

"Okay get some help, I'll be there in ten minutes. I'm on Ventura."

"Just hurry."

She couldn't believe what was happening as she stood in the bushes looking out on Lankershim Boulevard. When the rain began to fall a few drops at a time, she was dabbing at her head with the bottom edge of her dress.

"Damn it, you've got to be kidding me." She looked up and saw nothing but dark gray sky above her. The rain was slowly gaining momentum. Off in the distance she could easily see Andrew's Rover just off to the side of the intersection half-on the sidewalk. The horn was still stuck in the on position. The street lights made the window-glass that was scattered all over the intersection look like precious gems, diamonds or sparkling stones. Not a single soul, as far as she could see, was coming or going up Lankershim. The whole Earth felt deserted. '*Thank God*' were the only other words that she could mentally put together. She wanted a cigarette more than anything, but quickly deduced that she had left hers on what was left of the console back with Andrew. Going back to get them was out of the question, as was going inside the store. The Police would surely ask the clerk later if they saw the accident or if anyone had come in injured. The last thing she wanted was to be on closed-circuit television.

When Layden finally got there, it felt much longer than ten minutes. She wanted to yell at him and ask where the fuck he was, and why he took his sweet time, but she thought better not to.

"Holy Shit, Qian! You're bleeding from your head and you're covered in blood."

"Yeah, no shit, Layden. Tell me something I don't know. Please tell me you have cigarettes."

"No. Sorry, I don't." he stared at her, mortified.

"Christ, just take me home."

"Why don't you please explain to me what the hell is going on. I pick you up in the middle of the night from some random street in the valley, and you say you've been in an accident, but I don't see your truck anywhere," he was foaming, Qian cut him off abruptly.

"Look," she was pointing her finger straight up the street at the intersection in the distance. Layden could see the truck demolished off to the side. A car was now slowly going through the intersection, it wasn't a cop, but it looked like an unmarked vehicle. They both watched the car continue on after slowing for only a moment. It was Los Angeles, nothing more should've been expected. Layden turned the car around and headed in the opposite direction, taking a longer way around to get back to her house than was needed, but necessary in order to avoid the accident.

"One moment you're telling me where to stick it, the next you're depending on me in the middle of the night, Qian. It's a good thing for you that I was out. If I had been at home I wouldn't have picked up."

"Save it, Layden. You haven't rescued me. Don't feel so flattered. I was dazed, I probably should've called either Brittsy or Sebastian. There's no prize because I called you." Qian looked ridiculous with her dress hiked up blotting the wound on her head. Layden saw that she wasn't wearing any underwear or a bra as usual. She was just trying to stop the bleeding, and being exposed didn't seem to bother her in the slightest. The landscape outside seemed to pass slowly, but Layden was probably crossing the Valley back to Burbank as fast as he could. She was trying to block Layden out, but he continued to talk. She focused in on the sound of Michael McDonald singing *'What a fool believes'*, floating around quietly from the radio. She felt as if she was in a dream and then a moment later suddenly felt as if she was going to be sick.

"Stop the car. I'm going to puke," she commanded.

"Wha … ?" Layden seemed more dazed than she was. The car was still moving when she pulled on the handle and started to get out. He immediately hit the brakes and pulled to the side. Qian collapsed to her knees and began retching on the sidewalk with the door open, it was only then that they fathomed that she was half-naked in public and hadn't looked to see how busy it was. Before she had an opportunity to pull down her dress from around her head, she heard the squeal of the squad car and the flashing lights coming up quickly from behind. Her heart sank with the realization that she was probably about to be arrested once again. The sidewalk seemed to get closer as she continued to dry heave down on her knees. Nothing was coming up. She considered that it must have been a reaction to the drugs and not the loss of blood at all. She dry heaved for what felt like an eternity. She could hear the cops talking with Layden. She was having a hard time responding to the female cop standing beside her asking her questions and trying to put pressure on her head.

The rain started falling a little quicker but hardly noticeable despite the rest of the way she felt. She was soaking wet sitting handcuffed on the curb having her head-wound attended to by a paramedic. She watched Layden get arrested and put into the back of another car that had come some moments later. Most likely for solicitation or leaving the scene of an accident. Everything she was seeing was passing by in clumps and was unclear, the last foggy thought she had was *'why is this strange man putting his hands under my nose'*. It was then that everything came alive and she realized that he'd snapped something similar to an amyl-nitrate under her nose to bring her around. When everything cleared it was only then that she could feel how tight the cuffs really were. Everything began to suck harder than it ever had before. She had quietly wished that she had called Brittsy instead. She saw Layden's face from the backseat of the cruiser pull away as she was stood up and was herded into her own backseat. When the door slammed shut the only thing that she could register was how much she was regretting her whole damn life. None of it seemed worth any of this.

The wise man has the power to reason away ...

I didn't see Qian again for quite some time after that long night with Andrew and Layden. I had watched the whole thing unfold from the concealment of my cruiser and felt more than compelled during several moments to intervene, but I knew that it was probably best not to. When I saw the Volvo slam into Andrew's Rover up in the distance, I was mortified and accelerated to get to the scene faster. Half-way, something was telling me that I was about to make a mistake, so I killed my lights and parked on the side of the street and blended in to the concrete. I saw Qianqian emerge from Andrew's SUV bleeding and dazed, I saw the Volvo driver desperately trying to restart the car and I didn't even bother to take down the license plate. I wondered if he was going to get out and see if they were going to live or not. I shook my head as he pulled away. I felt that I was witnessing something that I wasn't supposed to see and every fiber in my body wanted to help, but a quiet voice in my ear told me not to. I felt conflicted, but I had to let it be.

When the rain fell, and she was bobbing around in handcuffs sitting on the curb crying again, I felt like emerging from the car and straightening the whole situation out with the uniformed patrolmen. It would've been hard to explain, but I could've gotten them both off. It was just better that I didn't. The image of her bloody, with her dress around her head in the rain, dry-heaving on the side-walk made me realize that she was probably supposed to be going through that, and I wouldn't have been really helping her at all. That was the moment that I knew I was powerless to help someone who wouldn't even help themselves. It was also the moment when I felt as if I had failed her completely as a friend. I felt shitty about the whole damned thing.

I decided not to call her again after that, and I didn't expect her to call me. She was probably too embarrassed and most likely wanted to forget everything that had happened. She probably already surmised that I was aware and thus would have made any further meetings between us awkward. I was at the station when her parents showed up to take her out of custody. I was in uniform and Su-Ying was upset frantic and in tears. I told them it was best if she didn't know that I was there and so I stayed behind two-way glass drinking coffee and feeling sheepish.

Apart from looking though the most basic of sources some time later, I made almost no attempt to find out what she doing and how she was. I ran her address information through the county database and discovered that she had moved on two occasions, both times closer to her girlfriend, Brittsy. I didn't want to know if she was still stripping at the club or not. I didn't want to know if she was still receiving her money from Layden and leaving the country on his dime. I didn't have any more room inside me to know. Her lifestyle choices were now beyond my judgment. Knowing that she didn't return to her parents home in San Diego after her father had bailed her out from the custody of the North Hollywood Division, didn't bode well. She had seen the inside of that jail a total of three times and so I had believed that she had hit bottom, but the more I thought about it, the more I realized that she was probably far from it.

Within several months, I was reassigned full time to an administrative post at the Bradbury building and shortly after had decided to resign. I had stayed long enough, learned more than I needed and had long suffered enough bureaucracy and uniforms. If I continued, it would've only been unhealthy and I would end up doing something stupid. A person has to know when to quit. I knew there was a lesson in there somewhere.

Having wrapped up business at the weekly, giving no more new information to the grindstone of public opinion, I had received my severance pay from the editor and had abandoned my desk to the rising tide of hack writers. I didn't care for journalism almost as much as I didn't care for police work. In my opinion, they were both one in the same, self-indulgent masturbation. I had made a decision to get out of Los Angeles, move back East, and possibly go back to school. With the way that I saw the city, and how much I hated everyone around me, I knew I couldn't stay. I was no-good for it anymore and had I poison surging around inside me. I knew that I had reached my high water mark and that the passing time would only see me sink further into the abyss of depravity that awaited if I stayed. I had no intention of being swallowed whole by the death-grip of living in an over-priced fashion show. I was hoping to find something more pure and meaningful.

As for my feelings for Qianqian, they never changed. I still loved her and always would, but I had no ability to console her. Not a day would ever pass where I wouldn't think of her at least once. It was my curse, if anything. I loved her for her capacity of self-destruction and her lack of remorse. For her, it had no bottom.

Although, I had several things that I wanted to say to her, a few pieces had congealed in my mind over the last many weeks regarding the things that had very little to do with the previous events, and more to do with life in general.

I wanted to tell her that even though she probably hated me, I had missed her. I also never got the opportunity to say goodbye properly. The last time we had spoken, she busted out the front door leaving me in a wake of distaste.

Even though I believed our fates were intertwined, I doubted if we would ever cross paths again. She was probably spending a lot of energy putting a distance between us that I would never cross. She had once told me that she had absolutely no regrets, but I knew that if I asked her now, she probably say "our relationship". I didn't hold any grudges about what had happened, but I knew that things would never be the same between us, separated or not. My guess was that she would stay the same and unfortunately everybody hits rock bottom at different depths.

With her gone, I could still sense her presence. Once, I thought I passed her traffic at a red light, going in opposite directions, which was symbolic in itself. Another time, I saw her at a restaurant having sushi with Brittsy. I didn't yet have the strength to see her then and I was caught unawares. I had frozen up, turned and left without saying a word.

A few times I had actually woken up in the morning and felt her lying next to me in bed, realizing but a moment later that I had imagined her. A product of wishful thinking. Several times, I had also woken in the middle of the night after a dream, having a very lucid and seemingly real conversation with her. Each time she had seemed pleased to see me and filled me in on things that had been going on. When I contemplated the dreams later, I had wondered if she was trying to tell me something, or if she missed being with me as much as I did her. The cold truth was probably neither. One night, I ended up watching *The Princess Bride* again for the hundredth time and couldn't help but think of her and how much she hated it. I was engrossed in the scene with 'The Man in Black' examining the sword. Stuck out, he said: *'I have never seen its equal'*. I had already accepted that I would never meet another woman like her either. Sometimes beauty itself can do ugly things to people, the product of the way I felt being no exception. I had been taken prisoner, and badly handled like a blade run through the guts of an innocent victim. I was having a difficult time getting past it all, but time was the only medicine and it would have to take its toll. Breaking up with Qianqian created a different form of grief within me. A form of grief that didn't want to fade or go away. Sometimes people try to offer advice, and say that it gets better, but most of time they're wrong. Grief changes shape, but it never ends, and that's what I was finding out. When people you love, leave you, you're not going to be better about it, you're just going to be alone.

On the chess board, the game ends when the king is isolated and has nowhere else to run, Queens have often long since retired. Such is the game and so it was. So it happened.

Yellow Fever

"It is the finest blades that are most easily blunted, bent or broken. He withdrew from his fellow man after he had given them everything and had received nothing in return. He lived alone because he found no second self."

Excerpt from the eulogy of Ludwig van Beethoven delivered at his grave by Franz Grillpazer. March 26th, 1827

STEFFAN PIPER

Steffan Piper currently lives on the outskirts of Los Angeles
with his family. Most of his writing occurs in the dead
of night unlike the bulk of his contemporaries.

www.ingramcontent.com/pod-product-compliance
Lightning Source LLC
Chambersburg PA
CBHW031119030726
47496CB00002BA/597